No Escape:
The Sweetwater Tragedy

No Escape:
The Sweetwater Tragedy

Jean Henry Mead

Medallion Books
Glenrock, Wyoming

Published by Medallion Books and printed in the United States of America. No part of this book may be reproduced in any manner without the express permission of the publisher, with the exception of brief quotes used in critical articles and reviews.

Library of Congress cataloging pending

First edition published in March 2013

Book cover design by Bill Mead

ISBN: 978-1-931415-41-5

Other Medallion Books by Jean Henry Mead

A Village Shattered

Diary of Murder

Murder on the Interstate

Gray Wolf Mountain

Escape

Mystery of Spider Mountain

Ghost of Crimson Dawn

The Mystery Writers

Casper Country: Wyoming's Heartland

Wyoming's Cowboy Poets

Westerners: Candid and Historic Interviews

Wyoming Historical Trivia (as J. J. Hammond)

Dedicated to the late
George W. Hufsmith, whose research
helped me complete this novel.

"In a Victorian era that placed women on alabaster pedestals, to jointly agree to garrote a helpless young woman and an innocent man on the flimsiest of evidence, and to carry out a sentence of death in the face of millenniums of law to the contrary, is altogether beyond the comprehension of this author."

~George W. Hufsmith

Acknowledgements

I first became interested in the "Cattle Kate" controversy in 1985 while researching a Wyoming centennial history book by reading 97 years' worth of microfilmed newspapers over a three year period. I was mystified when I read that cattlemen had hanged a young woman homesteader and her husband, falsely accusing them of running a bawdy house in exchange for rustled cattle. I attempted to research the subject intermittently over the years and was pleased to read the late George W. Hufsmith's nonfiction book, *The Wyoming Lynching of Cattle Kate 1889.*

Hufsmith spent more than twenty years researching and interviewing residents of Sweetwater Valley, Wyoming, who had accurate knowledge of the events and aftermath of the hangings of Ellen Watson-Averell and her husband James in July 1889. I'm dedicating this book to Hufsmith for all his hard work in dispelling the rumors and bringing the truth to light.

I had originally planned to write this novel solely about Ellen"Ella" Liddy Watson-Pickell-Averell, but didn't want to end the book with her tragic death, so I researched single women homesteaders and have written the book from a composite of some 200,000 single women who attempted to prove up on homesteads of their own. Some successful, some not. So the book is written primarily from my protagonist, Susan Cameron's viewpoint.

My thanks to Rick Young, director of the Fort Caspar Museum and Pattie Morrell of the Wyoming Railroad Interpretive Center in Douglas for their help.

~Jean Henry Mead

Chapter One

Wyoming Territory: June 10, 1889

Susan Cameron awoke from her nap to the sound of gunfire. Bolting upright in her seat, she was surprised when two men rushed past as the train came to a jarring halt. Handguns were drawn and at the ready. Across the aisle, a small boy screamed in his mother's arms. The woman glanced at Susan with frightened eyes as her young daughter crawled beneath the seat.

The connecting door burst open and an aging conductor signaled for silence. "Train robbers blocked the tracks. When they come aboard, give 'em whatever they want or somebody's liable to get killed. You men keep your guns holstered. There's women and children on board."

Heart pounding, Susan removed most of the money from her reticule. Loosening the laces of her high topped shoes, she slipped the bills inside each one. Her dress was then pulled down over her ankles.

Gunfire ceased as three men entered the coach. Sweat-stained hats hung low over their brows, bandanas hiding all but their squinting eyes. They were dressed like photographs Susan had seen of working cowhands.

"Hands up if you wanna live," the first man yelled.

The children screamed as their mother attempted to comfort them on the floor between the seats. She pulled their faces to her chest when one of the bandits shouted, "Shut them kids up."

Demanding that everyone stand, two of the disheveled men moved down the aisle, flipping open canvas sacks and ordering them filled. Susan got to her feet and glanced at the other passengers, whose hands were held aloft. She and Amanda Turner were the only women occupying the coach. The remaining seats were filled with men of every description, including a number dressed as cowhands. She wondered if they were members of the gang.

"Empty your pockets," the first bandit demanded. "And you ladies open your bags." He offered his canvas sack in one hand while waving his gun with the other. Susan sighed with relief when he walked past to the middle of the coach.

"Guns, money and jewelry," the second man said as he approached Susan's seat. His body odor made her recoil before he came opposite her. Holding her breath, she emptied the contents of her reticule onto the seat.

"No jewelry?"

"Single women can't afford jewelry." He wasn't much taller than Susan and she resisted the urge to grab his gun.

"Where's the rest of your money? Maybe I oughta search ya."

"While you're doing that, I assure you the men in this coach will disarm you." Susan hoped her voice didn't belie her bravado.

Grunting, he turned to demand cash from the young

woman across the aisle. When she released her children, their screaming increased in volume until passengers' upraised hands were covering their ears. Placing the sack beneath his arm, the burly bandit stooped to reprimand the boy, who promptly bit his hand.

"What kind of monster are you, slapping that child?" Susan cried.

"Didn't do nuthin' to the little brat." Shaking his injured hand, he moved on to passengers in the next row. The Turner woman dipped her head and smiled her gratitude.

Susan drew a sharp breath. While the bandits were collecting their bounty, she wondered what had happened to the passengers who rushed from the train. Imagining them lying on their backs, bleeding from multiple wounds, she shook her head to dislodge the disturbing image.

A third bandit stood guard at the front of the coach, watching as passengers were relieved of their possessions. When his companions left the coach, he fired a shot through the roof and ordered everyone down on the floor. Moments later passengers were back in their seats, watching the bandits skirt sagebrush as they rode toward the mountains. Taking her seat, Susan heard a chorus of men's low-voiced curses.

The conductor stood and mopped his perspiring brow. "Stay in your seats. We're lucky no one was hurt. Nobody but the bandit, that is."

Susan yelled above the din. "Where are the missing passengers?"

The conductor turned back at the connecting door. "Gang members, ma'am. I just watched 'em ride off with the rest of the bunch."

"Why didn't they stay and rob us?"

"I reckon they didn't want anybody to recognize 'em. They boarded the train down the tracks in Douglas, and probably robbed the adjoining coach. They were wearing masks when they left but I recognized their clothes." He turned and grumbled his way back through the connecting door between the coaches.

Susan pulled the money from her shoes and returned the bills to her reticule. No one had warned her about train robbers. What had she gotten herself into? She thought of homesteading as a peaceful venture and knew that other single women had proved up on their own land. Could she carve out a living on her homestead, without being robbed?

Wyoming Territory seemed a panacea for single women seeking independence. The territorial government had granted women suffrage more than twenty years earlier, allowing them to not only vote, but serve on juries as well as hold public office. Those privileges alone had brought her to the territory.

Less than an hour later, the train whistle shrieked, signaling the conductor to announce their arrival in Casper. Tired of traveling, Susan rose from her seat, lifted her reticule and made her way to the outer door. Standing on a makeshift platform were more than a dozen men, most of them wearing dusty, wrinkled clothing that apparently had been worn for quite some time. Several had missing teeth and stringy, shoulder-length hair. Horrified, she drew back when one of them offered his hand.

"Welcome to Casper, ma'am."

Susan hesitated, then realized the hand belonged to a tall, neatly dressed man with perfect teeth.

"Michael O'Brien at your service," he said as he helped her down the steps.

Susan withdrew her hand. "What kind of service are you offering, Mister O'Brien?"

A puzzled expression etched his pleasant face.

"Whatever I can do to help you get settled, ma'am."

"Show me to the hotel, if you please."

He indicated a two-story building some distance away. A sea of sagebrush stood between them and the hotel. Smiling, he nodded toward a large, stained canvas structure resembling a circus tent. "I don't suppose a lady like you would want to save money by staying in the tent hotel."

Susan gasped as she surveyed her surroundings. A number of aging wagons were parked in the vicinity. To the south a nearly flat-topped mountain dominated the barren landscape, like a giant ridge.

"Where's the land filing office, Mister O'Brien?"

"In Rawlins, more than a hundred miles southwest of here. I'm headed that way in the morning. You're welcome to ride along."

Susan shook her head. "I'll take the first stage tomorrow, thank you."

"No stages in this area, ma'am."

"*Miss* Susan Cameron," she said as she swiveled to survey the area. "You can't mean this is all there is?"

"I'm afraid so. The Carey Brothers and the railroad are selling city lots to anyone with the cash. Not homestead land, you understand, but twenty-five by hundred foot lots for two hundred dollars to two-fifty. I've got mine staked out." He pointed westward.

"But who are all these people?" She nodded toward those who still stood near the train.

"Mostly railroad followers waiting for the tracks to lay further west."

"The wagons and tents are their permanent homes?" *That's no way to live in this barren wilderness.*

"Railroad gypsies," he said.

"How do they earn a living?"

"Any way they can. Be careful, miss. Some of these

people are hungry."

Susan shivered in the warm afternoon sun. "I need somewhere to spend the night."

"As I said before, there's Walt Beaker's hotel tent but I think you'd rather stay at the hotel in town. I'll be happy to escort you there."

Behind them the young family disembarked from the train, the small boy still crying. Susan turned to help them, realizing that she should have offered sooner. She had been too anxious to begin her new adventure. Petite, dark-haired Amanda Turner shifted her young son to her left shoulder. She smiled when introduced to Michael O'Brien.

Michael picked up their baggage but when Amanda took one look at the emptiness of their surroundings, she refused to move another step. "We'll stay on the train."

The conductor had just climbed down to close the coach door. "Can't do that, ma'am. Train's gotta be cleaned and turned around for the trip back to Nebraska."

"It's not going on to Utah?"

"No, ma'am. This here's the end of the line for the Fremont, Elkhorn and Missouri Valley Railroad."

Amanda's lovely face fell and Susan thought she was going to cry. "My husband's waiting for us in Utah."

"I'm afraid you boarded the wrong train in Omaha, ma'am. You can return there and board a westbound Union Pacific train. Or you can hire someone with a buckboard at Orin Junction to take you over some rough country to Wendover and catch a train to Cheyenne. I wouldn't advise it with the children."

The young woman gasped. "All the way back to Omaha?"

The conductor nodded. " Unless you want to wire your husband to come and get you. That would mean staying for weeks in Casper."

Susan wondered whether Amanda's children had distracted her, causing them to board the wrong train.

"Come with me," she said. "We'll stay at the hotel and I'll help you with the children." She took the small girl's hand, who couldn't have been more than four.

Amanda's expression said she had arrived on the fringes of hell. Michael O'Brien led the way and they trailed along behind.

When they reached the large tent, a paunchy, pit-faced man greeted them at the entrance. His stained brocade vest was missing a button and his battered stove pipe hat appeared to have been creased by a wagon wheel. The only clean thing about him was the white silk garter worn on his dingy sleeve.

"Welcome," he said, a gold tooth gleaming in the afternoon sun. "I was just on my way to offer accommodations." He doffed his battered hat and gestured toward the tent.

Amanda Turner gasped. "Is this the hotel?"

Susan groaned when she glimpsed the tent's interior. The canvas shelter wasn't fit for animals, let alone humans. Stained and threadbare, the cots had been used by unwashed men. How could anyone sleep there?

"The ladies are staying at the hotel in town," Michael said, beckoning them to follow.

Susan heard the tent owner swearing as they left. No matter how primitive the hotel was in town, it had to be a vast improvement over the greasy tent. Perhaps that's why Michael O'Brien had shown it to them.

When they reached the hotel with its clapboard exterior and plain, unattractive appearance, Susan brushed back a long strand of blond hair that had escaped her chignon in the increasing wind. At least the building was new. Led into the small lobby, both women were assigned rooms on the second floor. Their escort causally mentioned that his own room was below Susan's.

"I'd be pleased to have you accompany me on the trip to Rawlins," he repeated at her door. "I need to buy supplies before I open my office."

"Office?"

He nodded. "I'd appreciate some company on the trip."

"That's unacceptable," Amanda Turner sputtered. "You can't go without a chaperon."

"The societal rules are different here in Wyoming Territory, ma'am. Women are men's equals. In most respects, that is."

"But what about Miss Cameron's reputation?"

Susan sighed. Her mother would require smelling salts if she knew that she was considering his offer. She envisioned the assemblage of railroad followers and knew she couldn't stay there alone.

"We'll be leaving early," he said, his expression hopeful.

"I'll let you know in the morning." She quickly closed the door behind her.

Wyoming Territory was far worse than anything Susan could have imagined. A wagon trip with Michael O'Brien was probably her only option. Was she making a mistake by accompanying him on the trip? He seemed a decent sort but her dealings with men in the past had made her wary. She prayed she could weather the trip without incident, confident her father's self-defense training would keep her safe, despite her small stature.

Chapter Two

Sweetwater Valley, Wyoming, June 10, 1889.

"Something I can help you with, Mister Jones?"

The wiry little cowpoke grinned. "Jimmy's a lucky man. I wish I had me a big, purty woman like you."

Ella abruptly turned her back to busy herself at the shelves. She wasn't used to that kind of adoration.

"Where'd he find you, anyhow?"

She glanced over her shoulder at the dusty rider, who was leaning across the counter for a better look. They couldn't afford to lose a customer so she decided not to slap him.

"I was cooking at the Rawlins House when Jimmy came for dinner." Perhaps she shouldn't have told him that. Her husband wanted to keep their history secret.

Harvey Jones scratched his chin through a month's worth of whiskers, his expression hopeful. "Maybe I oughta ride on over to Rawlins."

"The replacement cook's married, Mister Jones. She took my job when I moved here with Jimmy."

Apparently crestfallen, he mumbled, "She might be a

widder by now."

"Still married the last time we were there."

"When was that?"

"Last month when we rode in for supplies."

The cowpoke's attention was flattering although it embarrassed her. He slumped across the counter, his lip so low he could have almost stepped on it. She wondered why a pint-sized cowpuncher was enamored with a larger woman. Ella's height had always been a source of shyness. At five feet-eight, she was taller than her husband and outweighed him a good thirty pounds. Increasingly uncomfortable with the customer's admiration, she sighed with relief when her husband entered the store. Jimmy stopped long enough to acknowledge Harvey Jones, then promptly delivered his message.

"Annie Masters has taken sick and her husband wondered..." He nodded toward a middle-aged man standing in the doorway.

"Of course." Ella removed her apron. "I'll take the buggy, if you don't mind me going." She knew he didn't but felt she had to ask. When he smiled his approval, she hurried to their living quarters behind the store to pack some clothing, relieved to be rid of Harvey Jones. Gazing about the room, she sighed. The cowpoke was wrong in his assessment of her husband. *She* was the lucky one. Before she left, she jotted a note telling him that she loved him.

Jimmy had already hitched Old Blunder to the buggy when she entered the store. She found him pouring Harvey a mug of beer at the store's makeshift bar. There were few customers in Sweetwater Valley, although the emigrant trails had been heavily traveled several decades earlier. An occasional wrangler would stop for a drink and settlers imbibed when they picked up their mail, if wives weren't along. Jim Averell's road ranch stocked a few staples, razors, stockings, and other frontier necessities. The small bar featured beer from the brewery in Casper, which was poured into foaming mugs. The bottled brew was kept cold with frozen blocks cut during winter from the Sweetwater River, and stored in their small ice house.

His boot propped on the railing, the cowpoke had his finger aimed at Jimmy. "Bothwell's none too happy that you homesteaded on his meadow land."

"The land was legally filed on," she heard Jimmy say. "Bothwell and the other cattlemen have used this range for years, without paying for it."

"I reckon they think they own it."

"They'll have to abide by the law."

Harvey lifted his mug as though saluting the bartender. "Gov'nor Moonlight shore knowed what he was doin' when he appointed you postmaster and justice of the peace."

Jimmy smiled and poured him another beer. Ella had heard the conversation countless times before. Clearing her throat, she signaled her husband to follow.

"Sure you don't mind?" she asked again once they left the store.

"Of course not. Just don't stay too long."

She leaned to kiss him, then held him to appraise at arm's length. Slender, handsome, dark-haired and intelligent, he was the answer to Ella's prayers. She shuddered, recalling Bill Pickell, her abusive first husband. There was little to compare the two.

"You'll see to the boys?" she asked, knowing that he would.

Jimmy smiled. He was as fond of their three young charges as she was. "I'll bring them down from your cabin and make sure they're fed."

Ella had gathered the boys to her like a mother hen. Eleven-year-old Gene Crowder's mother had died and his father was a drifter. Jimmy's nineteen-year-old nephew Ralph was staying with them as well as John DeCorey, who was fourteen and had been hired to work her homestead and tend to twenty-eight footsore cattle purchased from an emigrant. The small herd had increased to forty-two. All had recently been imprinted with the LU brand, which she had purchased from Gene Crowder's father and promptly registered in Rawlins. The papers had been stored in a bank safety deposit box.

"Be careful." Jimmy kissed her again and helped her into the buggy. "Harvey'll help himself to another beer if I leave him alone too long. It's nearly time for another trip to Rawlins for supplies."

She promised to hurry back. Lifting the reins, she clucked to Old Blunder, her stomach queasy when she considered the Masters family. They kept to themselves like most homesteaders. Annie Masters must be terribly ill for her husband to ask for help. She didn't know the woman well and wasn't sure how she felt about her. Some wives shunned Ella, thinking her a divorced woman living in sin with a widower. She understood why Jimmy insisted they keep their marriage secret. They could lose the adjacent homestead land she had filed on.

Thanks to the Desert Land Act, they owned half a section together, but if word got out they were married, cattlemen could force them to forfeit half their land. She wouldn't mind, as long as she had Jimmy, but her husband was adamant in his efforts to prevent cattlemen from gobbling up Sweetwater Valley. Their combined homesteads blocked Albert Bothwell's access to Horse Creek, and *her* homestead had been legally filed on in Bothwell's former hay meadow.

She was well aware of the stockmen's resentment and worried about her husband. Although the governor had appointed him postmaster as well as justice of the peace, cattlemen had little respect for his authority. Jimmy's titles could not protect them from the cattle barons' wrath.

Storm clouds lay on the horizon. Clucking again to Old Blunder, she steeled herself for what lay ahead.

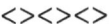

They left the following morning, after accompanying the Turner family to the train. Seated beside her escort, Susan scanned the high plains, wondering how long the wagon trip would last and what their sleeping arrangements would entail. She should have asked before they left the hotel. Their luggage had been stored in the wagon bed, along with a tent, food, and water.

Dark clouds appeared on the horizon at mid-day, which had her worried. The storm raced across the high plains, leaving them drenched and shivering. Too tired to care how she looked, Susan was grateful when Michael built a campfire that evening near the tent, which he had purchased from a railroad follower. She accepted his offer to sleep in the tent, but with no small amount of uneasiness. Her body ached from the long wagon ride, and she wondered whether she should have returned to Nebraska with the Turner family. The thought of another train ride with screaming children was more than she could bear. Taking the blanket he offered, she settled in the tent. Sometime during the night an animal howled nearby and she awoke gasping.

"You all right in there?" Michael asked from outside the tent.

"What are you doing up at this hour?"

"Thought I'd stir up the fire in case you're getting cold. The high desert nights can get chilly this time of year. I've heard that it's even snows in June."

Susan encased herself in the blanket and peered through the open flap.

"You're welcome to sit a while, Miss Cameron."

"Call me Susan." She returned his smile as she crawled from the tent.

"Want to talk about the reason you came out west?" He leaned to drop a handful of woodchips in the fire. "You're not having second thoughts, are you?"

"Well ... perhaps." The fire roared and crackled, casting strange shadows across his face. Not a truly handsome face, but one she felt she could trust.

"Where's home, by the way?"

"Missourah." She stared into the flames for long moments before the words came tumbling forth. "My friend Mary Lynn and I used to talk for hours about the freedom women have in Wyoming Territory, and how we could hold public office."

"Still can."

"But before we planned to leave, Jeffrey Baskin proposed marriage and Mary Lynn wasted no time accepting. So I came alone."

He frowned. "Didn't your friends and family try to talk you out of it?"

"Of course, but I couldn't convince even one of them to come along."

"Most people aren't cut out for this kind of life, Susan."

"Well, I certainly am. Don't let my small stature fool you. I'm equal to any man."

He coughed and attempted to hide his grin.

"No one's going to tell *me* how to live."

"I'm not going to try."

Susan sighed. "I'm worried about Amanda and the children."

"Why? We saw them off safely on the train."

"I should have gone with them and taken a train to

14

Rawlins."

"And miss this wonderful trip with me?"

"Don't go getting any notions about me, Mister O'Brien."

"Michael."

"I'm going to homestead a place of my own. On my own."

"I wish you'd tell me why that's so important."

"I might tell you, someday."

Standing, he said, "I'll let you get back to sleep. I'm sure you'll tell me when you're ready." He smiled as he made his way back to the wagon.

The fact that he was amused infuriated her. Abruptly leaving the fire, she crawled back into the tent, securing the flap so that even a bear would have been frustrated in its attempts to enter. It was a long while before she fell asleep.

Next morning, light was filtering into the tent when she caught the scent of coffee. Hastily brushing her hair, she left her cubbyhole in time to watch him disappear behind the horses. Rushing to the wagon, she insisted on helping him hitch the team.

"Not a woman's job, Susan."

"I'll be homesteading soon. Don't you think it's time I learned my way around horses?"

He glanced at her, apparently unconvinced.

"I'll need a team of my own."

"There's bacon in the wagon. Why don't you—"

"You brought me along to cook?"

Michael sighed. "All right. I'll cook breakfast while you hitch up the horses."

"A little instruction would be helpful."

"While we're standing here arguing, the land office in Rawlins is busy signing up homesteaders."

Susan bit her lip.

"I'd hate to see those pretty little hands get blistered."

"Mister O'Brien, we both know I'm as plain as an unbuttered biscuit."

"Hardly."

"The lack of women in this territory has obviously lowered your conception of beauty."

He simply shook his head.

"Show me how to hitch the horses and I'll gladly prepare your breakfast. Tomorrow we can trade off chores."

Michael grumbled but set about demonstrating the necessary techniques. As she watched him straighten the reins and tighten cinches, an apprehensive chill passed through her. For all her determination and bluster, she wondered whether she could actually manage alone.

"Allow me to help," she said, gripping the gray's halter. Standing on her toes, she worked to set it straight.

Michael laughed as they headed back to the fire. "All right, wilderness woman, let's see how well you cook."

Sweetwater Valley hid in twilight when Ella reached the Masters' ranch. The unlighted house had her worried as she drove around to the barn. Tom Masters was waiting and wordlessly unhitched her horse. His refusal to acknowledge her presence caused a colony of ants to march down her spine. Dismounting the buggy, she made her way to the house, glancing about to determine where the children were. The dark house was forbidding and she groped about the back porch for an oil lamp. Increasingly apprehensive, she was retracing her steps when she noticed a lantern bobbing toward her.

"The wife's asleep," he said, failing to even glance at her.

"Where are the children?"

"With their aunt in Rawlins." He held the lantern low, his face in shadows as Ella tried unsuccessfully to blink back the darkness. "Go inside," he said, his voice unusually gruff.

Ella pushed the door aside and cautiously stepped inside. Her senses told her to turn back and run, but his hand gripped her arm and propelled her forward.

"Annie's in the bedroom."

She balked when they entered a short, narrow hall. Reaching around her, he pinned her against the unopened door. Ella recoiled not only from his touch, but the combined odors of tobacco and sweat.

When the door opened, the lantern illuminated the bed and she saw that it was empty. "Where's your wife, Mister Masters?"

"In Rawlins."

In one swift move, he set the lantern on the floor and shoved her down on the bed. A dusty quilt muffled her cry of shock. Unable to breath, she fought to free herself of his weight on her back.

"Everybody knows you take mavericks for your favors. His large calloused hands roughly caressed her hips. "You'll not get so much as a copper penny outta me."

Ella managed to lift her head and scream.

Masters jerked her onto her back to rip the buttons from her dress.

This can't be happening, her mind railed as she struggled to hold him off. For a moment in the strange, lantern-lit room, it was her first husband abusing her again in a drunken rage. While Masters groped to free her breasts, she balled her fist and struck, targeting his nose.

It was his turn to scream. He let go long enough for her to roll from the bed. Struggling to her feet, she managed to get as far as the bedroom door before he caught her. Taller than Ella, he was as stringy as barbed wire and equally hurtful. Nose spurting blood, he jerked her back toward the bed.

Ella kept her balance as she stooped to grasp the lantern bale. Swinging it in a wide arc, she struck him on the side of his head. Glass shattered and Masters' hair caught fire. Shocked by her own violence, Ella jerked the quilt from the bed. When she tried to smoother the flames, she was struck by the screaming man's fist. Dazed, she fell against the wall.

"Dear Lord, what have I done?"

Still on his feet, Masters revolved in a slow death spiral, his clothing engulfed in flames. When he fell, she tried again to smother the fire, but soon realized the room was ablaze. Escaping into the hall, she could hear the flames' roar, which heightened her sense of urgency. She frantically searched for an outer door. Shadows danced menacingly in the reflected light, ghostly hands reaching for her everywhere she turned. Where was the entry door? Groping along the wall, she tripped over furniture and sprawled onto the rough-hewn floor. Groaning, she tried to pick herself up but pain in her wrists made her fear they were broken.

A timber fell and flying sparks burned holes in her dress. Blinded with smoke and tears, she managed to get to her feet to feel her way along the wall until she at last found a door. Smoke filled her lungs and she feared she would die.

"Jimmy, help me!" she pleaded, although she knew she had to save herself. A coughing spasm overcame her as she managed to wrench the door open and fall across the threshold. She wasn't sure how long she had lain face down on the wooden porch before night air revived her. Stumbling from the porch, she escaped the heat and deadly smoke. Somewhere in the darkness horses whickered.

Ella collapsed again in the dooryard, coughing. The

house was burning like straw and would soon be nothing more than embers. She wondered whether neighboring ranchers had seen the flames, and if anyone would come to her rescue. Pulling the remnants of her bodice across her ample breasts, she was afraid that she would be blamed for the fire, as well as Master's death.

She desperately needed Jimmy.

Disoriented, Ella listened to the sounds of frightened horses. She then noticed the barn in the fire's reflected light. Moving cautiously in that direction, she prayed she could find Old Blunder. Calling to him when she reached the barn, she worried she would further agitate him.

"Where are you, old boy?"

Ella recognized his whicker and continued talking to him as he replied to her calls. When she reached his stall, she spent long moments stroking his muzzle and whispering to him. He at last quieted and she tore off a strip of her ruined dress to blindfold him and lead him from the barn.

She knew she couldn't hitch him to the buggy in the darkness, but Jimmy would retrieve whatever she left behind. Blunder was nearly sixteen hands and, despite her height, she was unable to mount him from the ground. She then remembered a flat rock she had passed in the yard and led him in that direction. Cringing as she watched the Masters' house disintegrate, the memory of what had happened brought nausea and she fell to her knees and retched.

She had to get away.

Ella had only ridden sidesaddle but would have to straddle Blunder. Carefully climbing the rock, she hitched up her long dress and pulled herself astride the old horse. He was as skittish as a young colt and it had taken more than one attempt to mount him. Ella's body trembled as she wrapped her long legs around his ribs. Why had Masters lured her there? She'd never given him or any man reason to mistreat her. What was it he had said as he abused her? That she had taken maverick calves in exchange for her favors? How had he come to that conclusion?

Ella pulled up short as she escaped the flaming ruins, unsure what she should tell her husband. He was a good man but what would he do when she told him what had happened? The culprit was dead but most men would want revenge.

It was then she heard approaching horses. Circling Blunder to determine their direction, her heart rate increased to the point of pounding. When she decided the horses were coming from the east, she urged the horse north toward the Averell's Road Ranch.

She was halfway up the rise when she remembered the buggy, still parked in the Masters' barn.

Chapter Three

A crescent moon didn't provide much light, but Blunder seemed to know the way. What should she tell Jimmy? Already infuriated that local cattlemen were illegally grazing cattle on homestead lands, he might do something irrational, if he knew about the terrible lie that was spreading about her virtue. Drying tears on her sleeve, she decided to withhold the truth.

What if someone had seen her following Tom Masters to his ranch while his family was in Rawlins? If rumors were circulating that she was a loose woman, her reputation was ruined. She might even be charged with the fire and Master's death. *How could this have happened?*

She halted Blunder when light from their cabin came into view. Envisioning her husband sitting in his rocker, she knew he was reading. Books and newspapers were their main source of entertainment. Jimmy always stopped whatever he was doing when the weekly mail wagon arrived from Rawlins.

Slowing Blunder to a walk several hundred feet from the barn, she hoped Jimmy wouldn't hear her approach before she could ride to her own cabin to change clothes. She then remembered that the boys were staying there. As she sat astride the horse deciding, the cabin door opened and Jimmy yelled, "Who's out there?" She heard the click of his rifle as he pulled back the hammer.

"Don't shoot," she yelled.

"Ella? Is that you?"

"Help me down." She tried to calm her voice but a large lump had formed in her throat. She watched a dark form race toward her and nearly lost her perch, so eager to find herself in Jimmy's arms. When he lifted them to help her down, she heard his worried voice.

"My God, what happened?"

Bursting into tears, she sobbed uncontrollably as he led her to the cabin.

Holding her at arm's length, he gasped. "What happened to your dress? Tell me, Ella. Did Masters—?"

"There was a fire and the house ... the house burned down."

"Was anyone hurt?"

"I-I don't know, Jimmy. I tried to help but—"

He stared at her tear-streaked face. "Tell me what happened."

"It was awful. I tried to save him."

"Him? Masters?"

She nodded, unable to speak.

"What about his family?"

"In Rawlins." She couldn't lie to him.

"I'll kill him."

"He's dead, Jimmy. I hit him with the lantern when he tried to—"

Her husband dropped his arms and reached for his rifle. He was halfway to the door when she screamed. "No! I need you here."

His face crumpled and tears slid down his cheeks.

22

Dropping the rifle he gathered her into his arms. "Forgive me," he whispered. "Tell me everything that happened."

<><><>

Susan's teeth rattled as they traveled the bumpy trail. Michael had spoken little all afternoon and seemed immersed in his thoughts.

"How long before we reach Rawlins?" she asked, attempting to draw him into conversation.

"A few miles less than the last time you asked, Miss Cameron."

She drew a sharp breath. "I apologize if I've said something to offend you."

He turned his head to glance at her, the reins held taut in his hands. "Not at all. I was just thinking about all the single women who tried their hands at homesteading."

"And?"

"Some successful, some not. Quite a few get married before they prove up on their land."

"That's not my plan." *Marriage is the last thing on my mind.*

"Women are scarce in the territory and single men consider them a prize."

"Even if they look like me?"

He sighed and glanced back at the trail. "I don't know why you'd say that, Susan. I find you quite attractive."

She laughed. "You'll not get me into your wagon bed with flattery, Mister O'Brien."

"You must have had a bad experience with a man back home."

"That's hardly any of your business." *I'll not tell you a thing about it.*

Shrugging, he said, "Anytime you want to talk, I'm a good listener."

Gazing in the opposite direction, she watched a herd of animals race across the uneven ground, their white tales bobbing in the distance. She asked what they were.

"Pronghorn antelope. Actually not antelope at all, but members of the Antilocapridae family."

"Antilocapridae?"

"Believe it or not, pronghorns are closely related to the giraffe and the European okapi."

Susan laughed. "They look nothing like giraffes."

"They're an extinct species of giraffe that resembled large deer and the okapi has striped legs like zebras. Many animals are related."

Susan stared at him for a long moment. "You're a curious man, Michael O'Brien. Why would someone with your education come to Wyoming Territory?"

"A long story. Probably not unlike your own."

"Ah, an unrequited love?"

"No. Is that what brought you here?"

Susan felt her face flush and lowered her eyes. "You must be a psychiatrist or a circuit preacher."

"Neither. I'm a veterinarian whose father was a storekeeper."

"Is this a journey to study wildlife?"

"No, I'm here to establish my practice in the territory."

"Why? There's nothing here but sagebrush." She imagined him chasing deer with a butterfly net.

"Trades and professional people are needed to settle the territory. I thought I'd help the cause along."

"I'm impressed."

"No need for that ... What about you? Why did you decide to homestead on your own?"

She hesitated. "I guess deep down I'm a hermit. I've had a few courtships that didn't work out. Now, I'm only searching for independence and freedom."

Michael sighed again as he snapped the reins.

Susan fidgeted on the wooden seat and looked off into the distance. She then asked about various species of wildlife. While he rattled on about elk and deer, she focused on the future. Was there any land worth homesteading in Wyoming Territory? Could she grow enough food to sustain herself? Another thought kept recurring. Was she a fool to think she could homestead on her own? If only Mary Lynn had come along.

Michael must have noticed that she wasn't listening. "Are you planning to hire someone to build your cabin?"

"No, I plan to build it myself."

I assume you've built one before."

"How hard can it be to build a one-room cabin?"

He smiled. "Not hard at all if you're twins."

"I'm sure I can manage." *I'm more capable than I look, Mister O'Brien.*

"Winters here get mighty cold. Thirty to forty degrees below zero, or so I'm told. Think you can chink logs so snow won't blow inside?"

"I can do anything I set my mind to." *I'm sure I can.*

"I'll be glad to help."

"What about your veterinary practice?"

"No hurry with that. People who've arrived so far don't seem to need my services."

"Then why the trip to Rawlins?"

"A retiring veterinarian has office supplies for sale. A good way to start my own practice inexpensively."

Glancing at Michael's appealing profile, she wondered why he wasn't married. "Have you practiced elsewhere?"

Shaking his head, he said his father had been in poor health and that he'd taken over management of their general store until the elder O'Brien died. When his mother passed on, he decided to travel west to start his practice.

"I'm sorry for your losses, but I'm glad you came to

the territory." Susan felt her face flush. He must think she was interested in him.

"You are?" His brows raised in surprise. "I'll need an assistant when my office opens in Casper. Could I interest you in the job?"

"Is that why you invited me along?"

"The thought just occurred to me."

Susan sat as tall as her small frame allowed, crossing her arms across her slender midsection. "I'm sorry, Michael. I'm not interested. The reason I've decided to homestead on my own is because I've had my share of domineering men."

"Domineering?" Michael shook his head.

"Always saying what's best for me from the day I was born."

Michael grinned. "Has anyone ever accused you of being headstrong?"

She shifted in the seat to face him. "Is that what you think? That I'm a stubborn female?"

Michael avoided the question. "Once your cabin's built, you can rule your own little world." Glancing up at the western sky, he frowned.

"You'd help me build my cabin before you start your practice?" *As much as I hate to admit it, your help would come in handy.*

"I'd be willing to do that."

"I couldn't pay you until my first crop comes in."

"I wouldn't accept pay and this isn't farm land, Susan. Unless you're lucky enough to draw land with river frontage or other source of water, your best plan is to raise sheep or cattle. This is dry land with very little rainfall. Perhaps eight inches a year."

Lightning streaked the sky in the distance, followed by a clap of thunder

Michael halted the wagon and tied the reins. He then

ran around the wagon to help her down.

"But it's only a thunderstorm."

"It's worse than that. Look at that cloud bank and the color of the sky. Tornado weather."

They talked until dawn. Ella pleaded with her husband to keep the disaster quiet, but he insisted on retrieving their buggy from the Masters' barn before someone discovered it. She worried that a neighbor would see him. How would he explain?

"We'll say that Masters borrowed the buggy."

"With his family in Rawlins?"

Jimmy paced their small living quarters, repeatedly striking his palm with a closed fist. "Harvey Jones was here when you left. He must have heard me telling you that Masters' wife was sick."

"What condition was he in when he left?"

"I was afraid he'd fall from his saddle. He kept laying down money and insisting on another mug of beer."

"He might have forgotten about Mister Masters."

"Maybe for a few days until his hangover wears off."

"If he remembers, will he tell anyone?"

"He's moon-eyed over you, Ella. He wouldn't do anything to harm you."

Ella wrung her hands. "I don't feel right keeping this secret, but no one will believe what really happened."

"I know, Sweetheart. I want you to stay here while I ride to the Master's place to get the buggy. Old Blunder's worn down so I'll take Big Red."

"No, Jimmy. He never pulled a buggy. That could be dangerous."

"We'll be fine." He grabbed his cap from the hat tree and placed it on his head.

"Please be careful." She kissed him and resisted letting go.

Jimmy assured her that he would and insisted that she get some sleep before it was time to open the store.

<><><>

The wind picked up, blowing dust and particles of unknown substances. Susan's sun bonnet sailed from her head and Michael prevented her from chasing after it.

"Help me turn the wagon over," he yelled above the wind's roar.

They braced their feet to help them push the wagon onto its side. Susan didn't think she was accomplishing much until a strong gust of wind aided their efforts. A splinter stabbed at her palm, which she ignored as the wagon began to tip.

He yelled, "Push harder."

The horses were rearing, jerking the wagon. She could hear their frightened whickers and noticed their efforts to free themselves. What if they ran away? How would they reach Rawlins? Even worse, what if the tornado lifted them into the sky and dumped them on the prairie.

Susan pushed with renewed effort. The wagon finally capsized and he gripped her arm. Pulling her away from the spinning wheels, he towed her to the other side.

"What if the wagon falls on us?" she shouted.

"It'll protect us from the wind."

"The horses!"

Michael ran to quiet them. They had jerked the wagon until it plowed furrows in the dry, cracked earth. Wind tore at her hair, ripping it loose from its bun. An opaque wall of rain abruptly drenched her clothing as she frantically searched for Michael. Shielding her eyes, she saw that he was freeing the horses from the wagon and attempting to picket them to prevent them from running. Rain was so intense that they disappeared from view.

"Under the wagon," he yelled when his hand found hers.

The roar sounded much like a train rushing toward them. Daylight disappeared as Michael found the space in the wagon box where the seat lifted it from the ground. He urged her to crawl inside. Wind sucked at her clothing as she tried to seek shelter among the contents of the overturned wagon. She felt Michael's hand pushing her forward, and used her dwindling strength to escape the wind and rain. Holding her breath, she prayed the wagon wouldn't lift into the sky, leaving them exposed to the storm.

Crawling alongside, he patted her back reassuringly as a loud tapping sound announced the arrival of hail. Rain blown into the wagon through their crawl space made Susan shiver until Michael moved closer to cradle her in his arms. She at first resisted but the warmth of his body changed her mind about the impropriety of his action. It was comforting to have someone to hang onto during the deadly storm.

"If we're lucky," he said near her ear, "the main part of the storm will pass us by entirely."

"And if it doesn't?" she said through chattering teeth.

"We won't have anything else to worry about, will we?"

Chapter Four

Dawn streaked the horizon as Jimmy led Big Red from the barn. Saddled and ready for the trip to the Masters' ranch, he waved to Ella, who stood watching from a store window. When he mounted the horse, he blew her a kiss. She needed him but protecting her from suspicion was even more pressing.

Big Red pranced in anticipation, almost unseating Jimmy when he leaned from the saddle to close the wire gate. The last thing they needed was for their few horses to leave the corral. The big sorrel switched gaits as they headed south. Immersed in his thoughts, Jimmy's anger grew as he envisioned what Ella had told him. Damn whoever was spreading rumors about his virtuous wife. He would repay them. Somehow.

The sun had begun its arc across the late spring sky when he slowed Big Red to a walk. A group of horsemen stood in the distance near the ruins of Masters' house. What would he say to them if they asked how he knew about the fire?

Trotting into the dooryard, he raised his hand in greeting. When they turned to acknowledge him, he uttered a cry of surprise. "What happened here?"

A grey-bearded neighbor squinted at him. "Don't know what caused the fire but somebody musta set it?"

"Why would anyone do that?"

"Beats the hell outa me. Masters kept to himself. Didn't believe in bein' neighborly."

"Where's his family?" Jimmy hated his own deception.

"Nobody seems to know, but we found a body in the ashes."

"Who?

"Masters himself, I reckon. I don't think his wife wears a belt buckle."

Jimmy dismounted and led Big Red to the circle of horsemen. "Let's see." Turning the tarnished buckle over in his hands, he told them he recognized it from Master's last visit to the road ranch.

"When was that?" an overalled man asked.

"Week or so ago. He came in asking if we needed anything repaired. I told him the buggy needed work so he took it with him. He said his tools were here in the barn."

"That right?"

Jimmy snapped his fingers. "I just remembered. He said his family was visiting relatives in Rawlins."

"Then his wife don't know nothin' about this," a third man said. "Poor woman. And her with that brood of kids."

"Yeah. Nothing to come back to."

Jimmy shook his head as sympathetically as he could manage. Edging back toward Big Red, he said, "It's a real tragedy, all right ...Well, I'm gonna check the barn to see if my buggy's been worked on." Tipping his hat in leaving, he heard grumbling behind him as he led the horse toward the barn.

"Hold on there, Averell. I'll go with you."

Jimmy felt his stomach flutter, but managed a thin smile.

When they entered the barn, it was several moments before their eyes adjusted to the dim light.

"Where do you s'pose he'd work on a buggy?" the bearded man asked.

"I don't know. He said he knew how to fix anything with wheels and that he needed the money, so I took him at his word."

"Masters wasn't doing so good, last I heard." Jimmy's companion pointed to the back of the barn. "Ain't that a buggy?"

"Yeah, looks like mine. I'll just hook up Big Red—"

"Hold on. We better wait for a lawman to git here."

"I don't see why. We need the buggy to visit a sick friend."

"How'd I know it's your's?"

Jimmy chewed his lip while he thought. Afraid his face would betray his embarrassment, he said, "There's a heart carved on the seat back with some initials."

The bearded man laughed. "Let's pull 'er out and take a look."

Tying Big Red's reins to a post, Jimmy helped him pull the buggy from the barn. A moment later, the man called to his companions to have a look. They then all shared in his amusement.

"Guess I'll take it on home now, if you gentleman don't mind."

Still laughing, they waved him on. Wasting no time, he hurried back to hitch up Big Red, who wasn't the least bit cooperative. Whispering to him, Jimmy said, "A bag of extra feed's waiting for you as soon as we get back to our own barn."

The gelding wasn't impressed and danced away from the traces. He should have brought another horse, but he would still be on the trail to the Master's ranch. Big Red was probably the fastest runner in Sweetwater Valley. Too bad he wasn't buggy broke.

"Need some help there, Averell?" one of the men called.

"No, thanks. Red's just feeling his oats this morning."

Glancing skyward at roiling clouds, James Averell silently prayed for all he was worth. "Please settle Red down and make him gentle. And forgive me for my stupidity."

It was several moments before the horse calmed long enough for Jimmy to hitch him to the buggy. When they started back down the trail, he could hear laughter in his wake. Doesn't matter, he told himself, as long as Ella's safe.

Big Red attempted to distance himself from the buggy as he bucked and crowhopped along the trail. Jimmy thought he might have to hide the buggy and return for it later with Old Blunder. The horse must have had similar thoughts because he ignored Jimmy's reins and ran off the trail. A ravine loomed ahead, large enough to swallow a good-sized ox.

Tugging at the reins and yelling for the horse to stop, Jimmy jumped before the buggy reached the gully. Big Red ran along the edge and came to a sudden stop. Turning his head to stare at his owner, who lay crumpled on the ground, the horse neighed as though he'd had the last laugh.

Dusting himself off, Jimmy said, "Okay, you win." After testing to make sure none of his appendages were broken, he hobbled to the buggy, which sat precariously on the edge. Even a slight breeze would send it careening into space. He tried pushing it forward but something was blocking its path. When he investigated, he saw that sagebrush trapped one wheel. If not for the plant, the buggy would have fallen into the ravine.

Glancing at his lack of shadow, he determined it was midday. He decided to leave the buggy where it stood and return with Old Blunder. Pulling a scrap of paper from his pocket, he used a stubby pencil to write a note stating that he would return to retrieve the buggy. Hopefully, no one would decide they needed it more.

The roar seemed to last forever, the wagon inches above their heads, trembling violently in the high wind. Why had she taken the chance of traveling with Michael when she could have ridden the train? Now she was going to die with him beside her. What would people say when they found their bodies together, entwined as though they were lovers?

She pushed him away.

"What's wrong, Susan?"

"How dare you force yourself on me."

"I'm only trying to protect you."

"I can take care of myself."

"So you've said." He angrily scooted backward through the crawl hole.

When she realized what he was doing, she tried to stop him. Too late. He was gone.

Pushing herself back through the hole, she knelt in the downpour and tried to locate him. A lightning flash provided enough light for her to see something dark on the ground and she crawled in that direction. Blinded by the rain, she reached out to touch what appeared to be a log. The tips of her fingers felt something wet and hairy. Horrified, she jerked her hand back. Was it an animal killed in the storm? She then heard a groan.

"Michael?" she shrieked.

"Get back under the wagon."

"What happened?"

"Something hit me."

She squinted into the wind and rain. Debris of every description was blowing past. Crouching over him, she noticed blood seeping from a wound on his forehead, which washed away in the rain.

He groaned again as he tried to get to his knees.

She screamed when something slimy slapped her face. Scraping it off with the back of her hand, she turned and crawled to the wagon. The hem of her dress caught on a sharp object, which tore when she pulled it free.

"Hurry," Michael yelled from behind her.

Safe for the moment under the wagon, they lay panting from exertion.

"Why in heaven's name did you go out there?"

"To check on the horses ... I need something to bandage my head."

Rolling onto her side, she pulled her knees to her chest and found the tear in the hem of her dress. Tugging, she ripped a long strip and handed it to him. "I'm sorry. If we live through this storm—"

"We will. I think the tornado passed us to the south, but not by much."

"Thank heavens, Michael. Are you badly hurt?"

"I'll live, but I'll never touch you again."

The late afternoon sun had already disappeared behind the highest peak of the Seminoe Mountains when Jimmy approached the corral. As soon as he dismounted, the cabin door flew open and Ella ran into his arms.

"The buggy?"

"I've got to take Blunder back to get it." He stooped

to brush dirt from his clothing and refused to meet her eyes.

"What happened?"

"You were right, as usual. Big Red refused the hitch."

"It'll be late before—"

"Doesn't matter. I'll grab a handful of jerky." Leaving her standing in the yard, he lifted the wire from the gate and led the gelding into the corral. Ella dashed into the store to grab whatever she could find. Before long he returned with Blunder.

"Be careful, Jimmy." She accepted a brief kiss and watched as he rode out of sight. Shivering, she relived Masters' assault and the resultant fire. Why hadn't she fought him off sooner, when he dragged her down the darkened hall? She had been in shock, she told herself, and it hadn't occurred to her that he would lie about his wife. She had believed him until she saw the empty bed.

Shrieking, she ran to their living quarters in the back of the store where she threw herself across the bed. How could she have been so stupid? What if someone had seen her in the buggy following Masters to his ranch? What if Jimmy was waylaid by angry neighbors before he could bring the buggy home? Ella banged her fists into the mattress. It was all her fault. She should have refused to go. No, she couldn't have done that, either. Helping neighbors was a way of life in Wyoming Territory.

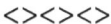

<><><>

When the rain stopped, Michael left the safety of the wagon to look around. Susan followed and was shocked to find a large amount of soggy sagebrush piled high atop the wagon.

"Where are the horses, Michael?"

"Do you see them?"

She shrank from his anger.

"How will we get to Rawlins?"

"We'll walk."

"What about our things?"

"Unless you want to carry them, we'll have to come back for them."

"But—" It was useless to argue so she followed him through the storm's debris.

"How far?"

"A few days unless we meet someone on the trail," he flung over his shoulder.

"What about food?"

Michael patted his hip where his pistol rode. "I've got lucifers in my pocket to start a fire."

"That's all we have to survive?"

He stopped to pull a knife from his boot.

"Everything we need."

Susan hitched up the torn hem of her dress and trudged after him. His long legs soon outdistanced hers and she was forced to run to keep up. It wasn't long before sunset. Where would they sleep?

A huge orange-red butte rose from the sagebrush to their right, not far from the North Platte River. Susan stopped to wonder at its beauty. Light from the setting sun streaked the western horizon when Michael decided to rest. Gathering sagebrush that had escaped the storm, he stomped them into something resembling pallets. Indicating one for her, he told her to try it on for size.

"You expect me to sleep on this?"

"You can sleep on the ground, if you choose."

Susan sat on the edge of the pallet and tried to make herself comfortable. Her legs ached and her feet felt as though she had walked across a bed of glass. "You're still angry with me, aren't you, Mister O'Brien?"

"You've made it quite clear that you don't need help from anyone."

She glanced at the ground. "I'm not accustomed to close proximity with a man."

"You can't be serious." He stopped collecting sagebrush and dropped down on his own pallet. "Were you raised in a nunnery?"

"Not quite. My family lived on a spur of the Ozark Mountains with no close neighbors. My father ran a sawmill and hauled wood to a railroad stop, so we didn't see many people, my sisters and I. When he died, Uncle Jacob, my mother's brother, helped us move to a small town on the Arkansas border. That's where I met my friend, Mary Lynn."

"But you speak so well. I thought you must have an education."

"My mother was a teacher. She made sure that we girls had plenty of books to read. After we moved to town, she arranged a scholarship for me to attend the university. That's where I met a horticulturist who took me under his wing."

"I see. So that's why—."

"Don't think you can take advantage of me because I'm—"

"Naive? What kind of man do you think I am?"

Susan rose from her sagebrush pallet to stand over him. "Someone with a terrible temper. Someone I should be afraid of."

Michael started to rise but she stopped him. "Keep your distance, O'Brien. Come near me again and you'll regret it."

He laughed as he got to his feet. "And just what will you do if I touch you again?"

"My father taught me the art of self-defense and I won't hesitate—"

He reached to pull her into his arms, but doubled over when she stomped on his instep and twisted to elbow him in the stomach. Gasping, he fell across his sagebrush bed.

Folding arms across her chest, she said, "Isn't it time to shop for dinner?"

"Fine way to treat your benefactor." Getting to his feet, he started off in the direction she had pointed. A small herd of deer stood watching them.

"I hope you brought along some salt and pepper." she called after him.

Chapter Five

Rattling panes woke Ella from her nap and she rushed to peer from the nearest window. The air was filled with sand and debris and she couldn't see past the frame.

Jimmy!

Rushing to open the road ranch door, she lifted the timber from its casings. A loud thump sounded as though someone were knocking. It had to be him. When the storm came up, he must have decided to return home. Unlatching the heavy planked door, she almost lost her balance when it blew open. Sand and grit pelted her as she tried to push it closed. Bracing her feet, she leveraged her weight against the door, but not before rain had drenched her clothing. Turning her back, she pushed with all her strength, crying out in relief when she heard the door latch click. She'd glimpsed the corral posts leaning toward the east, the wire fence snapping in the wind. What should she do? The boys were at her homestead, too far away to help. She prayed they'd had enough warning to reach her cabin before the main storm struck.

Where was Jimmy? Had he taken refuge from the

storm? Tears blurred her vision as she fell to her knees on the gritty floor to pray.

The store had a window facing south and she tried to scan the trail, but found the glass coated with sand and prairie dust. Frantic, she pulled on her old winter cap to protect her from flying objects. Opening the window little more than a crack, she peered out, debris instantly assaulting her. Cupping her hands to protect her eyes, she leaned further into the yard, the wind jerking the cap from her head and rain splattered her hair. Visibility was near zero.

Struggling to close the window, she heard the door open to their living quarters. She screamed when she noticed what appeared to be a ghost. Coated with alkali dust, he brushed it from his arms and shook it from his hair. He, too, had lost his cap to the wind.

"Tornado," Jimmy said. "Looks like it took out one of the sheds."

"Doesn't matter as long as you're safe." She hugged him, despite his coating of dust.

"I've got to make sure the boys are all right."

"Don't go until the storm passes. There's nothing you can do until then."

Jimmy hung his head. "I know, Ella. This is all Masters' fault."

"Masters?"

"If he hadn't tricked you, we'd have been prepared."

"Big Red?"

"In the barn. The funnel cloud seems to have passed just to the north of us."

"But the boys—"

"With any luck it passed between the store and your cabin."

Tears streaked Ella's face. "They've got to be all right."

He turned and started for the door.

"Wait, I'll go with you."

"It's too dangerous. You might want to start cleaning up the mess." He stomped his feet to show her how much sand had filtered into the log dwelling. "The boys and I will help when we get back."

She watched as he made his way to the door. The wind seemed to have calmed considerably and she prayed she'd soon see the boys again.

Michael shot a young doe, then cut its throat to bleed it out. After he had skinned the hindquarters, he cut off a chunk of meat. When told to start a campfire, Susan began gathering sagebrush, the only fuel in sight. When she had an armload of the gray, bitter-smelling branches, she dropped them and struck a match, placing it on top of the pile.

"Don't waste lucifers. That's no way to start a fire."

She stepped back, appalled by his disgusted expression. Telling her to prop up the deer to keep it from the dirt, he rearranged the sagebrush with bloodied hands and sheltered a small blaze with his body.

"This is the way it's done. How you're going to survive on your own is beyond me," he grumbled. Michael twisted a branch from a sage plant, which he used as a spit to cook the meat over the campfire. They said nothing while the venison roasted. Susan made a face when she bit into a small offering once he deemed it done. She laid it aside, deciding she wasn't hungry.

"Better eat," he said. "We don't know when we'll find more food. The meat wouldn't be so tough if I was able to hang it up for a while before we cooked it."

She shook her head. "I can't. It tastes terrible. And that poor deer—"

Michael laughed. "The Lord provides us with food on the hoof. Why do you think they're here?" Still smiling, he handed her another small slab of venison.

Closing her eyes, she took another bite and forced herself to swallow.

"That's better. You'll make a frontier woman yet."

Susan sighed, thinking the trip had been one of her worst decisions.

Michael added more sagebrush to the fire and she then helped erect the tent. She was vaguely aware that he had kept the fire burning during the night. Exhausted from little sleep, she arose the following morning and scanned the horizon.

"Did you hear the coyotes howling last night?"

"No, Michael. Did you?"

"They were serenading us and you missed it?"

She stood and dusted herself off. "I'm surprised you didn't cook one for breakfast."

He chuckled. "If that's what you want." He started off into the sagebrush.

"No! I'll eat venison." She cringed at the thought. What she really wanted was water. She found the canteen on the opposite side of the campfire and shook it to determine how much was left. Unscrewing the cap, she tilted it to take a drink. Before she had satisfied her thirst, he grabbed it from her.

"Just a sip. We don't want to run out of water."

"We're going to die out here, aren't we, Michael?"

"Of course not. If we follow the trail, we should arrive in Rawlins within four or five days."

"If some animal doesn't attack us. Or the Indians."

He laughed. "This is eighteen eighty-nine. Most Indians are on reservations. The only animals we have to worry about are wolves."

"Wolves?" She shaded her eyes and gazed in each

direction. "Are they out here?"

"That's why I kept the fire burning last night."

"Why didn't you warn me?"

"Because you wouldn't have been able to sleep."

They forced down as much venison as they could eat, then started back on the trail to the southwest. The small town of Rawlins was out there beyond the morning haze.

When the sun was overhead, Susan thought she heard a rattling noise. Michael had already turned back to face the east. A battered wagon pulled by two mismatched horses was coming toward them on the trail. They stepped aside and waited. When the wagon was opposite them, a grizzled old man tipped his hat and asked why they were walking in the middle of nowhere. He introduced himself as Montana Dan.

The wagon driver wiped mid-day sweat from his brow. "Musta been a short touch-down 'cause I shore didn't see no twister."

Michael frowned. "Unfortunately for us, it wrecked our wagon and we lost the horses."

Susan stepped closer and gave the old man her best smile. "Do you have room for us in the wagon?"

"Shore, missy. One a you can ride up front with me."

She asked Michael to help her into the wagon bed. He then took a seat next to Dan. Seating was uncomfortable and she tried to find a bare spot. Something was hidden beneath the tarps and she lifted an end flap once they were on their way. To her dismay, the wagon was loaded with guns—pistols, rifles and shotguns. Her father had been a gun collector and she was well acquainted with firearms. She planned to buy several of her own while in Rawlins.

Was the old man a gun runner? Where had he purchased guns in this desolate part of the country? Montana Dan must have acquired them in his home state. Billings, perhaps. She studied his back, noticing a long diagonal tear in his plaid shirt. Leaning forward, she saw one of his boots propped on the foot rail. It was well scuffed and looked as old as the man himself. Gun running must not pay well in Wyoming Territory. Then again, maybe someone had hired him to deliver the weapons.

"Where are you going, Mister Dan?"

He half turned to stare at her. "Rawlins."

She nodded and continued to survey the road they had just traveled. Red dust swirled into the wagon, making her cough. "Mind if I cover myself with one of these tarps?" she yelled.

"Go right ahead, little lady. Just don't let the dust get on them guns."

That gave her pause. He must be transporting them legally, if he didn't mind that she saw them. Then again, maybe he planned to use one to rob and shoot them both. Susan felt like slapping herself. She'd read too many dime novels about the west. The old man must be trustworthy or Michael wouldn't be sitting beside him. Or would he? She wasn't sure about Michael, either. She turned to stare at the back of his head. Were the two men in cahoots? No, her imagination was running away, like the horses. Clutching her reticule to her chest, she resigned herself to a bumpy, uncomfortable ride. At least it was better than walking.

She anxiously watched the sky, concerned there might be another storm. This time they had tarps to keep them dry, but what would the old man do if his guns got wet?

Jimmy returned with the three boys. His nineteen-year–old nephew, Ralph Cole, had arrived from Wisconsin in April to spend some time at the ranch. His mother hoped that his health would improve in Wyoming.

Eleven-year-old Gene Crowder had a thatch of hair the color of hay and fourteen-year-old John DeCorey's unruly mop resembled blackbird feathers. Ella rushed to hug them before leading them to the wood stove where she had prepared a pot of cocoa.

"They made it back to the cabin all right," Jimmy said, removing his dusty coat, "but I'm afraid your cabin took some damage."

"All that matters is you're safe." Ella wiped a tear from her eye.

"You shoulda seen what happened, ma'am." Young Gene's eyes appeared as large as his cup. "The wind picked up a calf and throwed it over the fence."

Ella bit her lip. "I'm glad it wasn't one of you boys."

"I tried to help the calf up but I think it broke a leg."

"I'll take care of it." Jimmy shoved his arms back in the sleeves of his coat. "We can't let the calf suffer."

Ella nodded sadly. "Looks like we'll have veal for supper sometime soon. We haven't had that in a while."

The boys smiled and licked cocoa from their upper lips.

"Where we gonna sleep tonight, Miss Ella," Johnny asked. "A post broke a winda outa the cabin and we tried to stuff a board in the hole but—"

"It's all right. You can help Jimmy board it up tomorrow. And you can all sleep in the guest cabin."

They camped that night along the North Plate River. Montana Dan had a small tent that wasn't large enough for two, so they slept along the sandy bank. Too exhausted to worry about their comfort, Susan used her reticule for a pillow and promptly nodded off in Michael's tent. During the night she heard an animal howl nearby and tensed, hoping the men were prepared for a possible attack. She drifted off again and awoke with faint daylight filtering into the tent.

"Time to rise and shine," a gruff voice said.

Susan sat up and yawned. Twisting her long blond hair into a bun, she held it in place with a tortoise shell clasp from her reticule. Her dress was wrinkled, torn and dirty but she was beyond caring. She would wash up in the river while the men prepared breakfast. The late spring morning was warm with a hint of summer in the air. The river gurgled and danced over large rocks as it flowed northeast toward the railroad town of Casper.

Michael was busy fueling the campfire. He glanced up and smiled when she left the tent. "Good morning, Miss Cameron. Sleep well?"

"I did until the wolf howled."

"Just a mangy ol' coyote," Dan informed her.

Susan walked down the river bank and knelt to scoop a palm full of water.

"Careful, miss," Dan warned. "The river's cold as a snow bank."

Susan agreed as she splashed the icy water on her face. She was ready for a steaming cup of coffee one of the men had prepared. Michael held out a mug as she approached.

"Your turn," he said. "We've each had a cup."

Susan looked from the cup to each of the men, wondering whether they had washed it.

Dan must have read her thoughts, "Dipped it in the river after your pardner used it."

"Partner?" She glanced at Michael, who lowered his head.

"Shore. He was tellin' me 'bout his vet's office in Casper and that you was gonna help him get it started."

She placed both hands on her hips and glared at Michael. "Really? That's news to me."

Michael rose to his full height, a good foot above her. "Unless you're independently wealthy, you'll need to work during the winter months. You're only required to spend seven consecutive months on your homestead and most of the women homesteaders teach school during the winter. That's how they can afford to buy necessities."

His speech over, he sat down to feed small branches to the campfire.

"You're presuming a lot, Mister O'Brien. What if I don't want to work in your office?"

"Where else will you find a job, Miss Cameron?"

"In Rawlins, perhaps."

Montana Dan muttered as he walked back to his wagon. "That's why I never got hitched. Never liked no danged arguin'."

They apologized to their host and sat glaring at one another across the campfire.

Men! They always know what's best for women. Like Dan, she'd never marry. She could make it on her own. No wonder so many single women decided to homestead alone.

Chapter Six

Next morning they rode to Ella's cabin in the supply wagon to assess the damage. The prairie was littered with sagebrush and all manner of trash. She spotted several worn leather halters and a woven basket from a nearby Indian encampment. The barbed wire fence had collected its own souvenirs from the storm and would keep the boys busy setting things straight.

Inside the broken cabin window was a splintered fence rail. Ella sighed, thankful the boys had not been hurt. The roof had received some damage but it wouldn't take long to make repairs. Overall they had been lucky. Thank goodness Jimmy had arrived home unscathed the previous evening. It didn't matter if the buggy had been blown into the next county. They would buy another when they could afford one.

While sweeping sand from the cabin, she overheard men's voices. Peering from the broken window, she recognized Harvey Jones from the nearby ranch owned by Albert Bothwell. His excited voice told Jimmy that his boss was plotting to run all the homesteaders out of Sweetwater Valley.

"We've talked about this before," she heard her husband say.

Harvey cleared his throat. "I know, but he's gettin' the other cattlemen together for a meetin'."

"They have no legal right to run homesteaders off their property. Bothwell and the other cattlemen don't own the land. They've just been using it to graze their cattle."

"I'd be plumb careful, Jimmy. When you blocked Bothwell's access to Hoss Crick with your fences, you made a dangerous enemy. And your woman's cabin is smack dab in the middle of Bothwell's hay meadow. He aims to get it back."

"It's not Bothwell's hay meadow. Ella filed a legal homestead claim on government property, just as I did. The cattlemen have no right to claim ownership of seventy-five miles of the Sweetwater River."

"Well, I gotta get back to the herd. Just thought you oughta know."

Jimmy thanked him and shook his hand, warning *him* to be careful.

A chill crawled down Ella's spine as she went about cleaning up the cabin. She worried the cattlemen would take their anger out on all homesteaders. They would probably collectively hire an entire army of gunslingers to accomplish the task.

Susan gasped when she glimpsed the rugged beauty of Sweetwater Valley with its nearly level plain, which seemed to stretch into infinity. Occasional rocky hills rose from the sagebrush-studded land as though monuments to nature, the Seminoe Mountains hovering in the background. They had crossed over a North Platte River bridge after they left Casper. Once in Dan's wagon, they forded several creeks when they entered the Sweetwater Valley. Dan said they were traveling the Oregon-Mormon Trail, which had served as a major thoroughfare for some half a million emigrants as late as 1870. Few travelers now followed the same route although deep, permanent ruts made by covered wagons were still clearly visible.

When Dan turned the horses south toward the Seminoe Mountains, Susan noticed several log buildings in the distance. She sighed, anxious to leave the wagon as well as the rough trail.

"Some nice homesteaders run a road ranch along Hoss Crick," Dan said. "We'll stop in and I'll introduce you. It ain't far and maybe they can tell you where's the best place to file a homestead."

They had just stopped in the dooryard when another wagon pulled in behind. Jimmy jumped down and helped Ella from the wagon. The younger boys were already running toward the store when the driver of the other wagon raised his hand in salute.

Jimmy walked over to shake the older man's hand when he dismounted the wagon box. "Good to see you again, Dan. Headed for Rawlins?"

The bewhiskered man nodded. "Thought I'd stop by to wet my whistle and introduce you to a young lady who's interested in homesteadin' on her own."

Jimmy nodded at Susan as Michael helped her from the wagon. She appeared delicate with small bones, blond hair, fair but sunburned skin, and large blue eyes. She resembled a porcelain doll left out in the sun too long. He knew Ella would be more than willing to befriend her.

Ella welcomed them as though they were old friends

and invited them into the store. They always left the door unlocked in case someone was in need while they were away. Jimmy's young nephew Ralph Cole was seated in the store reading. At the small bar against the far wall, Jimmy poured the two male visitors foaming mugs of beer to wash the trail dust from their throats. Ella, meanwhile, asked that Susan accompany her to the small café cabin where she prepared a pot of tea. She wondered why Susan had decided to homestead in Wyoming Territory.

Susan stretched her arms and legs, grateful to be standing upright after the long wagon ride. "I've been reading about the freedom and equality offered here to women. Holding office and serving on juries. That's something unavailable in Missourah."

Ella smiled. "So it's freedom and independence that you're seeking?"

"I need to be my own person, without some man telling me what to do or how I should think." When she noticed the expression on Ella's face, she said, "I'm probably telling this to the wrong person. You seem happily married."

Ella hesitated. "Women who marry before they prove up on their land can lose their homesteads, so—"

"That's not fair."

"You won't tell anyone?"

"Of course not. That's discrimination of the highest order."

"I'm glad you agree."

"Forgive me for asking, but your accent makes me wonder where you're from."

Ella lowered her eyes as though embarrassed. "I was born in Canada and my parents are Scottish and Irish immigrants. I guess I still speak my family's brogues."

"It's lovely. Don't ever lose it."

Nodding her thanks, Ella asked, "Where do you plan

to homestead?"

"I love this beautiful valley. Do you know of good land nearby where I can file a homestead claim?"

Ella's smile waned. "I think there are a few Desert Land acres still unclaimed—"

Susan waited for the rest, but Ella busied herself gathering tea cups and cookies. At last her hostess said, "The land has been illegally grazed for years by cattlemen who want to rid the valley of homesteaders."

"Then why are *you* here?"

"We have half a section of land between us that was legally filed on. And we also love it here."

"I understand."

"I'd like to have you as a neighbor, Susan, but you'd have to be prepared for trouble."

Susan said that her father had taught her to use both handguns and rifles. And that she planned to arm herself in Rawlins.

"We'll be close by if you ever need help."

Susan sighed and briefly closed her eyes. She had been on the verge of returning home until she met the Averells. Now homesteading might be possible. It was all going to work out and she wouldn't have to depend on Michael O'Brien.

Jimmy drew a rough map of the available land and repeated Ella's warning. Dan was ready to leave and Susan took the map, thanking them for their hospitality. Boarding the wagon, she waved goodbye until the Averells were out of sight.

Dan later halted his wagon for a mid-day meal at Independence Rock, where hundreds of thousands of emigrants had stopped to rest during several decades of travel along the California-Oregon and Mormon trails. It was a place to camp and carve their names in the huge monolith on their way to Utah and the West Coast.

Susan thought the rock resembled a large overturned bowl. Climbing down from the wagon, she made her way through sagebrush to have a closer look. Running her hand over the granite surface, she read countless names and inscriptions left by travelers as early as 1813.

Dan told her that a group of rowdy emigrants had blown off a section of the rock with dynamite one Fourth of July, destroying some of the names and carvings. But more peaceful gatherings had also taken place, including marriage ceremonies and baptisms in the nearby Sweetwater River.

They ate canned beans and Susan resumed scanning the sky for another possible tornado. But the sun shone brightly, the temperature rising close to what she imagined was a hundred degrees. How she wished she had the sunbonnet she'd lost in the storm.

While rinsing the dishes in the river, she overheard the two men discussing her plan to homestead in the area. "That little missy shouldn't be out here on her own," Dan said. "Settlers ain't welcome in this part of the country. The cattlemen are dead set on runnin' 'em off."

Michael turned to determine whether Susan was listening. She pretended not to hear.

"Where's the best land for homesteading?" Michael asked him.

"Sweetwater Valley's a good place for crops, if that's what she has in mind. Land along the Sweetwater River might still be available under the Desert Land Act."

Susan made a mental note to ask about the valley when they reached Rawlins. She would listen to everything Montana Dan had to say. He must travel regularly through the territory, picking up various bits of news and information. She could be happy in this valley but the Averells' warning about the land-grabbing cattlemen had her worried. She needed to arm herself against invaders and hoped that she could file a claim near the Averell's properties. It would be nice to befriend Ella and have a store nearby to buy some of her supplies.

A lone rider approached at a gallop as they were preparing to leave. Dark-skinned and curly-haired, he smiled beneath his heavy mustache when he recognized Montana Dan. Dismounting, he grasped Dan's hand and patted him on the back. Dan introduced him as Tom Sun, who grazed large herds of cattle in the area. His ranch house was located a few miles down the trail to the southeast near Devil's Gate, a deep V-shaped split in the granite formation at the end of the Rattlesnake Range. Dan later told them that dozens of Mormon handcart emmigrants had died in the vicinity during an early fall snowstorm.

Tom Sun was friendly and charming until he learned that Susan was on her way to Rawlins to file for homestead land "This is cattle country," he said, his thick, dark brows lowering over deep set brown eyes. "Not enough water for both farming and grazing."

"But the Sweetwater River and the creeks—" Susan said.

"Cricks can dry up in the summer." He remounted his horse and, with a wave to Dan, headed back in the direction he had come.

"French Canadian," Dan told them. "Nice fella but he has quite a temper when he gets riled."

Susan's stomach churned and she wondered whether she should look for land elsewhere. Gazing about the valley she thought no, this was where she wanted to build her cabin and live forever. Cattlemen be damned.

Chapter Seven

Two days later they arrived in Rawlins during early
evening. After supper at the Rawlins House, they climbed
the stairs to their rooms. Susan resolved to be first in line
at the filing office the following morning, so she cleaned
her dress as best she could at the small wash basin. She
then smoothed it out on the other narrow bed in her
room. Covering herself with a quilt, she settled in for a
few hours' sleep. It wasn't long before someone banged
on her door.

A woman's high-pitched voice called, "I have another
guest who needs to sleep in the room."

Susan rose, wrapping the quilt about her. Light from
the saloon across the street cast eerie shadows on the
walls as she made her way to the door. Opening it wide
enough to peer into the hall, she saw a woman with
frizzy red hair holding an oil lamp. Her scandalously
skimpy dress didn't manage to cover her knees. One
eye was swollen and she limped into the room on a shoe
with a broken heel.

"Good heavens." Susan gasped as she noticed the
rooming house manager retreating down the hall. "What

happened to you?"

"Saloon fight." The words were clipped, her voice husky.

Susan hurried to the bed to snatch up her dress before the woman sat on it. Looking about she spotted a rickety chair and draped the dress over it.

"You were fighting—?"

"No, I wasn't fast enough to get out of the way."

"But what are you doing here?"

"Somebody took my room."

Dan and Michael, most likely. The saloon girl—although she was much too old to be called a girl—stood half a foot taller than Susan and a good many pounds heavier. She wasn't about to argue with her. Susan asked if there was anything she could do for the woman, which she immediately regretted when the woman eyed Susan's reticule. Picking it up and pretending to locate something inside, she reclined on the bed and placed the drawstring bag beside her. Wrapping the quilt securely around her, Susan rolled onto her side and pretended to sleep as she watched the woman through narrowed eyes.

Her companion had nothing with her and Susan wondered where she had left her things. She watched her toss her shoes at the wall, blow out the hurricane lamp and climb into bed without undressing. She must be in pain.

Susan debated whether to offer to get something for her discolored eye but decided against it. The bartender had probably applied an ice pack after the fight took place. She shuddered when she considered what the other participants in the fight must look like. Before long she heard the woman snoring and covered her ears with the quilt. She knew she'd get little sleep that night and worried she wouldn't wake in time to take her place at the head of the filing office line.

<><><>

Sunlight filtered into the room when she awakened. The other bed was unoccupied and Susan panicked. Unrolling herself from the quilt, she found her reticule where she had left it. Sighing, she looked for her dress, which had fallen to the floor. Attempting to shake out the wrinkles, she gave in to frustration and allowed herself a few tears. Dashing her face with cold water from the wash basin, she dried off and dressed.

No time for breakfast. She hurried to the filing office and was surprised to find no line awaiting her. When she went inside, a hollow-faced older man stood alone behind the counter. When told where she wanted to file a homestead claim, he frowned.

"Sure you want to live there, miss?"

"Certainly. Why do you ask?"

"That's grazing country. Big cattle herds in Sweetwater Valley."

"So I've been told."

His expression was sympathetic. "Not the place for a young lady such as yourself."

Susan fumed. "I can take care of myself."

He shrugged, his expression suggesting, *Don't say I didn't warn you.*

A 160-acre unclaimed parcel was located southeast of Jimmy's homestead. Together with Ella's acreage, they formed a three-sided square around Albert Bothwell's illegal ranch. She told him she would take it. When the papers had been filled out, signed and the $1.25 an acre fee paid, she hurried over to the general store to buy a handgun as well as another dress and undergarments. Excited, she hoped she could hire someone to take her back to retrieve her luggage.

Taking her purchases to the Rawlins House, she spotted Michael and Dan at a table near the window. Michael stood to pull a chair for her when she approached.

He then offered to take her back to the wagon and her homestead land. She refused, saying she would hire someone. She wouldn't allow him to talk her into returning to Casper as his veterinary assistant.

"It's no imposition, Susan. I have to retrieve the wagon so I can load up the supplies I bought from the retiring veterinarian."

"But the wagon is broken."

Michael laughed. "Nothing I can't fix."

"But how will we get there?"

Dan wiped his mouth with a napkin. "I'm headed back that way tomorrow mornin' early. You're welcome to come along."

Susan groaned. She didn't relish riding in the back of the wagon again. Hesitating, she said, "Thank you, Dan. I'd be pleased to ride along beside you."

Dan's grin spread beneath his large, bushy mustache. From the corner of her eye, she noticed Michael's frown. Before he could object, she told them about her homestead claim. Dan agreed that it was a good place to build a cabin. "But it's in Bothwell's grazing area," he said. "And there's no water on that piece of land that I know of."

"I think the Averells will allow me to dig a ditch along the edge of their land to water."

Dan shook his head, but said nothing more.

After breakfast, Susan hurried back to her room at the hotel to change clothes. The dress she had worn for days was ruined and she would dispose of it later. Uncertain what to do with her purchases, particularly the handgun and ammunition, she decided to ask if she could leave them with the hotel manager until the following morning. The woman who worked in the saloon might return and she didn't trust her.

Descending the stairs, she overheard men's voices from the main floor. Two working men by the looks of them. They were discussing building materials for a cabin. Susan stood at the foot of the stairs until they noticed her and dipped their heads in greeting. She asked if either man was willing to build her cabin.

The tall, burly man smiled and said, "When do you want us to start?"

"Next week would be wonderful. Are you available?"

"We are. Where do you want to build your cabin?"

"Sweetwater Valley near the Averell's Road Ranch."

His shorter companion coughed and glanced at his partner. "You forgot about that job we promised down at Point of Rocks, Carl."

"Oh, yeah, that should take a good six months."

"Six months? Is there anyone else who can build my cabin?"

Carl scratched his head and said that he didn't know of anyone. They turned on their heels and left when she accused them of fearing the cattlemen.

Susan returned to her room to change clothes, then descended the stairs and walked out onto the dusty street. Spotting the nearby newspaper office, she dodged between horses and wagons to reach the other side. A young man wearing an ink stained apron said the latest edition of the newspaper wouldn't be available until that afternoon. She then asked if he knew of someone who would build her a cabin.

"Only two that I know are in town at the moment," he said. "I saw 'em headed for the hotel."

Susan sighed. So everyone was afraid of the cattleman named Bothwell, or didn't want to antagonize him. She might have to accept Michael's help after all. Working in a veterinary office wasn't to her liking, but she didn't have the patience to teach school. Perhaps she could find a job in Rawlins during the winter months to earn enough money for supplies. She'd saved enough to purchase lumber for her cabin and other necessary items. But would she have water to grow the crops she planned to sustain her. Wyoming was arid and she knew there wasn't sufficient rainfall. Maybe she had been hasty in filing without getting permission from the Averells. What if they refused her a trench to bring water to her property? A slight chill of fear caused her to shiver in the morning heat.

She walked out of the office and spotted a young boy standing on the boardwalk holding a basket of puppies. He asked if she owned a dog. When she shook her head, he withdrew a squirming brown ball of fur. Susan reached to pet the puppy's head and it licked her hand.

"Cute, ain't he?" the boy said, grinning.

Susan took the puppy and cuddled it against her. "How much?"

"He's free, ma'am. Our dog Emma had ten pups and we can't keep 'em all." The boy's tattered shirttail waved in the breeze and his dingy pants were much too short above his tanned bare feet.

She handed the puppy back long enough to rummage in her bag. Withdrawing a large silver certificate with Martha Washington's image from her reticule, she gave it to the boy and reclaimed the puppy.

"What's your name, son?"

"Alexander, ma'am."

"Then I'll call my puppy Alex."

Smiling, the boy stubbed his toe on the boardwalk. She wished him luck in giving away the rest of his puppies, then crossed the street to the hotel. The balding manager immediately blocked her path, telling her in no uncertain terms that dogs weren't allowed in his establishment. Susan hugged the sleeping dog and turned to leave. She remembered Montana Dan's wagon. Surely he wouldn't mind an overnight guest.

She found the wagon parked near the livery stable and hesitated. Reaching over the rear of the wagon she discovered the bed was empty. Placing the puppy under the tarp, she decided to leave him there, but a moment later, Alex began to whimper. Before long he was yapping. Susan lifted him from the wagon and returned to the corner where the boy still stood.

"I'll give you more money if you'll keep the puppy until tomorrow. Come here early and I'll take him with me."

Alexander grinned and placed the puppy back with the rest of the litter. "He'll be a good guard dog, ma'am. Like his mama."

"I know he will. Now, don't forget to be here at sunup and I'll take Alex with me." She patted the boy's blond head and left again for the hotel. *A guard dog is exactly what I need. Maybe I should have taken two.*

Chapter Eight

No one shared her room that night and Susan slept soundly. Next morning while she was getting dressed, someone rapped at her door. Michael stood in the hallway grinning when she turned the glass knob moments later.

"Ready for breakfast, Miss Cameron?"

"Of course, Mister O'Brien." *Let's keep this relationship formal as long as possible.* "Where's Mister Dan?"

"Apparently sleeping off an overindulgence last night."

"Don't you think we should invite him to breakfast?"

"I thought we could spend some time together."

Susan stepped out into the hallway, slamming the door. "You're much too presumptuous, Mister O'Brien. I have no intention of sharing time alone with you." *Is that a smirk on his face?*

"We'll be properly chaperoned in the restaurant, Miss Cameron."

Her stomach growled before she could refuse. "Oh, all right." She obediently followed him down the hall.

A large platter of eggs, potatoes and ham appeared before her as soon as she was seated. "What's this?" she said. "Someone else's breakfast?"

"I ordered it for you, Susan."

She pushed the platter toward him and rose from the table. "This is exactly the reason I decided to homestead on my own. Men have always decided for me."

He stood, eyes pleading. "I was just trying to please you. Sit down and order whatever you like."

Hesitating, her hunger got the best of her. When she resumed her seat, Michael waved the waitress over. "I'll have half of what he's about to eat," she said.

Michael smiled. "That's what I like about you, Miss Cameron. You always know what you want. You'll make a homesteader yet."

When they finished breakfast, she asked how he proposed to help her build her cabin when there was nowhere on her land to stay.

"I'm sure the Averells will invite you to stay with them, and I can live in my tent."

"You won't try to shanghai me as your assistant?"

He sighed. "You've made it quite clear that you're not interested. I'm sure I can find another attractive young woman to fill the job."

Susan nodded. Michael didn't give up easily. She then remembered her puppy and bolted from her chair. Michael rose to follow. She found Alexander seated on the edge of the boardwalk, three puppies remaining in the basket on his lap. He seemed to be dozing. *Poor little fellow.* Susan touched his shoulder to wake him.

"I'm sorry to be late. I'll take another puppy to make it up to you."

Alexander's large brown eyes widened and his smile was so sweet that she wanted to take him as well. When she picked up the puppies only one furry ball remained.

"I'll take the other one," Michael said, handing him more money.

The boy whooped and ran into the middle of the dusty

street before turning to thank them both. Susan was afraid a wagon would run him over. Turning the corner, he disappeared from view.

"That was good of you, Michael."

He made a face. "This little fellow needs some medical attention. His litter mates have seriously chewed his ears."

"Will Dan mind three puppies littering his wagon?"

"I think the only thing Dan cares about this morning is surviving his night on the town."

They found Dan at the livery stable brushing his team. He growled a "good morning" when he noticed them. When he spotted the puppies, he managed a weak grin. "Better get them critters some scraps at the butcher shop afore we leave."

Michael placed them all in the wagon. "Good idea." He turned to Susan. "I'll help Dan with the horses while you—"

"I'll help Dan while *you* collect the scraps."

Michael's lips set in a firm line. Turning smartly, he started off down the main street.

"That was mighty plucky of you, Miss Cameron."

"Susan," she said. "Let's get the team ready, shall we?"

Jimmy took Ella in his arms. "Susan seems like a nice person."

"She is and I'm worried that Mister Bothwell will make life miserable for her. She doesn't realize the danger she'll place herself in by homesteading on what he considers his grazing land."

"He doesn't dare harm any of us, Ella."

"I hope you're right. But even Harvey Jones thinks he's up to no good."

"Harvey's an alarmist and he's afraid something will happen to *you*."

Ella felt her cheeks burn. She hoped the cowpoke would transfer his infatuation to Susan. Perhaps Harvey would volunteer to help build her cabin.

"What about our fence that was torn down."

"The boys repaired it. It could have been an elk that ran through it."

"But Jimmy—"

"Stop worrying. Bothwell doesn't have a legal leg to stand on."

Ella tried but was unable to set her worry aside. She had only seen Bothwell twice but his eyes frightened her. He looked at her much as Masters had done. She shivered in the early summer heat, unable to block the memory of Master's attack and the subsequent fire. What was it about her that attracted that kind of attention from men? Her long brown hair and dark eyes were ordinary. She viewed her matronly figure in the mirror and shook her head. Ella made her own clothes and was conservative in her dress. She had never flirted with any man, other than her husband. Tears threatened and she gave into them.

The trip back to the damaged wagon was uneventful with Dan telling stories of his adventures in Montana and Wyoming. Susan wondered whether he was exaggerating about the Indian attacks. His hands and face were scarred, including a six-inch welt along his left cheek, so he was probably telling the truth. His long white hair and beard flapped in the wind and she wondered why he didn't visit a barbershop. What bothered her most was the sympathetic expression on his face when he looked at her. Did he consider her an imbecile who couldn't survive on her own?

When they left Dan's wagon, he said he'd stop by to check on her during his return trip. She bit her lip to prevent herself from telling him not to bother. She liked Dan and didn't want to alienate him, but she didn't need a caretaker. Michael was a different story. The less she saw of him the better. After her cabin was built and his animal clinic established, she never wanted to see him again.

The puppies and their purchases were lifted from Dan's wagon and Michael untied the horses he'd bought in Rawlins, which had trailed behind the wagon. He had ridden one of them bareback for a while but decided to ride in the wagon bed. Susan's stomach was queasy as she watched Dan's wagon pull away. She was alone again with Michael.

Once the puppies were placed on the ground, they scattered in three directions. Before she had a chance to catch them, Michael took her arm and led her to his own wagon, telling her to help him push it back on its wheels.

"The pups will come back when they're hungry," he said.

"But the wolves—"

"We'll put them in the wagon as soon as it's upright."

Susan watched over her shoulder as the puppies disappeared into the sagebrush. Stooping to lift the wagon box, she mustered all her strength but it didn't seem enough. She then heard Dan's wagon returning.

"Don't know why I didn't stick around to help right the wagon." he said, climbing down from his own.

Within minutes Michael's wagon was upright, although a little worse for wear. Susan ran to capture the puppies. She found one of them chewing on a dead animal that must have been killed by the tornado. Another had a sagebrush limb in its mouth. The third puppy was nowhere in sight. She carried two of them to the wagon, where Michael was repairing a wheel. She then skirted sagebrush in the opposite direction. Calling Alex, she searched for nearly an hour before she heard him yelping. She found him in a hole just large enough to hold him prisoner. Hugging him, she stroked his fur until he stopped crying and fell asleep.

When she arrived at the wagon, Michael announced they were travel ready and she climbed aboard clutching Alex.

"You're going to spoil that dog, Susan."

"That's my choice, Mister O'Brien. He'll make a fine watch dog."

"And the female?"

"She'll produce a fine litter of pups once she's grown."

Michael laughed. "Good luck keeping them apart until then."

Men! Was spreading their seed the only thing on their minds? And the very idea of a brother and sister mating made her ill. Perhaps she could persuade Michael to trade his male for her female.

They rode in silence until they reached a level riverbank that someone had cleared of sage. The owner had probably gone to Casper for supplies. Michael squinted at the setting sun, saying he doubted the homesteader would return that day.

Susan busied herself building a campfire and prepared a meal of dried biscuits and beans. She had been too tired to argue about chores and ignored the smirk on his face when he offered to cook while she unhitched the horses. Mentally preparing her homestead claim, she couldn't be bothered with his teasing. When the dishes were rinsed in the river and put away, she helped to erect the tent. She insisted that he sleep in the wagon with the puppies.

Next morning she awoke to the strong scent of coffee. Finger combing her hair and brushing the wrinkles from her new dress, she opened the tent flap to find Michael grinning at her.

"Hungry, Miss Cameron?"

She managed a smile. "What's on the menu this morning?"

"Biscuits and gravy."

She watched him season the flour and water simmering in a cast iron skillet. "Looks good."

He handed her a mug of coffee and asked that she take down the tent. She took a sip and set the cup aside before dismantling her sleeping quarters. Rolling the canvas into an oblong package, she stood to admire her work.

"Not bad for a tenderfoot," he said. "There's a lot of hard work involved in homesteading."

"I'm quite capable of handling it, Mister O'Brien."

"I'm sure you are. How about feeding our livestock?"

Susan lifted the tent into the wagon and climbed aboard. The puppies were yelping with hunger and she doled out their rations for the day. The horses were grazing nearby and she wondered whether she should feed them some of the grain Michael bought in Rawlins. They were his horses. Let him decide.

Michael was a better cook, but she would have plenty of practice, once settled on her homestead. After cleanup, they packed the wagon and set off down the trail. They left the mountains behind and should make twenty miles that day. Or so he said. She could still not believe he was willing to drive all the way to Sweetwater Valley to build her cabin, knowing that she refused to work for him. He probably thought she'd feel obligated after her home was finished.

Chapter Nine

They stopped at the Averell's road ranch that afternoon where Michael pumped water for the horses while Susan entered the store. She found Ella polishing the counter, her smile radiant when told of Susan's homestead. Dropping her dust cloth, she hugged her new neighbor.

"We'll help in any way we can."

Susan swallowed a lump in her throat. "I couldn't ask for better neighbors."

Led into the small log café, she watched as Ella prepared a pot of tea. When told of their encounter with Tom Sun, Ella appeared uneasy. "He's not a man to trifle with."

"I bought a gun in Rawlins and I know how to use it."

"Be careful, Susan."

"I also bought two dogs to protect me." She took Ella's arm and led her to the wagon. The puppies were wrestling and chewing each other's ears.

Ella laughed as she picked up Alex, who tried to wriggle from her arms. "Hopefully by the time your cabin's built, they'll be big enough to serve as guards. By the way, who's going to build your cabin?"

Michael stood upright near the wagon box. "I volunteered for the job."

Ella seemed relieved. "Oh, good. So the two of you are—"

"No." Susan stamped her foot for emphasis. "We're simply ..." She hesitated. "Friends."

He nodded his agreement. "I've tried to talk her into working in my veterinary clinic during the winter months to earn enough money to survive. But she refused."

Ella's expression was one of surprise. "Do you plan to teach instead?"

"No, I'll find a job in Rawlins."

Ella appeared perplexed. Turning to Michael, she offered him a cold drink. He agreed and followed the women into the store. Apologizing for her husband's absence, Ella poured him a foaming mug of beer. Susan refused a mug of her own, reminding her hostess of their tea in the café. Michael trailed along behind with his beer.

When they were seated, Susan asked permission to dig a trench along their land to water. Ella said she was sure her husband would agree. Jimmy had gone to help the boys repair damages caused by the tornado.

Susan's smile evolved to a frown. "Montana Dan said the cattlemen are angry because you fenced off their access to the creek."

"They can dig a well or water their stock in the Sweetwater River. They don't own this land."

"But you're worried, aren't you?"

Ella lowered her eyes and nodded. "There's no real law in the valley. The cattlemen have had their way for years and no one's here to stop them."

Susan envisioned Ella's husband, a slender man with a ready smile. He was certainly no match physically for Tom Sun. She hoped he was a good marksman. She then remembered Ella saying that he had served twelve years in the frontier army.

Michael suggested they leave after he drained his mug of beer. They were only halfway to Rawlins, which was another long wagon ride away. She reluctantly climbed back in the wagon with a promise to let Ella know when they returned.

When they reached Independence Rock, Michael was true to his word. While Susan prepared supper, he withdrew a hammer and chisel from his wagon toolbox and set about carving their names and the date in the huge granite rock. When he stopped to eat, he said, "I read some time ago that a priest by the name of DeSmet named this monolith 'the great register of the desert.'"

"It's certainly that. There must be thousands of names carved or painted on the rock."

"Four to five hundred thousand emigrants have traveled through here, or so I've read. Everyone traveling west."

She wondered how many had been single women homesteaders.

When he finished carving, he stood back to admire his work. He then suggested she make a list of building supplies they would need to construct her cabin. Retrieving a notepad and pencil from her reticule, she wrote as he rattled off a long list of building supplies. How did a veterinarian know so much about construction? Michael O'Brien was a curious man.

A lone rider approached whom Susan didn't recognize. Tall and lean with a neatly trimmed Van Dyke, he was scowling when he rode up to them.

"Back, I see." He didn't dismount to offer Michael his hand.

Michael stepped forward and reached to offer his, which the rider reluctantly clasped. He then announced that he was A. J. Bothwell.

After Michael introduced himself and Susan, he said,

"I'm planning to help Miss Cameron build her homestead cabin."

"And where might that be?"

Susan hesitated. "Southeast of the Averell's store."

Bothwell's frown deepened. "There's no water there to grow crops."

"I might run my own small herd of cattle."

His horse seemed nervous as it crowhopped to the right. Pulling his hat lower, he said, "Cattle need water and rain in the valley is scarcer than hen's teeth."

Her chin lifted as she crossed her arms. "I'll take my chances."

Bothwell touched the brim of his hat. "Good luck," was all he said as he wheeled his horse back in the direction of his ranch house.

Susan gnashed her teeth as she watched him ride away.

There was concern on Michael's face. "I don't like his attitude. And I don't think you'll be safe out here. Maybe you should reconsider—"

"And work as your assistant in Casper?"

"The job's still yours if you want it."

"No thank you, Mister O'Brien. I didn't come all this way to work in a veterinary clinic. I could have done that at home."

Next morning, they rushed through breakfast and loaded the wagon. The farther they bumped along the trail, the more uneasy she became. Was she making a terrible mistake homesteading in Sweetwater Valley? The fear on Ella's face was contagious. She needed to buy a rifle and more ammunition, if she were to survive. Clinching her jaw, she thought no cattleman was going to run her off her homestead, if she had to work in Michael's clinic to pay a full-time guard.

Michael flipped the reins and turned to smile at her.

"Pennies for your thoughts."

She glanced at him and shrugged.

"I was wondering if you'd consider helping me establish my office when we're finished with your cabin."

She said nothing for several moments. "Fair enough, if it can wait until this fall. I might even take you up on your offer."

He almost dropped the reins. "You would?"

"Maybe, just maybe." But would her homestead be safe while she was gone? A feeling of foreboding overcame her as the afternoon heat baked her already sunburned skin. She should have asked if there was a sunbonnet for sale at the Averell's store.

A group of riders sat on a nearby hill, watching them as they traversed the well-worn trail. Cattlemen or bandits waiting to rob them? She recalled the train robbers encountered earlier. Michael said they must be cowpokes out looking for stray cattle. She wanted to believe him but was so frightened she couldn't breathe. She stopped herself from clinging to him.

"Nothing to worry about. If they were going to rob us, they would have done so by now."

She would always carry a gun. Opening her drawstring bag, she located her Smith and Wesson revolver, a comforting handful of steel. She didn't know whether she could shoot to kill, but she certainly wouldn't allow them to take her captive. Her hand curled around the handgun hidden in her bag, where it stayed until the riders were out of sight.

"You're a skittish little woman."

"Really, Michael, weren't you the least bit nervous?"

He grinned but refused to look at her. "Only a fool *wouldn't* have been nervous. I just didn't want to worry you."

"How considerate of you, Mister O'Brien."

"Your sarcasm is wearing me down, *Miss Cameron*. Would you care to walk the rest of the way?"

"Certainly not. I'll keep my thoughts to myself." She didn't say another word until they stopped for the night. The open prairie made her less anxious. Not another soul was visible in any direction and she scanned the landscape for riders long enough to admire the distant mountains illuminated by the setting sun.

Michael startled her. "Are you cooking tonight or taking care of the horses?"

"I'll cook. I need the practice." She thought she heard him groan.

Michael unhitched the horses and tethered them so they could graze. He then fed the puppies and swept debris from the wagon. After supper and the dishes had been washed in the nearby stream, they bedded down for the night. The tent was stifling but Susan was afraid to open the flap to allow for a breeze. She could hear the faint howling of wolves and shuddered at the thought of them prowling about the tent. Maybe she would ask to sleep in the wagon the following night. She laughed at the thought of puppies crawling over Michael as he slept.

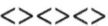

"What are you doing, Jimmy?" Ella leaned across the table to peer at what he had written.

"A letter to the editor of the *Casper Weekly Mail*."

"Why are you writing to the newspaper?"

He looked up and smiled. "To let everyone know what's happening in Sweetwater Valley."

"Which things?"

"The cattlemen's illegal grazing on homestead land and their threats against the settlers."

"Do you think that's wise, dear? Won't it make things worse?"

Jimmy's expression was one of anger. "They tried to stop the division of Carbon County to form Natrona County. Carbon County was too large to be properly developed."

"Or to protect law abiding settlers," Ella added.

"You're right about that, my love." Pushing his chair back, he pulled her into his lap. When she protested she was too heavy, he laughed. "I wouldn't trade you for a dozen skinny women, Ella Watson-Averell."

They arrived in Rawlins as the sun was setting. Susan walked to the hotel while Michael settled the horses at the livery stable. She hoped the puppies wouldn't create a ruckus. Finding a place for them the following morning would present a problem when the wagon was loaded with building supplies. The veterinarian could worry about that. She needed a good night's sleep.

Michael knocked at her door at sunrise. His face was drawn and she knew he'd had little sleep. The puppies had been yelping so he'd slept in the wagon to comfort them.

He waited in the hall while she collected her things and accompanied her to the restaurant, which was already crowded.

"Cowpokes fresh off a cattle drive," the waitress said when they had ordered breakfast. "Some of them are in bad need of soap."

Susan nodded her agreement. She was anxious to get back on her own trail to Sweetwater Valley. As soon as breakfast was over, Michael drove the wagon to the lumber yard, where he consulted with the owner about supplies. While they were negotiating, she walked to the newspaper office. The latest edition, fresh from the press, reported on the controversy over splitting the county in half. She bought a copy and walked to the gun shop where she purchased a Springfield .30-.40 Krag rifle with a 22 inch barrel. The rifle weighed nearly eight pounds and the gun shop owner questioned whether she could handle it. Insisting that she could rest the stock on a window sill, she marched back with the gun and ammunition to the lumber yard, where they were already loading the wagon.

"Did you know about this?" she asked when Michael returned to the wagon carrying a sack of nails. She showed him the front page article.

"I've heard about it."

"My land is halfway between Rawlins and Casper. Which county will I be living in?"

"Southern Natrona County. The cattlemen are dead set against the split."

"Why?"

"They want to keep the entire territory as a cow pasture."

"But that's unfair to people who want to settle here."

"That's why I'm worried about you homesteading on your own."

"I can take care of myself—"

"So you've said."

"Other women have proved up on their land."

"Not in Sweetwater Valley."

"Then I'll be the first."

Michael sighed heavily as he headed back to the lumber yard office. A few moments later, he beckoned to her from the door. In his hand was a foot long bill. "I hope you can afford to pay for this."

Susan gasped when she read the statement, knowing

she should have stayed while they negotiated the sale. "What's this for?" she said, reading each item.

"Women." The owner fumed. "They know nothing about building."

Susan demanded that he explain each charge. When he finished, she nodded and opened her reticule. Counting out nearly a hundred dollars, she left the office with Michael trailing behind. Without a word, he helped her into the wagon and took a seat beside her.

When she asked about Alex and his litter mates, he said they were sleeping in a box beneath her feet. She protested they might smother but he assured her it was well ventilated. "Speak quietly and they'll sleep for quite a while."

"And when they wake?"

"You can cradle them in your lap."

'All three puppies?"

"I bought some heavy twine. You can braid collars and make leashes to walk them for a while. That should tire them out."

"But—?"

"You have a better idea?"

Susan pursed her lips but said nothing more. It would be a miserable ride to her homestead land. Adjusting the sunbonnet she bought in Rawlins, she consoled herself with the fact that she was seated on the wagon seat with a full view of the trail, unlike riding in the back of Montana Dan's wagon. A growing sense of apprehension haunted her as they rode closer to Sweetwater Valley.

Her mother always said that she was too stubborn to face the facts. Had she been right and was Susan riding into a nightmare over which she had no control? She remembered the expression on Ella's face when she told her about her homestead. Was it fear that Susan would fail or that cattlemen would harm her?

Maybe Michael *was* concerned for her safety, not just that he wanted her to work as his veterinary assistant. It was too late to turn back. The lumber had been cut to her specifications and couldn't be returned. She was running low on funds and knew that she would have to find a job. She glanced at Michael, wondering what kind of a boss he would make. And did he want something more than a working relationship? She wouldn't allow him to ruin her dream of proving up on her own homestead land.

Chapter Ten

Storm clouds appeared on the horizon shortly after their noon meal. Frightened that it was another tornado, Susan pleaded with Michael to turn back. He looked at her as though she were a ninny, insisting that Wyoming tornados were rare.

"And what if you're wrong?"

"We survived the last one, didn't we?"

Stubborn, arrogant man! She dared not give voice to her thoughts.

The wind picked up, snatching at her new sunbonnet. Grasping it with one hand, she tried to hold down the hem of her dress with the other. Turning her head she glared at him. "You're going to get us killed."

"Storm's not my fault."

Tears hesitated on her cheeks before they were whisked away by the wind.

"Life's a gamble, Susan. You of all people should know that. You're gambling with your life by homesteading in Sweetwater Valley." His voice rose to thunder pitch to be heard above the roar of the wind.

Dark clouds raced toward them as the wagon bounced

along the trail. Before long they were assaulted with sleet. The frightened horses were ready to bolt. Yelling for her to pull a tarp from the lumber to cover the horses' heads, he jumped from the wagon box to prevent them from running.

She heard the puppies yelping in fear as she pulled a tarp loose from the windows. In the process, she heard a distinct crack. The sunbonnet wasn't much protection from the sleet as she climbed down and managed to throw the canvas tarp over the horses' heads. They were attempting to rear as Michael stood between them, struggling to hold them down.

He turned his head to shout at her: "Back in the wagon under the other tarp before you get hurt."

Frightened but undecided what to do, she turned instead to the horse called Briney. Tugging her halter, she managed to stay away from her stomping hooves. Hanging on with all the strength she could muster, she talked to the mare and tried to calm her. When he noticed her efforts, Michael concentrated on Dopler, the other mare. Exhausted, Susan realized the sleet had stopped but the horses continued to snort and prance in place on the ice-covered ground.

She didn't hesitate when told to climb in the wagon box and pull back on the reins. Placing her feet on the rail, she tugged as though her life depended on it. The horses gradually settled down and he removed the tarp which had slipped to their backs. Rewrapping the windows, he climbed back in the wagon and flicked the reins.

Tears streamed down Susan's face when he confirmed the windows were broken. How could the trip end well when it started out so badly?

"At least it wasn't a tornado."

How could he remain so calm? He knew she couldn't

afford replacements.

They spoke little that day as Susan worked to braid the puppies' collars. Camping that night along the North Platte River, he offered to prepare the evening meal as well as care for the horses. After she fed the puppies, she pulled the tent from the wagon and set it up, refusing his help. No longer hungry, she crawled in the tent and fell asleep. She awoke when he called her for supper but she ignored him and fell back asleep.

Susan woke again when wolves howled nearby, which set the puppies yelping. She knew that Michael was sleeping on a pallet beneath the wagon and wondered if he were awake. Sitting up, she heard something snap and noticed the fire flame up through the tent wall. He must be sitting there feeding the fire to keep the wolves away.

Next morning Michael was brusque and not in the mood to talk. He had to be exhausted and regretting his offer to help her build the cabin. She couldn't blame him. She was regretting it, herself. Susan set about cooking breakfast and offered to help him hitch the horses. When the wagon had been reloaded and the puppies taken for a walk, Michael announced that they were ready to leave.

"Not much longer," she said with a smile.

He muttered. "Not soon enough."

She considered apologizing but decided her actions were more important than words. She'd try to be more cheerful.

The sun baked through her sunbonnet before they reached an area south of Sweetwater Valley. That evening Susan sprang from the wagon and began preparing dinner. Michael's attitude was far from friendly and she considered sending him back to Casper once they reached her land. On second thought, she'd give him another day and a chance to visit with the Averells. That should put him in a better mood.

When they pulled onto her land late in the afternoon two days later, Susan climbed down and danced among the sagebrush, her arms spread wide. Michael must think she'd lost her mind as he sat watching her from the wagon box.

"Bring the puppies," she called. "Let them run for a while."

He obediently set them free and watched as they scattered. Smiling at last, he asked where she wanted him to unload the building supplies. She hadn't considered a location. Scanning the sage-peppered land, she decided to place her cabin within sight of the Averell's store. Michael walked what he decided was the dividing line between the two homesteads, attempting to locate the surveyor's stakes. He finally discovered small piles of rocks at the suggested boundaries.

"You should build your cabin back aways in case we're on the Averell's property."

Susan agreed but when she noticed cattle grazing nearby, she tried to shoo them away. They stubbornly refused to move.

"Those are steers," he warned. "Better keep your distance. You'll have to build a fence around your property to keep them out. And that's not going to make you popular with the cattlemen."

"I think I'll let the cattle roam here for a while to see what happens. I can't afford the fencing right now."

"Suit yourself, but you need to know your boundaries."

Climbing back into the wagon, they drove to the locaton she chose. The panoramic view was breathtaking with the Seminoes to the south and Rattlesnake Range to the north. She could be happy here with good, close neighbors. Michael was already unloading the lumber and she hurried to help him. The sun would soon disappear and she needed to prepare a quick meal of canned beans and dried biscuits. While gathering an armload of sagebrush for the fire, she noticed a rattlesnake nearby. Panicking, she frantically searched for the puppies. Dropping the sagebrush she screamed for Michael, who came running with a hoe. Deftly chopping off the snake's head, he told her she would have to kill them herself, once he was gone. Nodding, she rushed off to find the puppies while watching for another rattler.

Susan called to the pups, realizing she'd have to clear the sagebrush from her land to keep track of them. She didn't want to chain them up. Brody was in the process of relieving himself when she snatched him up, soaking the hem of her dress in the process. She spotted his sister Areola sniffing at a strange looking rock. She almost got away before she was caught.

Michael had unloaded the last of the supplies and started a campfire with the sagebrush she gathered. She returned with two puppies and tears in her eyes.

"I can't find Alex."

"Don't worry. He'll come back when he's hungry."

"But what if a rattlesnake—?"

"That's something you'll have to live with here in the valley, Susan. You'd better get used to it."

She had envisioned the peacefulness of living alone, without the presence of cattle or rattlesnakes. What else would she have to put up with? She would talk to the Averells about it.

"Don't forget the rabbits, Susan."

"Rabbits?"

"Jackrabbits will eat your vegetables and other crops."

She imagined herself chasing them away with a broom.

"Anything else I should know, Mister O'Brien?"

"I hope you're a good shot with a rifle because the

wolves will be coming around once they hear the puppies yapping."

"Speaking of the puppies, would you care to trade your male for my female? I don't want to raise another litter of puppies."

He pulled at his lip. "You may need a new litter if the snakes—"

"All right, I've heard enough." Turning, she marched off in search of Alex. It was already twilight and she had to find him soon. From the corner of her eye she noticed Michael unhitching the horses. He wasn't even going to help her.

"Alex," she screamed. "Where are you?" She imagined a large snake swallowing the puppy whole.

Michael yelled from the wagon. "You're going to scare him into running further away."

"Then come and help me find him."

She watched him rummage in the wagon before heading in her direction. What was that he was holding? Meat scraps?

"We'll make a trail back to the wagon," he said when he reached her.

"You think he'll smell the meat and eat his way back?"

"Pups are always hungry. He'll come back. You'll see."

"I hope the meat doesn't attract a larger animal. Or another snake."

"We'll know soon enough." He pulled a pistol from his holster and spun the chamber.

Alex still hadn't appeared when they finished supper. Susan ate little as she kept a constant watch beyond the campfire for anything moving about. She was thankful the moon was full. The two puppies were noisily playing in the wagon and she wondered why Alex hadn't missed his litter mates. Sighing, she picked up the tin plates to scrub with sand.

Michael's expression was sympathetic. "Some dogs are roamers. They're never satisfied to stay in one place until they're well on in age."

"Are you saying Alex's a roamer?"

Michael shrugged. The fire was burning low and he rose to gather more sagebrush. Night winds on the high desert were often cold, despite the season. Susan pulled her shawl around her shoulders. She wouldn't allow him to watch her cry. It would only increase his insistence that she return to Casper. She forced a smile when he returned with a huge pile of sage.

Feeding branches into the fire, he said, "We'd better bed down for the night, It'll be a long day tomorrow."

"Same sleeping arrangements?"

"Unless you want to share the tent."

Susan rose without a word and made her way to the wagon. Sliding the tent to the ground, she pulled it near the fire. When it was upright and staked to the ground, she crawled inside and closed the flap securely. How dare he suggest sharing the tent with her? She'd share her bed with no man unless she decided to marry. Homesteading on her own had taken on an uncommon glow.

She lay awake long into the night listening to the sounds of the high plains. Sometime later she awoke to a scratching noise and a pitiful whimper. Opening the tent flap, she was overjoyed to find Alex. Gently picking him up, she closed the flap and settled back with the puppy in her arms. She would never let him out of her sight again, if she had to carry him on her back like a papoose.

She awoke at dawn when Alex wiggled from her arms. She could hear Michael moving about and smelled freshly boiled coffee. Smiling to herself, she combed her hair and tried unsuccessfully to brush the wrinkles from her clothing. Scooping up Alex, she carried him to the wagon. After breakfast, she would finish braiding a leash to attach to his collar. He would have to learn to stay at her side.

During breakfast they noticed someone riding hard in their direction. Susan tensed as Michael drew his gun, which he held at his side. As the rider drew nearer they recognized Jimmy Averell. Something must be wrong, but if that were true, why would he leave his wife behind?

Breathless, Jimmy pulled up just short of the campfire, dust swirling around them. "Prairie fire," he said, gasping. "Heading this way."

"How'd you know that we—"

"Saw your campfire last night."

Michael took Susan's arm and pulled her to her feet. "Which direction should we go?"

"Wind's blowing to the southeast. Better follow me on north."

"But the building materials," Susan cried. "They'll burn."

Jimmy dismounted and ran to help Michael load lumber into the wagon while Susan hitched the horses. Moments later they were on their way. Flames were visible to the west of Horse Creek and she knew that sparks would jump the creek, igniting the dry grass on Jimmy's land before traveling to her own. Where was Ella and would the store burn too? Susan craned her neck to follow Jimmy's route. He seemed to be headed toward the store. Was he going back for Ella? If so, why had he left her in the path of the fire?

Jimmy didn't stop at the store. He dismounted several hundred yards beyond to unlatch a wire gate. Pulling it back, he waited for them to reach him. Waving them through, he closed the gate and overtook them as their wagon bounced across the pasture. He led them in a westerly direction, then veered north, traveling nearly a mile before they reached a small cabin squatting in an open field. Jimmy dismounted and hurried inside. The fire seemed well to the south of them now and Susan hoped it would miss the road ranch entirely.

When they pulled up outside the cabin, both Averells came out to greet them, relief etched on their faces. Susan thanked Jimmy for saving their lives and, at the very least, her own cabin. When asked what might have started the fire, Jimmy said they had their suspicions.

"What do you mean?" Susan asked.

Jimmy scowled. "We noticed yesterday that cattle had been moved north away from Bothwell's summer grazing range. The fire seems to have started on the Durbin Ranch to the west of here. John Durbin is one of Bothwell's friends."

"So you think they set the fire to burn you and Susan out?" Michael climbed down from the wagon.

Scare us all out is more like it. Otherwise, it was a bit premature. He could have waited until Susan's cabin was built."

"We won't have to worry about fire now," Ella said. "The grass will only burn once this year."

"And the grass will come back even more plentiful next year," Jimmy added.

Susan wrung her hands. "What will the cattlemen do next?"

Jimmy invited them into Ella's cabin. When they were seated at the dining table, he said, "I've written about the situation to Governor Warren. I hope he'll send an emissary to talk to the cattlemen. We need a marshal to patrol Sweetwater Valley."

"Will the problem with the cattlemen get any better?" Michael asked.

"We can only hope. In the meantime, the two of you will have to be careful."

Michael and Susan exchanged glances. How could they return to her smoldering land?

"You're welcome to stay with us," Ella said. "We're used to traveling guests." She refused their offer to pay for lodging, saying they were going to be neighbors.

Susan sighed. Her new life was anything but peaceful and her independence had been severely impaired. On the other hand, she could have lost her life without Michael and the Averells. Her homesteading adventure wasn't turning out at all as she had planned.

"What about your own buildings?" Michael asked.

"We splashed water on all of them before I rode down to your place. But the wind has dried them out by now. Would you mind lending a hand?"

Michael rose from the table. "Let's get over there. The wind might change directions."

Both men rushed from Ella's cabin and were soon mounted. Susan watched as they raced back south, praying their efforts wouldn't be needed. Her new neighbor placed a hand on Susan's shoulder, smiling down at her.

"Don't worry. We'll rebuild if our cabins burn. And we have mine to move into, if necessary."

"I've never met anyone so optimistic, Ella. I'm so glad we're neighbors." Both women walked outside to shade their eyes against the morning sun.

"I have to admit I'm worried," Ella said. "The boys haven't come back from mending fences again. I hope they're not trying to fight the fire."

Chapter Eleven

The three boys appeared to have crawled from a hole in the earth. Gene's blond hair matched the color of the log buildings, his face as red as the beets in Ella's garden. Johnny and Ralph were equally dirty. Scooping sandy soil with shovels, they had managed to extinguish small fires started from sparks blown across the creek. John's cap was singed and they all had clothing ventilated with small burn holes.

Jimmy knew their bodies had also suffered burns. Gripping the younger boys by the arms, he pulled them away from the fire. "Let it go," he said. "We'll splash the buildings down again and the ground around them. Miss Ella will tend to your burns."

The wind had changed directions, the fire now threatening the road ranch. Jimmy ran to the barn and emerged dragging a horse trough. Placing it under the water pump, he asked Michael to fill it with water. The boys were then told to dip anything that wouldn't leak into the creek upstream. Johnny, Ralph and Gene raced to the barn as Michael and Jimmy dragged a half-filled trough to the west end of the store. Using large pots they scooped water, which they threw on the low roof and against the outer walls. The trough was then carried back to be refilled. Their clothing drenched, they felt the heat of the fire as it burned along the creek bank. While the trough filled, Jimmy ran to continue the work the boys had started. Sparks burned through his clothing and singed his hands and face. Scooping a shovel full of dirt, he threw it over himself and backed away.

Michael was attempting to drag the heavy trough and Jimmy ran to help. They seemed to be losing ground as dry grass caught fire and burned around them. Turning the heavy trough on its side, they managed to drown the area adjacent to the west wall. Both men were coughing and smoke stung their eyes.

Grass was burning near the cafe cabin and they rushed to stamp it out. The fire seemed to be making more progress than they were. Exhausted, Jimmy knew that Michael was as well. From the corner of his eye Jimmy noticed the two women tossing canvas on the fire. Holding the hems of their dresses above their ankles, they stomped along the edges to prevent the tarps from catching fire. When the boys returned, Jimmy told them to take the wagon horses to the barn before they panicked and ran.

Maybe they could save the road ranch after all. The wind seemed to have shifted again and no further sparks sailed in their direction. Everyone smiled and renewed their efforts. By sundown the fire had been contained, but what had it done to Susan's homestead land? They could see smoke rising from the east and knew that building her cabin would have to wait. Not only had the windows been broken, the land wouldn't be fit to walk on for days. Perhaps a week.

Jimmy shook his head when he thought of Susan's cabin built along the border of his own land. The closer her cabin stood to his, the more danger she would place herself in. Albert Bothwell wouldn't hesitate to take his anger out on a defenseless woman. What was he planning next?

The two women had gone into the cafe cabin to prepare supper while Jimmy and Michael helped the boys soak the ground again around the buildings. Fortunately, there were no other homesteaders to the immediate east.

Despite the late afternoon heat, Ella was boiling potatoes and frying slabs of steak. Susan stood nearby chopping carrots and green beans from Ella's garden. They hadn't said much since the fire but Susan was aware of the stiffness in her companion's shoulders as she went about her cooking chores. She could stand the silence no longer.

"Ella, do you think someone set the fire?"

"I'm sure of it."

"Because I decided to homestead here?"

Ella turned from the stove to face her. "It's not just you. The cattlemen don't want anyone homesteading on their grazing land."

"But they don't own the land."

"It doesn't matter. They've been using the land for years and consider it their own."

"You mean like squatter's rights?"

"Apparently so."

Susan twisted a flower sack towel into a knot. "Then I couldn't have chosen a worse place to homestead."

"This is a wonderful place to settle, but you need to be careful. At least they can't set fire to the land again for a while. And maybe by the time the grass grows back, we'll have law and order here in the valley."

Susan nodded and returned her smile. She then

noticed the men returning. They had to be hungry.

During the noon meal they discussed building Susan's cabin. The land was still smoldering, but they could all work on the irrigation ditch along the border between the two homesteads, beginning the following day on land that had escaped the fire. Michael said he was glad he had purchased two sharp-nosed shovels in Rawlins.

When the discussion turned to sleeping arrangements, the Averells insisted that Susan stay with them while Michael bunked with the boys in Ella's cabin. Jimmy then mentioned that Old Blunder had been limping lately and Michael agreed to take a look. It was the least he could do to repay their hospitality.

Jimmy left the table to retrieve a flyer he'd found along the fence line the previous day. "Some out-of-stater by the name of McCoy is trying to sell lots at Bothwell's place. He intends to start a town named for himself in the area of his ranch house. It says here that the town of Bothwell will be the capital when Wyoming Territory becomes a state. Can you imagine that?"

Michael said, "I thought the only towns in this territory were built along the railroad lines and rivers."

"The Sweetwater's not far away so I guess he plans for the river to provide the town's water supply," Jimmy said.

"Then why's he all riled up about you homesteading along Horse Creek?"

"Our combined homesteads are on his former hay meadow. And he used to water his cattle in Horse Creek."

"Seems your neighbor has some mighty grandiose ideas."

"Wait until you meet him, Michael. That wife of his walks around all day in high heeled shoes—when she's here. She spends most of her time in California."

"We met him yesterday along the trail. Not a friendly sort."

"Unfriendly isn't the half of it," Jimmy said. "He has a den of wolves penned up behind his house."

Susan cringed. "Wolves for pets? Or for protection?"

"Nobody seems to know, but those sons of his have been seen playing with them. Seems Bothwell killed a female wolf and adopted her pups."

"That says a lot about the kind of man he is. During my veterinary studies, I learned about people who have unusual pets. Men who keep wolves are generally ruthless. Although if they're raised well as pups in captivity or the offspring of a dog-wolf pair, they can probably be as gentle and trustworthy as any other canine."

Jimmy rose again from the table. Patting the two youngest boys on their shoulders, he said, "Keep a sharp lookout for anything suspicious taking place at the Bothwell ranch when you go back to Ella's cabin. But don't let him catch you spying on him." He then explained that Ella's cabin provided a panaramic view of the entire area.

Susan said, "Would Mister Bothwell have endangered his own home, if the wind changed directions and blew to the north?"

Jimmy frowned. "Not if he wet everything down. But you're right. It would have been a fool move on his part. And Bothwell's no fool."

"Then who would have wanted to burn us out?"

Ella suggested that it could have been an accident.

"I have a hard time believing that, with so few people here in the valley." Jimmy nodded to Michael, who left his chair. They needed to determine whether any smoldering grass had reignited.

Susan helped to clear the table once the men had gone. "Don't you worry about the cattlemen trying to run you off your land?"

Ella sighed. "All the time, but Jimmy doesn't think they'll do us harm."

"What do *you* think?"

"I agree with your friend, Michael. Mister Bothwell is ruthless and will probably stop at nothing to rid the valley of homesteaders."

"Sweetwater Valley is a lovely place but it's so far from anywhere. Why would he think the state capitol would be placed here?"

"I've heard talk that he's insane."

<><><>

Harvey Jones arrived at the store early the following morning. He was so excited that he was difficult to understand. Stuttering, he said that another Bothwell cowpoke had set the fire but claimed it had been an accident.

"Said he dropped his qwerly in the dry grass and couldn't stomp the fire out."

A vein rose on Jimmy's brow "Then why didn't he warn us before it reached the creek?"

"I asked him the same thing. He said he thought it'd burn itself out when it got to the crick."

Jimmy muttered to himself as he led the way into the store. Harvey followed as though a whipped dog.

"Reckon I could use a drink."

"This early. What's wrong?"

"Got myself fired."

Jimmy looked up from behind the small bar. "What happened?"

"Bothwell found out that I took a swing at Rogers, the feller that set the fire."

Jimmy handed him a foaming mug of beer. "Sorry, Harvey. I'm sure you can find another wrangler's job. There's plenty of cow outfits in the valley."

Ella entered the store with Susan. "What's this about

a job, Mister Jones?"

When told of the firing, Ella suggested that he help build Susan's cabin. Introduced to the valley's newest resident, the cowpoke readily agreed, even when told he'd have to settle for room and board.

Jimmy wondered how Michael would feel about the arrangement. He seemed to have more than a friendly interest in Susan. Harvey Jones was hardly in the running for her affection but some men didn't like competition. Michael O'Brien seemed that sort.

Harvey slapped his palm on the bar. "Almost forgot to tell you. Bothwell's plannin' a town on his property. He invited some newspaper fellers to move to the town and set up shop."

"Newspaper?" Jimmy laughed. "There's not enough people in the valley to support a newspaper here."

"Bothwell thinks so. That McCoy feller he hired to get people to move here convinced him to do it. Says it's good advertisin'."

"What are they going to call the rag?"

"The Sweetwater Chief."

Susan said she didn't understand. Bothwell wanted to run homesteaders out of the valley but was inviting people to live in his town. It didn't make sense. Unless he planned for them to help him run off the settlers. What had she gotten herself into? Her homesteading dream had become a nightmare.

Chapter Twelve

Michael decided to stay at the road ranch so that Harvey would bunk with the boys at Ella's cabin. Susan wasn't happy with the arrangement but with two men working, it shouldn't take more than a few days to build her cabin. She didn't know how she was going to repay the Averells for their kindness, or the men and boys for that matter.

The morning after the fire, small patches of earth still belched wisps of smoke. Borrowing a pair of old boots from Harvey, Susan lifted her skirts to stomp the smoking areas until she was sure the embers were out. She heard a man's laughter and noticed Michael standing nearby. Irritated, she turned her back and continued working on the embers.

She ignored him as Harvey Jones joined her. "I hope I'm not ruining your boots, Mister Jones."

"Not to worry. Them's my old ones."

He grinned at her like a Cheshire cat. Walking ahead of him, she continued stomping until Harvey again came alongside.

"Are you married?" he asked.

She whispered, "You won't tell anyone, will you?"

His brows lifted as he shook his head.

She crossed fingers behind her back. "My husband's in Missourah. He'll join me in a few months."

Harvey looked puzzled. "How come he let a purty little woman like you come out here all by herself?" He stretched to his full height, a few inches taller than Susan.

She sighed. Was there such a shortage of women in the West that every bachelor in the territory was out to bag a bride? Smiling to herself, she realized that he was interested in her.

"Does your friend O'Brien know?"

"No, and you mustn't tell him?"

"Mustn't tell me what?" Michael's baritone voice startled her.

Susan laughed to hide her embarrassment. "That Mister Jones and I are engaged." She looked at the small man and winked. Harvey's face turned a deep shade of crimson.

"Engaged?" Michael roared.

"Engaged in putting out the last of the embers."

"So, you *do* have a sense of humor, Miss Cameron."

"Under the circumstances, it's better than crying."

"I'm afraid I have to agree. Now, how about selecting your cabin site so we can begin to clear the ashes."

"Right over there," she said pointing.

"Looks like it's on the property line."

"It will place me near the road ranch."

Michael frowned. "Not a good idea. It's too close to Bothwell's grazing range."

Susan defiantly raised her chin. "No greedy rancher is going to tell me where I can live."

Michael muttered to himself as he walked off toward the area she indicated. She thought she heard him grumble that he would have to bury her there.

"Mister Jones, we have work to do."

Harvey obediently bowlegged his way to the store to borrow two additional hoes. She waited for him, not wanting to be left alone with Michael. When he returned, she made him promise he wouldn't tell anyone she was married. That disappointed look crept across his face again and she felt sorry for him.

There was work to be done. Leading the way to Horse Creek, she lifted her hoe and began to chop at the blackened soil. How deep would the ditch have to be to carry water to her land? Harvey suggested eighteen inches and she went back to work. Before long her muscles ached and she was exhausted. She saw that the little cowpoke was still chopping away a few yards behind.

"Careful that you don't trip and fall in the ditch I'm diggin'."

Susan smiled, regretting she'd lied to him. He was probably holding on to the hope that her fictitious husband wouldn't materialize. From the corner of her eye she noticed Michael approaching.

Frowning, he said, "I thought we were going to clear a building site?"

"We have temporary accommodations. What we need most is water."

Michael laughed. "The way you two are digging, the ditch will wind up in Rawlins."

He trotted off to the store, returning with a hammer, bundle of stakes and ball of string. Siting down his long arm, he walked a straight line to the pile of rocks, which marked the edge of her property. Then, pounding a stake in the ground, he tied it to the end of the string and walked back toward the ditch digging crew. Halting every few yards, he repeated the process until he reached them.

"Now," he said, "you can dig a straight line." A curious expression then flitted across his face. "Hold on a minute."

Susan watched as he walked to the creek bank and sat on his haunches for long moments. When he returned, he said that the ditch would have to be excavated to at least six feet and that the land slanted uphill so there would be no gravity feed.

"Are you saying that I can't get water from the creek?"

He shrugged. "I'm afraid that digging a trench that deep would take at least six months. And the ground will be frozen long before then. You'll also need an axe to chop through the ice during the winter months."

"But Ella said—"

"Their cabins are located near the creek bank."

"I can't live here without enough water to grow food and the rules say that I have to have water on the land to prove up on it."

"We can excavate a well. We're close enough to the river that we won't have to dig too deep."

"How deep, Michael?"

"Probably not more than a dozen feet."

Susan imagined herself in the bottom of a twelve foot hole.

"I read that the aborigines in Austrailia have used timbers and spinifex grass to line their wells in sandy soil, like along the river bank. Fortunately, the soil has a lot of clay on your property. Most domestic wells are lined with rock and held in place with concrete."

"What kind of rocks, Michael?"

He looked about the property. "There are plenty of them on your land. We can load them into the wagon and bring them to wherever you want your well."

"I don't think I can afford a well *and* a cabin."

"Then you'll have to decide which is most important."

"You mean unless I work for you so that I can afford to do both."

"That seems the logical solution."

You're determined to entrap me, aren't you, Michael?
"'I think I'll talk to Jimmy about my water supply." She
dropped her hoe and walked back to the store.

When Jimmy confirmed what Michael had said, Susan
stepped outside and cried. She soon felt Ella's hands on her
shoulders.

"We'll help with the well and you can stay with us until
you leave to find a job."

That evening Michael expressed concern that Susan
was placing her life in danger, but Jimmy repeated that
they were lawfully homesteading. Harvey Jones looked
skeptical and Michael thought that he knew Bothwell
better than their optimistic host.

"Bothwell's plannin' somethin'," Harvey said. "And
it ain't gonna be good."

Michael forced his shovel point into the ground. "What
makes you think so?"

"His wife left for Californie and he's been holdin'
meetin's" with other ranchers."

"Is that unusual?"

"It don't happen much."

"So do you think he's planning an attack on the
homesteaders?"

"I wouldn't be surprised."

Jimmy shook his head, reminding Harvey that they
had discussed the possibility many times before and that
none of the cowpoke's dire predictions had come to pass.

"Bothwell's none too happy about them letters you been
writin' to the editor of the Casper newspaper. He told them
newspaper boys he hired to write stories about how you
and the other settlers are ruinin' the grazin' land."

Ella rang the dinner bell attached to the cabin wall,

so they trooped off to the café. It was too hot to begin digging Susan's well that day but Michael and Harvey volunteered to clear her building site of embers. They returned in time for supper, appearing as though they'd slept it in a coal furnace. Susan laughed when she saw them, and offered to wash their clothes.

"The least you can do," Michael grumbled.

Harvey tried to wipe a clean spot on his face as though he expected a kiss. "Few more days of diggin' and we'll start on your cabin, ma'am."

Susan gasped. "That's miss, Mister Jones."

"Oh, yeah, I forgot." He turned sheepishly to glance at Michael, and she wondered whether they had been discussing her while they worked.

Jimmy cleared his throat. "Ella and I need to make a trip to Rawlins for supplies day after tomorrow. Anything you need while we're there?"

"You can take the broken windows back and replace them." Michael opened his wallet and retrieved several bills. He knew Susan was running low on money.

Susan objected. "I pay my own bills."

"No problem. I'll take it out of your first week's paycheck."

Susan stormed from the cabin He was trying to ensnare her and she wouldn't stand for it. Ella followed her into the yard, attempting to reason with her, but Susan refused to listen.

"Michael just wants to help."

"It's his attitude, Ella. He's so pompous that I can't stand him."

"He seems good-hearted."

"He's not going to buy me. I've had too many men in my life who wanted to control me. That's why I'm here."

Ella's expression was sympathetic. "I understand. I too ran away from controlling men. I divorced a drunken husband who beat me, and a father who—" She hesitated. "Who wanted to tell me how to live."

"But you have Jimmy."

Ella smiled. "He's the best thing that ever happened to me. I hope you find someone like him."

Susan nodded. *I don't think so. I always attract the wrong kind.*

"Is there anything besides the windows that I can get for you in Rawlins?"

"An extra box of shells for my pistol and the rifle. Looks like I may be shooting two-legged rattlers."

"I hope not but it's always best to be prepared."

A colorful sunset distracted Susan and she leaned against the cabin to collect her thoughts. Her own cabin would be built soon and she could get on with her life as soon as she helped Michael organize his office that fall. He'd have to find someone else to take the assistant's job, someone he could charm into marrying him. The image made her smile.

Harvey emerged from the store and said good night. He and the boys were on their way to Ella's cabin. Michael followed them out the door and Susan immediately went inside to help with the dishes. She refused to be alone with him. While she was drying plates, she caught her breath, realizing that he might just ride off before the cabin was built. She would have to treat him better. But what would she do when the Averells left for Rawlins? Maybe she should go along. She weighed the prospect of riding in the back of the wagon with staying in the same cabin as Michael. Each seemed equally repulsive.

Next morning she arose at dawn to find Ella frying potatoes and slabs of bacon. When asked to gather eggs, Susan rushed out to collect them. She would soon need some hens of her own. There was a neat row of roosts with nests but it seemed the hens preferred only two of them, which were piled three deep with eggs. While she was collecting them, she noticed a fat white hen lying in the corner of the coop with both feet in the air. Not the way to start her day. She knew little of chickens and wondered if the hen could be cooked. Probably not.

When told, Ella said one of the hens had been laying unusually large eggs. That had probably killed her. Susan shuddered, remembering stories of women dying in childbirth. That would never happen to her. Another Jimmy or not, she would never marry.

After breakfast, Michael handed her his grimy clothes, requesting that she wash them. Why didn't he just wear them another day? They would get just as dirty. Harvey had the same clothes on for days and didn't mention having them washed. Cowpokes probably wore the same outfit for a month before they changed. At least Michael was scrubbed and recently shaved.

The men went back to work on the well as the women cleared the dishes. It would be a long, hot July day. She wished she had a pair of overalls to work in like the men. She had nearly ruined her dress with soot the previous day while helping to load rocks into the supply wagon.

Pulling on Harvey's old boots, she trudged out across the field with Ella in pursuit. The men were already taking a break and Harvey sat sprinkling tobacco from a pouch into a small square of paper. Licking the edge, he rolled paper around the tobacco, twisted the ends, and stuck it in his mouth. When he struck a match on his boot heel, she shaded her eyes with her hand to peer into the distance, noticing riders on the horizon. Tensing, she wondered whether she should run back to the sleeping cabin to retrieve her rifle.

Harvey noticed her distress. "Cowpokes lookin' for strays, miss. Nuthin' to worry 'bout."

Nothing to worry about? She would never relax again.

Chapter Thirteen

By the end of the day, the well was nearly as deep as Michael was tall, the pile of rocks higher than Harvey's knees. The men continued to work for another hour when the women left to prepare the evening meal. They had been trading off digging and hauling dirt in buckets to the surface most of the day when angry clouds appeared on the horizon. Ella and Jimmy worried they would have to postpone their trip to Rawlins. A heavy rainstorm could muddy the trail and they would run the risk of getting stuck. A bad storm would also mean halting work on the well. On the bright side, the rain would put out any remaining embers.

A day of rest was what they all needed. Jimmy pulled a checkerboard from a cupboard and invited Michael to join him. When the dishes were done, Susan accompanied Ella to the sleeping quarters. When they were out of the men's earshot, Ella said, "We can lay the sooty clothes in the dooryard and soap them down. The rain will do most of the work for us."

Susan laughed. "What an excellent idea, but won't the wind blow them away?"

"Not if we weight them down with rocks along the edges."

Susan hugged her new friend, her head barely reaching past Ella's shoulder. "I don't know what I'd do without you."

"Oh, you'd get along just fine. It just takes time to learn the ways of the wilderness."

"Like doing laundry? I wonder if Harvey has a change of clothes. The ones he's wearing can probably stand alone."

Ella winked. "I'll tell him tomorrow's wash day."

The wind picked up not long after Susan bedded down in her room. Windows rattled and wind shrieked like a banshee. A later roar sounded much like the train she had ridden into Casper and she feared another tornado. Then, all she heard was a downpour of rain. Shivering, she pulled the thin blanket to her chin and fell asleep.

Everyone was at breakfast the following morning when she awoke. Hurrying into her clothing, she tiptoed through the mud to the café cabin where she found the men discussing the day's work.

Apologizing for not rising in time to help prepare the morning meal, she asked if the Averells were going to make the trip to Rawlins. Ella shook her head.

"Too muddy," Jimmy answered for her. "The wind should dry the mud by tomorrow."

Ella later took her aside and asked if she would like the boys to stay as chaperones while they were gone. Susan sighed with relief. It would keep Michael and Harvey at arm's length as well as give her a chance to acquaint herself with the boys, who had worked all day loading rocks.

Digging in the mud was messy but it was easier than

hacking away at hard ground. She groaned when she noticed how caked with mud the men were, and knew she needed to wash their clothes.

During a rare break, Susan watched a herd of antelope race across the field several hundred yards away. Their white rumps disappeared into the distance, making her smile. She scanned the horizon, taking in the sharply-formed Seminoe Mountains and the nearly level prairie land which stretched for miles to her homestead. She felt caught between heaven and the cattle baron's hell.

That night after the evening meal, Michael handed Jimmy a list of supplies to buy in Rawlins, including two new windows and bags of cement for the well. Susan fumed but remained silent when Ella gave her a knowing look. If she had to work for Michael to pay off her debt, so be it, but he'd better keep the relationship on a professional basis.

When reminded it was washday, Harvey agreed to relinquish his clothes. His rolled, spare outfit was retrieved from a saddlebag. Grimacing, Susan agreed to wash the muddy clothing in the creek that morning. She knew she owed it to them for the work they'd done, but wished she had tried Ella's suggestion to wash them in the rain.

Would her cabin ever materialize? It seemed an eternity since she had stepped from the train. Her enthusiasm had dried up like parchment, but it was too late to retrace her steps. She had little money left but still wanted to make it on her own. A traditional marriage back home was as appealing as living in southern slavery.

The basket of soiled clothing was waiting and she marched to the creek to wash them. Ella had loaned her a scrub board, small tub, and lye soap, warning her to be careful. She apologized for the lack of a washtub with wringer rollers, saying she intended to buy one when she could. Susan soon understood Ella's warning.

Scraping a small area of ash from the creek bank, she knelt to fill the tub with water. She then poured in the lye soap and swished it around until it made suds. The shirt was rubbed repeatedly on the corrugated board. In the process she skinned her knuckles, which burned when they made contact with the harsh soap. Envisioning her mother's new crank washing machine, she bit her lip and dunked her knuckles in the creek water before continuing with the laundry. She vowed that the next time she traveled to Rawlins, she would buy a barrel and paddle to wash her own clothes, as though churning butter.

When she finished, she did her best to wring water from Michael's clothing. She then started back for the clothesline behind the sleeping cabin. She noticed a cloud of dust rising from the north and heard Michael yell as he and the others raced for the road ranch. A herd of cattle was stampeding in their direction. Dropping the clothes, she ran for the store.

Out of breath, they all waited for the herd to pass, trailed by men whistling and yelling from horseback.

Susan tried to peer through a window but dust coated the panes. "Does this happen often?" she asked Jimmy.

"First time since we've been here," he said. "I don't think our good neighbor likes the idea of a well dug on your property. That makes it less likely you'll leave."

Susan felt light-headed and took a seat on a stool at the bar. The expressions on her companions' faces echoed her own worry. Albert Bothwell was one determined madman.

Michael took the stool beside her. "I think we should return to Rawlins to see if you can trade your property for a safer location, don't you?"

Shaking her head, she said she didn't know. She loved the Sweetwater Valley and couldn't ask for better neighbors than the Averells. "When are lawmen coming to the valley?" she asked.

Jimmy frowned. "I wrote to the new governor asking for assistance, but he hasn't written back." He peered out the door before closing it. "The cattlemen can't be allowed to ride roughshod over the homesteaders. I'll write another letter to the editor of the *Casper Weekly Mail.*"

"I don't think that's wise," his wife said. "Look what's happened since the last letter you wrote."

"What else can we do, Ella? Form a vigilante group and run Bothwell out of the country?"

Harvey cleared his throat. "He's got too many men for that. Last I heard there's more on the way. A whole damned army of gunslingers." He apologized to the ladies for his language.

"Then you're putting your own life in danger by helping us," Susan said.

"Ain't got nuthin better to do." He smiled at her with the look of a school boy crush.

Jimmy said he still thought Bothwell was using scare tactics, and would give up when he found they didn't work.

Michael's laugh was bitter. "We could have been killed in the fire as well as the stampede. I think Bothwell is dead serious in his attempts to clear settlers from the valley."

"If you'll excuse me." Jimmy turned to leave. "I've got a letter to write."

Ella shook her head. "I still think it's a mistake. But if you think it will help ..."

"Sounds like the herd's gone by." Harvey started for the door. "Are you ready to go back to work?"

Susan slid off her stool. "Don't risk your life on the well. I'm going back to the creek to finish washing."

Later, when she had washed her own clothes, she noticed that everyone was back at work. Even Jimmy, who must have finished his letter. He probably planned to mail it in Rawlins. Susan still wondered whether she should accompany the Averells to Rawlins, knowing she was tempted to board the train for home. Sighing, she realized that she didn't have enough money for train fare, so the decision was made. She would stay.

She rushed to hang the dripping clothes on rope lines at the rear of the cabin. She then hurried over to take Ella's place at the well so she could prepare for the trip. The sun was nearly overhead and it would soon be time to prepare the mid-day meal. So much work to do before the autumn snow. And she had promised to help Michael get his office ready. Closing her eyes, she swayed on her feet. A moment later she felt Michael's hand on her arm.

"Are you all right? Why don't you go back to the store and help Ella?"

Jerking her arm free, she said she would help the boys gather rocks. "I'm fine, Mister O'Brien. If you're tired, sit down and rest."

Grumbling, he went back to work hauling dirt from the well as Harvey took his turn at digging.

Less than an hour later, Ella rang the dinner bell. Gratefully tossing down a heavy granite rock, Susan walked alone to the cabin. The heavenly scent of spicy mutton stew filled the room. Ella was an excellent cook and Susan doubted her own culinary skills would ever compare. She consoled herself with the fact that Ella had worked as a cook for two years at the Rawlins House before marrying Jimmy.

They lingered over their meal as a breeze blew through the open windows. Although tired, the men and boys rose from the table to return to work as Susan helped with the dishes. She then walked back to the well. Although the sunbonnet shaded her face, the temperature had to have been hovering close to a hundred degrees as she carried rocks to the growing pile. It wasn't long before she felt dizzy and bent at the waist to prevent herself from falling. Michael's hands were on her again. When she protested, he swept her into his arms and carried her toward the sleeping cabin.

Reclining on her bed she noticed Ella's worried face as she draped a cool cloth across her forehead. "Lie still and rest," she said. "You've been working too hard in the hot sun."

After a short nap, Susan went back to work. She couldn't expect the others to dig her well without her.

That evening at dinner they discussed visiting homesteaders in the area to form a vigilante committee when Ella and Jimmy returned from Rawlins. They concluded that it would take more time than they currently had. Getting Susan's cabin and water supply ready would keep them busy until early September, when the first snow would fall. Michael and Susan then needed to establish his veterinary clinic.

"What can we do?" Susan asked in desperation.

"I wrote several letters to the territorial governor and the editor of the *Casper Weekly Mail,*" Jimmy said. "I may have to write to President Harrison to ask for law enforcement in Sweetwater Valley."

"Harrison hasn't been in office long," Michael reminded him. "And he's a Republican, who will probably side with the cattlemen, especially after so many cattle were lost during the big freeze the past couple of years."

"That's what worries me. If Grover Cleveland had stayed in office we might not have this problem. But he appointed Thomas Moonlight territorial governor because he's a Democrat. Moonlight should have stayed in Kansas, where he belongs. He hasn't lifted a finger to help the homesteaders."

Michael frowned. "I wondered why Cleveland appointed

a Scottish Indian fighter to the territorial governorship. Political favor, no doubt."

Ella rose from the table to begin clearing dishes. "Governor Moonlight did something right. He appointed Jimmy postmaster and justice of the peace."

"Hear, hear," Harvey said, raising his empty cup.

Jimmy waved away the accolades. "Wyoming's going to become a state soon and I read in the dispatch that our new territorial governor, Francis E. Warren, will become our first state governor."

"Another Republican," Michael said. "That doesn't bode well for the homesteaders."

Jimmy replied that the cattlemen were panicking. "They've become ruthless after the big freeze. They've lost so much money that they had to close down their precious Cheyenne Club."

"From what I've heard, cattle rustling's on the rise and they're blaming it on the homesteaders."

"That's right, Michael. But it's their cowpunchers stealing cattle to start their own ranches."

"Are you sure?"

"They've let it slip when they stopped by for a mug of beer."

Michael stole a glance at Susan before he said, "Sounds like it's about to become all-out war between the cattlemen and settlers."

"You could be right. That's why we need to call a meeting of all the homesteaders in the Valley to form a defensive army, if it comes to that."

Alarmed, Susan said, "But digging the well and building my house is keeping you from it."

Jimmy smiled. "We've plenty of time for that. First things first. Let's get you settled on your homestead before we worry about vigilantes."

Susan wasn't so sure. What if cattlemen went on

the rampage, killing homesteaders, burning crops and stealing their animals? It could happen while she was in Casper helping Michael set up his veterinary practice. She shuddered, realizing that she would be obligated to him for her livelihood.

The Averells left before sunrise the following morning. High overnight winds had dried the mud into stiff ridges and Susan knew it would be a rough wagon ride. She was almost glad that she wasn't going along—almost, because she was tired of carrying rocks to the well site. Another few days and the excavation should be complete. They would then start on a holding pond near her cabin. She shouldn't refer to it as a cabin because she had no logs. She didn't want to call it a shack although she knew that's all it would be. She would make do, as long as the roof didn't leak.

The wind had blown away most of the ashes but the hem of her dress was black with soot. She should have asked her friends to buy her men's overalls to work her homestead. Societal rules be damned. She wasn't going to ruin her dresses here in the outback. Susan wondered how Ella managed to remain so crisp and clean, even while working in the dirt.

That evening Michael offered to prepare dinner and Susan was too tired to argue. They had completed all but the last few feet of the well and would start on the holding pond the following afternoon. Fortunately, there was a depression not far from where she planned to build her shack, so digging would be kept to a minimum.

After Michael had helped with the dishes, she trudged off to bed, falling asleep soon after her head touched the pillow. It seemed only moments later that someone rapped at her door. She recognized Michael's voice when he said breakfast was ready.

Stiff and sore from the previous day's work, she dressed and haphazardly arranged her hair. The menfolk were already seated at the table eating breakfast. They rose from their chairs when she entered the room.

Michael placed a plate of scrambled eggs and bacon before her and she ate as though ending a hunger strike. The digging team soon left to finish the well and she rushed to join them after clearing the table and washing dishes.

The day was bright and cloudless, the temperatures even hotter than the day before. She was tempted to take a nap in the morning sun. Shocked from her daydreaming, she heard men's voices yelling there had been a cave-in.

Hurrying to the well site, she saw Michael and Harvey in the hole frantically digging with their hands.

"What happened?" she shouted.

Michael continued to dig as he yelled that Ralph was buried beneath the soil.

Susan thought her heart had stopped. She heard Harvey say that he had found Ralph's head. Peering over the edge, she noticed dark hair protruding through the dirt. Michael dug like a madman, himself encased in dirt past his waist. Harvey must have jumped in after the cave-in took place or he would have been covered like Ralph.

The young man's face was quickly uncovered and everyone feared that he was dead until he coughed and blinked his eyes. When he was able to move, Susan realized that he had been crouched to fill a bucket when the cave-in took place.

"Held my breath," he said when he could talk. "I was about to pass out when you uncovered me." He then helped Harvey unearth Michael.

"We'll have to cement off the dirt as we dig deeper,

Michael said, "or this can happen again."

It was all her fault. She should not have insisted on digging the well. This entire venture was nothing but a fiasco helped along by their unfriendly neighbor.

At noon they set their tools aside and walked to the confluence of Horse Creek and the Sweetwater River, which was just south of Ella's homestead land. There the three boys jumped in to cool themselves. Susan sat on the bank to remove her boots and dangle her feet in the water. Michael and Harvey joined the boys, splashing water on one another as though they were as young as Gene. When she closed her eyes, she was jerked from the bank. A painful burning sensation attacked her nose when her head sank beneath the surface. Panicking and afraid she was drowning, she struggled to reach the surface. Pulled from the water, she heard Michael's laughter.

"Fell in, did you?"

Coughing and sputtering, she tried to scream at him that she couldn't swim but was unable to catch her breath. How dare he humiliate her and nearly cause her to drown? Stumbling when she tried to climb the bank, she lost her balance and sank back beneath the surface. A sharp pain on the side of her head turned the blue haze to black as she lost consciousness.

Chapter Fourteen

When Susan came to, Michael was straddling her on the bank, his mouth pressed to hers. She tried to push him away but only managed to turn her head and retch. When he got to his feet, she rubbed her eyes to squint against the sun. Rolling onto her side, she noticed five pairs of dirty trousers blocking her view of the river.

"Are you all right, Miss Susan?" Gene Crowder's wet hair dripped down the sides of his face.

She coughed but was unable to answer.

Michael knelt beside her, his face awash with guilt. "I'm sorry. I just wanted to cool you off."

Enraged, she attempted to slap him but found herself too weak. Harvey removed his wet shirt and rolled it to form a pillow. She noticed his red flannel underwear and vaguely wondered how he could survive in the heat.

"I'll carry you to the cabin—"

She managed to scream, "No, Michael" before he faded from sight. She awoke on her bed covered with a quilt, still wearing her wet clothing. Her head ached and she touched the side of her head where a lump had formed. Had she struck a rock when she fell? The near drowning came back to her and she muffled sobs in the pillow.

Moments later someone tapped at her door. Young Gene stuck his head inside to inquire if she were hungry. Drying her tears, she asked what was on the menu.

"Mister O'Brien is heatin' up some mutton stew that Miss Ella put in the ice house. It's right good, ma'am."

"Your Miss Ella is a very good cook."

He nodded agreement and began to close the door.

"Wait," she said. "How's Ralph? I'm not the only one to suffer a mishap."

"He's been blowin' his nose a lot and digging dirt out of his ears, but I think he's gonna be fine."

Susan sighed. Why were all of these things happening? Was someone trying to tell her to give up her dream?

When Gene left, she peeled off her wet clothing. Susan toweled herself dry and reached for an old dress hanging from a wall peg. The dress was tight because she had abandoned her corset the day after she arrived in the valley. A little more physical work and she might be thin enough to discard the corset permanently

The aroma of mutton stew seeped into her room, making her ravenously hungry. She found them sitting patiently at the dining table waiting for her. They rose when she entered the cabin and ducked their heads as though small boys caught stealing cookies. Harvey was the first to reward her with a lopsided grin.

Michael asked how she felt but before she could answer, he immediately filled her bowl with stew. Thickly sliced homemade bread and a pot of churned butter were already on the table, and they wasted no time digging in. Little was said during the meal and she thought the atmosphere was akin to a funeral. Her headache seemed to be lessening and she managed a weak smile.

"Cheer up, boys," she said, including Michael, Ralph and Harvey in her sweeping gaze. "It could have been worse. A lot worse. I guess I'm going to have to learn to swim."

Gene raised his hand as though he were in school. "I'll teach you, Miss Susan. I'm a right good swimmer but you should learn in the Sweetwater River. Not the crick."

"I'll take you up on your offer as soon as my shack is finished. I'm afraid we won't have much time until then."

He nodded happily and Michael insisted she rest while they cleared the dishes. When she protested, they helped her from her chair and escorted her back to her room. At first resisting, she soon relaxed. *Why not? I'll have to nearly drown again to get this kind of chivalry.*

She thanked them and quickly closed the door. Now what? Spotting her traveling trunk, she searched through the contents until she found a copy of Jerome K. Jerome's book, *Three Men in a Boat*, which she had purchased before boarding the train for Wyoming Territory. She read enough on the train to know that it was a comic novel about a man and his dog Montmorency.

The puppies came to mind. She hoped they hadn't wandered off or drowned in the creek. Laying the book aside, she left the cabin to look for them. A moment later she found Michael feeding the dogs the remains of the stew. She watched as he stroked each pup in turn and felt a lump form in her throat as she appraised them. Michael, she decided, had a gentle nature, especially when it came to animals. In fact, he was just a boy in men's clothing. But weren't all men that way?

Shaking her head, she thought, no, there were evil men like Albert Bothwell, who only cared about cattle, money and power. Could she and the Averells survive another of his attacks and had her arrival triggered his outrage? It was probably a waste of time to build her shack. Bothwell would burn it to the ground the moment she left for Casper with Michael.

Her lips trembled and she willed herself not to cry. When Michael noticed, he left the pups to rush to her side. "Are you all right? Why don't you go back to the cabin and lie down?"

He guided her back to her room, again apologizing for his playful mistake. She was too tired to argue and accepted his help to the cabin. Closing the door before he could say another word, she sat on the bed and picked up the book. It would be twilight soon and she needed to light the oil lamp. But before darkness arrived, Susan reclined on the bed and fell asleep.

During the night she thought she heard music. There was a pause and then the sound of a harmonica wailing in the distance. She didn't know anyone who played a mouth organ. Was it Harvey or Michael? Or one of the boys? The music was growing louder. She smiled. Was someone serenading her? She pushed up the sash and looked out. A tall man with his hands to his mouth stood outside her window. It had to be Michael. Harvey and the boys weren't that tall.

When he approached the window, she panicked and drew back the shade. What was he thinking? He knew she wanted to keep their relationship on a friends-only basis. A moment later the music stopped and she heard a pebble strike the glass. Ignoring his attempts, she blew out the lantern and began to undress in the dark. He would get the message soon enough.

Next morning everyone was up before the sun. Susan bustled about the kitchen preparing breakfast and ignoring Michael as best she could. The sun was unbearably hot that day and they rested more often than they had before. Susan glanced in the direction of the Bothwell ranch. She noticed the others doing the same. They were like fish trapped in a pond if cattle stampeded again in their direction. It was too far to run back to the Averell's store. Where could they go? She envisioned them all stuffed like sardines in the bottom of the well.

<><><>

Two mornings later they were back at work digging the holding pond deeper near Susan's homestead site. When she noticed dark clouds on the horizon, Michael said that it was just an early summer storm, but her hands trembled and she dropped her hoe. Remembering the tornado, she looked about for a place to escape the storm. She would have to dig a root cellar after the shack was built, but she wouldn't ask anyone to help, not even the boys.

Jimmy's nephew Ralph had been quieter than usual since the well cave-in, causing Susan to worry about him. He had come to Wyoming for his health and she didn't think he should be spending so much time working in the sun. But when she suggested that he rest, he assured her that he was fine. She suspected that it was a matter of pride to keep up with the younger boys. Concerned, she had asked Ella about him and was told that he was his own man at nineteen and didn't want to be coddled. He reminded her so much of Jimmy.

Late that afternoon as the sun was sinking behind the mountains, they heard the sound of a wagon approaching. Susan's heart leaped into her throat before she recognized Ella and Jimmy slumped in the wagon box. They must have traveled a great distance in the heat. Michael helped Ella from the wagon and soon had his arms loaded with supplies. The couple appeared worried but declined comment until they entered the store.

Seated at the bar with a mug of cold beer, Jimmy reported that there had been recent attacks on most of the homesteaders. "The cattlemen still think they own the entire county and can keep it as grazing land."

"But isn't the governor going to do something?" Susan asked.

Jimmy wiped his brow with a red bandana. "He hasn't done anything yet and I doubt he ever will. Warren hasn't been in office long and he has friends among the cattlemen."

"Doesn't he care about the homesteaders?"

He shrugged. "Some of the settlers are talking about forming an army to fight the cattlemen."

"There's not enough of 'em," Harvey said.

Susan noticed that Michael's expression was one of worry. "Maybe you should wait until next spring to build your house," he said.

"Next spring? I can't wait that long. I'll run out of money—"

"Not if you work for me this winter."

Ella took her arm. "Michael's right. It's too dangerous to stay here on your own before there's law and order."

"I can defend myself."

"I think you underestimate the lengths that Mister Bothwell will go to get rid of homesteaders."

Jimmy placed his arm around his wife's shoulder, rocking her gently. "Now, Ella, don't go scaring the girl. Bothwell wouldn't dare do her harm."

"I wish I had your confidence, dear. Mister Bothwell's a ruthless man who will do anything to steal back this land. Don't forget what's he's already done."

"The missus is right," Harvey said. "Bothwell aims to control the whole Sweetwater Valley."

Jimmy curled his lip. "He's gonna have a fight on his hands if he tries."

"I noticed that you didn't bring back the bags of cement we need to seal Susan's well," Michael said.

"The store ran out and doesn't expect another shipment for three days."

"Oh, no," Susan wailed. She then told them of the well cave-in.

"It may be an omen," Ella said. "A message from above that you shouldn't build until next spring." She urged her new neighbor to return to Casper with Michael until the valley was safe. But no amount of persuasion could change Susan's mind. Just let Bothwell and his men try to take her land. She would pepper them all with buckshot, if necessary. That would mean buying a shotgun, but she didn't think she could spare the money.

Hot and tired, she returned to the guest cabin. Washing her face with water from the basin, she then reclined on her bed for a while before returning to the store. Ella was waiting, her face ashen.

"What's wrong?"

"One of our regular customers just stopped by. He came to warn us that Bothwell's planning a way to get rid of all of us and soon."

Susan gasped. "If that's true, we'd better leave."

"We've heard it all before. Jimmy says it's just scare tactics."

"What can Bothwell do that he hasn't already done?"

Ella briefly closed her eyes. "I don't know and I'm worried.

Susan didn't sleep well that night. She lay awake for hours trying to decide whether to build her cabin or return to Casper with Michael until the following spring.

Next morning after breakfast, Jimmy said, "We can't let that man rule our lives" Grabbing a canteen, he led the male contingency back to the holding pond where they continued digging. The women followed after the dishes had been put away.

When they arrived at the pond, Jimmy straightened to look inquiringly at his wife. Wiping sweat from his forehead with a sleeve, he asked if something was wrong.

Ella shook her head and picked up a shovel. "Just more rumors about Mister Bothwell. We can talk about it later."

Michael must have overheard the brief exchange because he started back in their direction. Susan held up her hand, signaling him to stop. Glaring at her, he went back to work.

Within the hour they raced back to the store to escape a brief rain shower. While they were drying off, Jimmy mentioned that they had failed to buy some necessary supplies while in Rawlins. Ella had been worried about Susan and insisted they rush back home when they learned of attacks on the homesteaders. Would Michael mind taking his wagon and buying the supplies they needed? The cement should be delivered to the store by the time they arrived in Rawlins. Maybe Susan would like to go along.

Both Michael and Susan said that they couldn't leave. The pond needed finishing and Susan's cabin had to be built.

"You'll only be gone a few days," Jimmy countered. "And the six of us will have the pond finished in no time. You might pick up some information on whether the governor is going to provide us some law and order."

Before they could argue, he said, "Good. Then it's settled. I'll make a list." Turning to leave, he nodded for Ella to join him, leaving the two of them alone in the store. The boys and Harvey had already gone to the cafe to find some of Ella's cookies.

Susan stamped her foot. "Is this some sort of conspiracy

you cooked up with the Averells? You know I don't want to go to Rawlins with you."

"They're worried about you, Susan. They know that Bothwell's planning something even more sinister than he's already done."

"Then we need to stay here and fight Bothwell with them. Not desert them."

"I doubt they would send us to Rawlins if they knew Bothwell was going to attack."

"Harvey warned us about that, and the cowpoke that stopped by said so, too."

"Jimmy wants us to buy more guns and ammunition. He said he thought about it all the way back from Rawlins."

"That makes sense. But what if something happens before we get back?"

Michel's smile was one of obvious relief. "Then you'll go?"

"I don't understand why you can't take Harvey or one of the boys with you instead."

"They're needed here to help fortify the store and outbuildings after they finish the pond tomorrow."

"But—"

"I need you to help me keep watch along the trail in case there's trouble brewing. You said you're good with guns." He raised a brow as though her marksmanship was in question.

"Yes, I'm a good shot."

Michael sighed heavily. "We should leave tonight in case Bothwell has someone watching the road ranch."

"I'll go on one condition, Mister O'Brien. That we're nothing more than comrades in arms."

"You've made that quite plain, Miss Cameron. Believe me, I have no designs on you at all."

Why did that bother her? He actually seemed to mean what he said.

Chapter Fifteen

They left in the supply wagon at twilight. Although relieved the moon was a mere sliver, Susan worried they might run off the trail. It wasn't long before she realized that Michael had excellent night vision and the horses seemed to know their way to Rawlins.

Jimmy had suggested they spend their first night at an abandoned way station. All that remained was a partial stone retaining wall that had escaped an Indian raid some thirty years earlier. It would protect them from the ever present wind. They parked next to the wall and Susan decided to bed down in the wagon, allowing Michael to use his tent.

They were on their way again at daybreak. Michael talked incessantly about politics and she turned a deaf ear, concentrating instead on when to build her cabin. She knew it would probably be burned to the ground as soon as she left. But if she decided to wait until spring, should she haul the materials to Casper or leave them with the Averells? She was afraid the store and outbuildings would be destroyed, if Bothwell continued his rampage. She finally decided. She would wait to build until after her indentured service to Michael was at an end.

He smiled when she told him her decision. "I think you're wise to wait. There should be law and order in the valley by next spring, so you won't have to worry about masked marauders."

"Masked marauders? Aren't you being overly dramatic?"

"After all we've been through, aren't you worried what the madman might do next?"

She nodded but said nothing more.

"Since you've decided to return to Casper, we might as well get started a day or two after we rest up at the road ranch."

"But what about the Averells?"

"We'll invite them to come along, but I doubt they'll want to leave."

"Perhaps when Bothwell learns I'm leaving, he'll ease up on his attacks."

"It's possible. He might even use your holding pond to water his cattle."

Susan frowned at the thought, wondering if her pond would appease the madman. Something told her that he would step up his attacks on all the settlers, thinking his tactics had frightened her away. Sighing, she closed her eyes and tried to imagine her one-room shack with its view of the majestic Seminoe Mountains. Would it ever become a reality?

They finished the pond by late morning and retired to the cabin café for an early meal. Jimmy told them to take the afternoon off, so Harvey decided to go fishing and trekked off down the creek with Johnny. They were warned to keep a watchful eye. Jimmy decided to take a trip to Casper, and was loading a supply wagon with empty bottles to be filled at the Casper brewery.

Ella had gone to her cabin to retrieve some clothes for the trip to Casper. Her husband was hesitant to let her go, but agreed when she promised to hurry back if she noticed anything unusual happening at the Bothwell ranch.

While Ella was sweeping out her cabin, young Gene rushed in to tell her that a group of Shoshones were camped nearby in the river bottom land where Horse Creek emptied into the Sweetwater River.

"They're the ones that make them purty moccasins you like, Miss Ella."

She smiled. Surely there was time for a quick walk down to the encampment before it was time to leave. Retrieving her reticule, she followed Gene across the meadow to the temporary Indian village. There she bought a lovely pair of beaded moccasins made of fine deerskin with multi-colored beads. Removing her shoes, she decided to wear them back to the cabin. As they crossed the field with her cabin in view, she noticed a buggy with a white surrey top parked nearby. Five men on horseback surrounded the buggy.

When she approached the cabin, a tall, lean man with a manicured beard said, "We need you to come with us." She gasped when she recognized him.

"Where?" she said, her heart pounding. "And why should I go with you?"

He dismounted and blocked her path to the cabin. Grabbing her arm, he pushed Ella into the two-seated buggy.

"I need to change my clothes," she cried. "They're dirty from cleaning the cabin."

"Doesn't matter where *you're* going," the tall man said.

She heard one of the men snicker. The buggy jerked forward before she could escape. It was headed toward the road ranch store. Would Jimmy see them coming and grab a gun? And would they shoot at him? Jimmy had been in the frontier army for twelve years and was a good marksman, but there were too many of them for one man to defend himself. Harvey had gone fishing with Johnny, and Jimmy's nephew Ralph had never fired a gun, so there was no one to help. She could hear Gene screaming as he rode his pony to warn Jimmy, but one of the men grabbed his reins.

"Don't hurt him," Ella cried.

They soon came in sight of the road ranch store, where Jimmy was loading the wagon for the trip to Casper. He had planned to talk to the news editor and others about the dangerous situation in Sweetwater Valley. He didn't say, but Ella knew he was worried about her safety and would try to talk her into staying in Casper.

She screamed Jimmy's name, yelling for him to take cover, but the man driving the buggy turned to slap her hard across the mouth. Another man on horseback leaned from the saddle to harshly inform her they would shoot her husband if she didn't remain quiet. Afraid he would carry out his threat, her fears turned to racking sobs.

Jimmy had stopped the supply wagon near the corral gate and was watching them as they approached. If he had a gun he didn't try to use it. She knew he would never fire in her direction. Two of the riders dismounted and pulled him from the wagon box. He was a small man and easily forced into the buggy with Ella. The procession then headed back toward the Bothwell ranch with three of the men aiming their guns at them.

"Where are you taking us?" Jimmy demanded. "And what's this all about?"

They laughed when the tall man said, "I guarantee you won't be writing any more letters to the editor."

Ella's hand sought Jimmy's and squeezed so hard that

he flinched. The buggy made a wide arc around a huge steepled rock formation, which blocked them from the road ranch's view. Passing within site of the Bothwell ranch house and the small, hastily constructed Sweetwater Chief's newspaper office, Ella noticed two men standing on the roof of the building, watching with field glasses, which reflected the morning sun. The procession then headed toward Independence Rock but veered off into canyon country filled with boulders.

"You're not going to get away with this," Jimmy yelled, sweat beading his forehead and trickling down his face in the hot July sun. When their abductors refused to answer, he pleaded with them to let Ella go.

"They're just trying to scare us so we'll leave the valley," he whispered to Ella. "Don't let them know you're afraid."

The procession continued forward into Spring Creek Gulch, sparsely forested with junipers and pitch pine trees. It was slow going for the buggy on the rocky incline.

"The governor knows what you're up to, Bothwell," Jimmy said in apparent calm. "I've written letters to him about what you cattlemen are planning."

The tall man laughed, "My wife and I visited Governor Warren in Cheyenne last month. He won't do a damn thing about it."

About what? Despite the heat, icy chills ravaged Ella's body. Jimmy was wrong. They were going to die and no one would find their bodies out here in the canyon. She knew Jimmy would jump from the buggy and try to escape, if she weren't there. But he'd never leave her. When they heard her sobs, she was told to stop her blubbering.

"Our homestead land doesn't belong to you," Jimmy said. "We filed on it legally. Maybe we can work something out—fence the meadow land so your cattle will have access to Horse Creek."

The tall man's laugh was bitter.

Jimmy hugged his wife to him and tried his best to comfort her until the procession came to a sudden stop and they were ordered to leave the buggy. He continued to argue with the men as guns were jammed into their backs and they stumbled forward over sloping, rough terrain. When they came to a scrub pine tree, they were forced to climb a large flat rock. Ropes were quickly slung over a limb and nooses placed over their heads. Ella bobbed and weaved to avoid the rope but was finally subdued.

Before she could cry out, she watched as the tall man pushed her husband from the rock. The limb bent so low that Jimmy bounced off the ground with booted toes. As he struggled, one of the men pushed Ella and she swung against her husband's body in her attempt to touch the ground. Her new beaded moccasins fell from her feet as the rope tightened and she could no longer breathe. Clutching at the rope with both hands, she bumped into Jimmy whose face was turning blue from lack of oxygen. Their terrified eyes met an agonizing moment before a gunshot sounded and her world darkened. She heard nothing more.

<><><>

They arrived in Rawlins before dusk the following afternoon. The dusty streets were filled with ranchers, cowpokes and homesteaders. Women with children in tow were boarding wagons and buggies for the trip home after a day of shopping. Piano music floated on the breeze from various saloons, and Susan realized that her stomach was growling. Michael pulled the wagon alongside the livery stable and jumped down to unhitch the horses. Susan knew she should help but was exhausted. All she could manage was supper at the Rawlins House and an early soft bed.

During their meal they overheard other patrons discussing the county split as well as cattle rustling. Before they finished their meals, a heated argument evolved into a fist fight. Michael grabbed Susan's arm and led her out to the boardwalk. When he returned after paying for their suppers, he hurried her off to the hotel.

"Old ways die hard," he said when they reached the hotel.

"Do the cattlemen actually think they can force out all the homesteaders?"

"It's a matter of survival for the cattlemen. If they don't continue to get free grazing, they'll go bankrupt. The recent freezing winters killed off entire cattle herds. That, coupled with declining cattle prices, has them in a panic. They're still blaming their misfortune on the homesteaders and the territorial legislature for splitting the county in half."

"How many expenses can there be, Michael? Harvey said his wrangler job only paid twenty-five dollars a month."

"Cattlemen have been living high on the hog. Fancy ranch houses, trips to Europe, hob-nobbing with politicians and high society, the Cheyenne Club—"

"So they've only got themselves to blame."

"Apparently so, and they're hanging on for dear life."

Susan made a face. "What I don't understand is why the government set aside homestead land for unsuspecting settlers, if they knew the situation here."

Michael shrugged. "Why did they throw two warring tribes—the Arapaho and Shoshone—together on the Wind River Reservation just north of here. The government has its own agendas."

Susan sighed. Her dream of living independently was fading fast. She couldn't sell her homestead because she hadn't proved up on the land, and she couldn't afford to abandon it.

Claiming exhaustion, she climbed the stairs to her room, leaving Michael standing in the lobby. Hoping she wouldn't have to occupy the same room with another saloon girl, Susan quickly undressed and climbed in bed. The mattress was lumpy but she soon fell asleep.

Gunshots woke her during the night. Crawling out of bed, she crept to the window, which faced a saloon. A crowd had gathered in the street and two men were pacing off, back to back, when a lawman arrived. Firing another shot in the air, he herded the two men down the street. Susan hoped it was to jail. This never would have happened back home. Was lawlessness the price one had to pay for independence and freedom?

She lay awake for what seemed hours, frightened a stray bullet would lodge in her bed. When she at last fell asleep, a knock at her door awakened her. When she asked who was there, she heard Michael's voice telling her to get dressed. They needed to leave town. He was waiting for her when she opened her door.

"Why so early, Michael?"

"We need to get back to the road ranch. I've got a bad feeling about Bothwell's next assault on the homesteaders. I overheard some cowpokes talking about a planned raid in Sweetwater Valley. It sounded like the Averells might be the next victims."

"Where was this, Michael?"

"I stopped in at a saloon to listen to what people were saying."

"Then we'd better leave now."

"As soon as we have breakfast and gather up the supplies on Jimmy's list."

Over breakfast at the Rawlins House, Michael told her about the duties he expected her to perform as his assistant at the veterinary clinic.

"Cleaning cages? I don't think—"

"All right, I'll hire a young man to take care of it."

"I don't mind doing the paperwork and making appointments. Or feeding the animals."

Michael nodded. "I should have asked sooner. Are you sure you like animals."

"Of course I do, especially puppies."

He grinned. "That's what worries me, Susan. You're going to spoil my patients."

"My main concern is living in a frontier town. I hope they've built more stores and houses."

"I'm afraid they've concentrated on building saloons and broth—"He hesitated.

"And what, Michael?"

"Uh—just before we left Casper, I heard they were planning to hold classes in the First Congregational Tabernacle Church until they can collect enough money to build a brick school house."

"So the town is becoming civilized." She noticed a dubious expression on his face.

"You saw the clothing and dry goods store. The hotel, grocery and feed store. And don't forget the Demorest Home Restaurant, where we ate supper the night you arrived. I understand they're planning to build more churches."

"You don't have to convince me, Mister O'Brien. They've probably added a few more businesses while we've been away. I'm sure I'll make friends and survive."

He set his coffee cup aside. "I heard they built a boarding house not far from the hotel. You might want to stay there."

"Why?"

"I'm sure it's less expensive than the hotel."

"I see. So you're not planning to pay me much for my hard work."

"I think twenty-five cents an hour is more than fair

wages," he said. "You should be able to save at least half your income to buy supplies for next year."

"What about my lumber and building supplies?"

"We'll haul them to Casper for safe keeping. Fortuntely, the Averells didn't replace your windows or purchase the concrete bags."

This might work out after all. She hated the thought of leaving her new friends but the road ranch was crowded. She and Michael needed to leave so the Averell's could charge travelers for their accommodations. She dreaded the thought of loading everything back into Michael's wagon along with three puppies, and Michael's veterinary supplies. At least she wouldn't have to worry about breaking new windows for a while or her house burning down. Smiling, she looked forward to a new adventure in the railroad town along the North Platte River.

But a nagging thought told her they should stay at the road ranch to help defend their friends?

Chapter Sixteen

They stopped by the newspaper office for the latest edition as they were leaving Rawlins. The headline was larger than usual and seemed to shout in bold print: DOUBLE LYNCHING. The prominent article said that James Averell of Sweetwater Valley had been hanged with a prostitute who had been living with him. Averell had been operating a hog ranch—a rural brothel—and Ella Watson, also known as Cattle Kate, had been accepting stolen calves in payment for her services. The article went on to say that Ella's corral held fifty head of newly branded steers, which prompted the cattlemen to act. Ten to twenty men had sneaked up on the Averell's cabin at night while they were drinking whiskey and playing cards.

Susan gasped as Michael swore beneath his breath.

The newsman shook his head and sighed. "I thought Ella Watson was a nice lady. She used to cook at the Rawlins House where I ate my meals when I first came to town."

"No!" Susan grabbed the newspaper and continued to read. "This isn't true. Ella wouldn't steal cattle."

Michael took the newspaper from her and led her to

a chair near the door. Turning back to the editor, he said, "This is a mistake. We just left Ella and Jimmy at the road ranch. And I agree with Miss Cameron. Ella Watson was *not* a woman of ill repute and would *never* accept calves in exchange for her favors. And Jimmy Averell's a good man who would never operate a brothel."

"Sheriff got a telegram this morning from Casper. Seems the bodies were left hanging for two days before they cut 'em down."

"No!" Susan shrieked again, ripping the newspaper from Michael's hands.

"Do they know who hanged them?" Michael asked.

"Nobody seems to know. Seems there was a customer in the store by the name of Frank Buchanan who took off after them. He claims to have shot at the men but couldn't stop the hangings."

Michael's face turned crimson with rage. "I'd advise you to print a retraction in your filthy rag about the Averells."

"I don't know why you keep calling them the Averells. Everybody knows they were living in sin."

"That's not true," Susan cried. "They were a wonderful married couple and my good neighbors."

The newsman lowered his eyes. "All I know is what the sheriff told me."

"Let's go," Michael said, taking Susan's arm. "We've got to get back to the road ranch."

Susan was forced to trot to keep up. Tears clouded her vision and she nearly fell before she reached the wagon. When he had helped her onto the wagon seat, Michael suggested she keep her pistol handy on the trip back to the valley.

"If the story's true, it's not safe for you to stay in the valley, Susan. If they've actually hanged the Averells, you're their likely next victim."

She was too busy grieving to argue. The news report

had to be untrue. Tenting her fingers, she prayed that someone else had been the victims of the cattlemen's wrath, but deep down she knew.

"I've heard the name Cattle Kate before," Michael said that night as they were preparing their evening meal. "She's rumored to be a ..." He hesitated before saying the words, "soiled dove. She's also a suspected cattle rustler."

"Not Ella?"

"No, a rough-looking woman who lives near Casper."

Susan felt buoyed by the news. "Then it wasn't Ella they hanged."

His expression was sympathetic. "Don't get your hopes up, Susan. The area where the couple was hanged isn't far from the road ranch. And they found a new pair of beaded moccasins under the woman's feet."

Susan bit her lip, remembering that Ella had said she wanted some beaded moccasins. Her throat seemed to close as tears refilled her eyes. She should have stayed behind when Michael left for Rawlins. She would have shot them all, if she'd had the chance.

Michael covered her hand with his own and she didn't pull away. She was engulfed in the worst nightmare of her life and knew that she needed him, no matter how repulsive he could be at times.

When Susan and Michael arrived at the road ranch, they found that the boys had excavated a large hole on the edge of the pasture. Underground water had seeped into the bottom of the five foot hole from Horse Creek and the Sweetwater River. The bodies had been placed in roughhewn caskets and the lids were in the process of being nailed down when they arrived. Susan hurriedly climbed from the wagon, glad that they had reached the road ranch in time. Jimmy's young nephew stood back from the grave, the boys all with tear tracks on their stricken faces. When eleven-year-old Gene noticed her, he ran into her arms.

A number of shoulder-slumped men stood nearby as Justice of the Peace B. F. Emery conducted a coroner's inquest. Frank Buchanan, Ralph Cole and Gene Crowder answered his questions and it was determined that the men guilty of the hangings were Albert Bothwell, Tom Sun, Robert Connor, John Durbin, Robert Galbraith, and Earnest McLean, all cattlemen, with the exception of McLean, a dairyman.

As members of the coroner's posse lifted the pine boxes the boys had built and started toward the hole, Ralph rushed over, insisting that he carry one end of Jimmy's coffin. After they were placed in the sodden hole and covered with dirt, two oak wagon wheels were rolled onto the graves to serve as headstones.

Gene returned sobbing to Susan's side. "We didn't have a chance to say goodbye."

Unable to speak, Susan hugged the boy to her. She then noticed a small hunched figure walking toward them from the corral. Harvey was holding something. When he reached them, he handed Susan a tiny, roughly-carved wooden horse. He said he would place it on the grave to speed Jimmy on his way to Heaven. "I cut it from an upright post," he said apologetically.

"What about Ella?"

Harvey walked over to a rock where a pair of beaded moccasins rested. "Them's winged moccasins. They'll fly her there with Jimmy."

Susan reached for them. "Why weren't they placed on her feet?"

"'Cause their bodies smell real bad after hanging in the sun and they're crawling with maggots—"

Susan fainted, falling before anyone could catch her. When she regained consciousness, she was lying on her bed with a damp cloth across her forehead. Michael sat in a chair beside the bed holding her hand, a concerned expression on his face. The boys stood at the foot with Harvey, who looked equally worried.

Harvey's lower lip quivered. "Sorry, Miss Susan. I shouldna told you—"

"It's all right. Don't blame yourself." Closing her eyes, she shivered in the mid-day heat although her companions were soaked with sweat. When she tried to sit, Michael restrained her.

"Better take it easy for a while.'"

"But I want to say a prayer for Ella and Jimmy before—"

"It's been done, Susan. We couldn't wait any longer in this heat. We can eulogize them right now." He bowed his head and recited the Lord's Prayer. They then all took turns saying a few words of praise for the Averells. Susan was so distraught that her words were unintelligible. When she at last opened her eyes, she realized they had all filed from the room—everyone except Michael, who still held her hand.

"I talked to Frank Buchanan. He jumped on his horse and followed the killers after they forced Jimmy into the buggy. When he saw what they intended to do, he fired at them from a distance, but it was too late. They had already pushed Ella and Jimmy off a rock and returned his fire. When he emptied his revolver, he got out of there before they killed him too."

"Poor Ralph. He's not well—"

"Frank said when he came back to tell Jimmy's nephew what had happened, Ralph rode out in a hurry and didn't tell Frank where he was going."

"Thank the Lord he came back to the store before they killed him."

"We need to leave for Casper as soon as you're feeling better. It's not safe to stay with those madmen riding roughshod over the valley."

"We can't leave the boys."

"Harvey said he would stay with them until we get back."

"But, Michael—"

"We need to talk to the sheriff in Casper to make sure that justice is done."

"Are they going to arrest the cattlemen?"

"The posse left for Tom Sun's place. The Justice of the Peace said he's going to talk to all the suspects."

"But those evil men might try to harm the boys before they're arrested."

"With the news of the Averells' deaths in all the territorial newspapers, they won't dare chance another raid on the road ranch."

"Then I'll stay here to care for the boys."

"I'm not leaving without you, Susan. We need to make sure the killers are taken into custody. When they're all in jail, I'll help finish the well and build your house."

"Is that a promise?"

Michael released her hand to cross his heart. "Promise. I know how important your homestead is to you. I won't let you down."

Despite his protective hand, she sat up in bed. "How dare they spread lies about Ella and Jimmy?"

"All they care about is stealing their land. They don't care how many lives they ruin to do it."

"They're not getting *my* land, if I have to shoot every one of them."

Michael's worried face told her everything she needed to know.

<><><>

Michael talked to the boys the following morning, exacting a promise from Harvey that he would stay to protect the boys until he and Susan returned. They then rode to Ella's cabin to make certain it hadn't been ransacked. When they returned to the road ranch, they cooked enough food to last the boys for several days while they were gone. Leaving them behind was going to break her heart and she hugged them often.

"Can we keep one of the puppies while you're gone?" Gene asked.

"Of course you can. If you promise to keep them safe, we'll leave all three." That brought smiles to sad faces.

"I wish we had enough room in the wagon to take you all with us." Susan wiped a tear from her cheek.

"We'll be fine," Ralph said, stretching to his full height, a few inches taller than Harvey. He reminded her so much of Jimmy that she turned her back to choke back tears.

Michael took her arm and led her to the wagon, the others trailing behind. When she had managed to compose herself, she hugged them all goodbye and allowed Michael to help her onto the wagon seat. The boys all waved as the wagon left for Casper.

They said little during the trip, both grieving in their own way. Susan was heartened by Michael's determination to bring the killers to justice.

She was surprised by all the building that had taken place when they arrived in Casper. A number of streets had twice the amount of businesses than she had witnessed earlier. Riding down Center Street, Susan saw that one entire block was filled with saloons. The alley between David and Center streets housed a row of cribs behind the saloons.

"This is one area you'll want to stay away from," Michael warned. "The women on this street are not those you'd want to associate with."

"Really? Why?"

He glanced at her as though she were the most naive person on earth. "We'll talk about it later."

After they arrived at the livery stable and taken care of the horses, they walked to the lot where Michael planned to build his veterinary clinic. They then found the sheriff's office where Michael questioned the deputy about his plans to apprehend the killers.

Casting his gaze to the toes of his boots, the deputy said, "Sheriff hasn't filled out warrants for their arrests yet."

"What's the hold up?"

"Can't say. He has to talk to all the witnesses."

"Where can we find him?" Susan asked.

"He's over to the newspaper office."

They thanked him and left.

The sheriff was leaving when Michael opened the office door to the *Casper Weekly Mail.* "We'd like a minute to talk to you," he said.

"Make it quick. I'm on my way to Sweetwater Valley."

"That's what we want to talk to you about. The Averells were our friends and Miss Cameron filed on the neighboring homestead."

"That right?"

"Our friends were murdered while we were on a supply trip for them to Rawlins," she said.

"Friends, huh?" He looked her up and down. "You seem a decent sort."

"And so were Ella and Jimmy Averell."

"That's not what I've been told."

"Lies. All lies by the cattlemen to cover up their heinous crimes," Susan said heatedly. "They tore down her fences and stole the cattle she bought from an emigrant before they hanged her and her husband."

"I heard she was running a hog ranch and taking calves—"

"A bald-faced lie," Michael roared.

"We'll see about that." The sheriff turned on his heel and left.

Susan wrung her hands. "No one believes us, Michael. What can we do?"

"I think we'd better head back to the valley and bring the boys here with us."

As much as she hated the thought of another bumpy wagon ride, she shook her head in agreement. They needed to talk to Frank Buchanan before he left the road ranch. They should not have left the boys alone with Harvey. Although the cowpoke was well meaning, he wasn't the smartest wrangler in the valley.

The horses needed to rest overnight before they returned to the road ranch. They ate supper at the Demorest Restaurant and took rooms at the hotel. They then left at dawn the following morning before breakfast. Susan was worried about the boys, especially Ralph, who seemed inconsolable since his uncle's death.

Michael stopped the wagon at Red Buttes for a quick mid-day meal and they were on their way again after watering the horses in the North Platte River. Susan's lower lip was swollen from the numerous times she'd bitten it while worrying about the boys. What were they thinking, leaving them at the cattlemen's mercy?

"Are we halfway there?" she asked at dusk when Michael pulled the wagon under a cottonwood near the river.

"Not quite. Quit worrying, Susan. Bothwell and his men aren't stupid enough to risk another raid this soon."

"Now you sound like Jimmy. Look how wrong he was."

Michael hung his head and said nothing more as he set about preparing the evening meal. Needing to be alone, she walked to the river to wash away her tears. She felt responsible for the calamity that had befallen everyone. If only she hadn't insisted on homesteading in the valley.

Chapter Seventeen

They arrived at the road ranch when the moon was full, as exhausted as their lathered horses. Susan's heart rate increased when she noticed no lantern light in the cabin.

"Maybe they covered the windows so no one would know where they are," Michael said.

Susan released the breath she was holding. "I hope you're right. I couldn't bear it if something happened to the boys."

Michael climbed from the wagon and hurried to the door. No one answered when he knocked. "It's Michael O'Brien," he said. "Open up."

Susan glimpsed brief muted light at the window and knew someone was inside. Seconds later the door opened a few inches and a pair of eyes peered out at them. Michael pushed the door open and turned to beckon to Susan.

When she entered the cabin she saw that Harvey stood near the door with his gun drawn. Johnny, Gene and Ralph were seated on the floor, a lantern between them, each with a handful of cards. When Susan was safely inside, Michael bolted the door behind them. He was right. Dark blankets covered the windows, apparently nailed in place.

"Mister Buchanan just left," Johnny said. "He's feedin' the puppies and bringing us some food from the ice house."

Susan squinted in the lantern light. "What have you been up to while we were gone?"

Johnny said, "Gene was so mad about the hangings that he rode over to the Bothwell ranch to tell them what he thought of 'em."

Susan gasped. "Didn't anyone try to stop him?"

"I went after him," Harvey said. "They pulled guns on me and told me not to come back or I'd wind up like the Averells."

"Oh, no." Susan collapsed into Jimmy's rocking chair.

The angry expression on Michael's face intensified in the lantern light. "What about the deputy? Did he stop to question Gene and Frank?"

"Yes, sir," Gene said. "I told him about the bad men who cut Miss Ella's fence and stoled her cattle. When I tried to ride to the store to warn Mister Jimmy, one of 'em grabbed my pony's reins and stopped me."

"Did the deputy arrest Bothwell?"

"Don't know," Harvey said. "He left before the boy rode over to Bothwell's ranch."

Susan rose from the chair. "You all need to come to Casper with us. It's too dangerous to say here."

"Bothwell has a whole army of gunslingers at the ranch," Harvey warned.

"Is his wife at home?"

Harvey shook his head. "I heard she left for Californie a coupla months ago. He's got a good lookin' housekeeper stayin' there now."

Susan sank back in her chair. "Gene and Frank are the only witnesses who can testify against the cattlemen."

Ralph informed them that he had also seen the men who kidnapped the Averells.

"Did they see you, Ralph?"

"I don't think so. I watched them from inside the store."

"Thank goodness," Susan said.

Ralph got to his feet. "A cowpoke came into the store yesterday. He said those two newspaper men from the *Sweetwater Chief* were standing on their roof with field glasses watching the whole thing happen."

"Did you tell the deputy?"

"Yes, but I don't think he believed me."

Susan looked to Michael. "What can we do?"

He lifted his shoulders but didn't reply.

"I wouldn't go over there," Harvey said. "Bothwell's got guards posted all along what he calls his property line and they've been told to shoot everybody that don't shout out his password."

Susan asked how Harvey knew and was told that he still had friends among Bothwell's crew, but that they wouldn't allow him on the property. It would cost them their jobs and maybe even their lives.

"What kind of men work for someone like Bothwell?" Susan asked.

"I heard his gunslingers are paid a hundurd bucks a month."

Johnny whistled. "That's a lotta money."

"Don't go gettin' any ideas about workin' for Bothwell," Harvey said. "He'd just as soon toss you down a well as look at ya."

"But *you* worked for him," Johnny protested.

"Not for long. When I found out what he was up to, I left."

"I thought you was fired."

"When I punched that feller that started the fire, it was my way of quittin'."

Susan said it didn't matter. She was glad Harvey was no longer in Bothwell's employ. He hung his head, saying he wished he hadn't gone fishing before the men had kidnapped the Averells. Johnny agreed. By the time they returned to the road ranch store, everyone except Ralph had disappeared.

She glanced about the cabin. "Where are the puppies?"

"In the barn," Johnny said. "We got tired of cleaning up after 'em."

A knock sounded and Michael called, "Who's there?"

"Buchanan. That you, O'Brien?"

Michael opened the door a crack before he allowed Frank to enter the store. Moments later they gathered in the Averell's cafe where Frank Buchanan told them what had happened.

"I was talking to Ralph in the store when I heard a bunch of horses ride up. When we looked out the window we saw Tom Sun's new white-topped buggy and Bothwell and some other ranchers on horseback. They grabbed Jimmy and pushed him in the buggy and left."

"Are you sure it was Bothwell?"

"It was him, all right. I recognized the rest of 'em too. Durbin had the reins of Gene's pony but he let him go when they turned the buggy around and headed back toward Bothwell's ranch. There were too many of 'em to take on myself, so I mounted my horse and followed at a distance to see what they were up to."

Buchanan cleared his throat before he continued. "Instead of going to Bothwell's ranch, they headed west toward Independence Rock. I could hear loud voices arguing but I couldn't tell what they were saying."

When the procession stopped in Spring Gulch Canyon, Frank had dismounted his horse and removed his boots so that he could sneak up close enough to hear their plans.

"That's when I saw the Averells standing on a rock and Bothwell looping a noose around Jimmy's neck. Ella was ducking and weaving to stop McLean from doing the same to her. I drew my gun and started firing. I hit one of them in the hip and he fell down."

"And that didn't stop them?"

"No. When my gun was empty, I started to reload. Bothwell had already pushed Jimmy off the rock and Ella was shoved right after him. I fired again till I was outta bullets and they were firing back with rifles. So I had to hightail it outta there."

"Are you absolutely certain of the men's identities?" Michael asked.

"That I am."

Susan placed a hand on his arm. "We know you did your best, Frank. It's not your fault."

When asked what he had done next, Frank said he rode back to the store to tell Ralph and then headed toward Casper to report the crime. He had gotten lost in the dark and came upon Tex Healy's small ranch on Fish Creek. When Healy realized how exhausted Frank was, he volunteered to ride to Casper to report the hangings. Frank acknowledged that his own life was in danger and Michael insisted that he and the boys accompany them to Casper the following day.

Susan asked Johnny what he had done when he discovered the Averells missing.

"They cut down Miss Ella's fence and ran off her steers, so I was tryin' to round 'em up." Johnny then said he had relatives in Steamboat Springs, Colorado, and planned to leave before dawn the following morning, before Bothwell knew he was missing.

Ralph also declined the trip to Casper. "If I don't stay here, they'll burn down the cabins and steal the supplies."

Michael admonished him by saying that the road ranch wasn't worth dying for. He wondered if anyone had notified the Averell's families. If not, he would do so when they reached Casper.

Ralph said, "After Frank told me what had happened,

I rode to Sand Creek to send word to my family after I told the justice of the peace about the murders."

"We need to notify Ella's family." Michael looked about for a writing desk that might contain the address.

"I wouldn't tell them about the bodies hanging in a hundred degree heat for over two days before they were taken down," Frank said.

The others agreed.

Frank said that Deputy Phil Watson and the coroner's posse arrived at the road ranch two days after the hangings and that Frank had led them to the grisly scene. He and the three boys had been awakened in the middle of the night by the posse who insisted they cut the bodies down before daylight. Susan was grateful that Frank didn't describe how the bodies appeared by moon and lantern light. The expression on his face was enough.

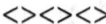

The procession left early the following morning, Michael driving his own wagon and Frank the Averell's supply wagon. Ralph had steadfastly refused to leave his uncle's property and they reluctantly left him behind. Susan prayed that he would remain safe until they returned the following spring to build her cabin, although the thought of living alone in the valley, without the Averells, had nearly convinced her to abandon her homestead.

Chapter Eighteen

News of the hangings had spread through Casper like a spring flood. The two wagons pulled into town at dusk and stopped at the local livery where a small crowd of residents were talking about a harlot called "Cattle Kate." According to the *Douglas Budget*, she'd been hanged with a saloon keeper and hog ranch operator in Sweetwater Valley.

Susan heard one of the discussions and rushed over to correct the men standing nearby. Several laughed and turned their backs on her. What did a little woman with trail dust on her clothing know about such things? Michael pulled her away before she further humiliated herself. Struggling, she stopped yelling and disengaged his hand from her arm.

"How dare you embarrass me like that?"

"You're wasting your breath on them, Susan. They obviously believe whatever they've read in the newspapers."

"But the people who knew Ella and Jimmy won't believe the lies spread by the cattlemen."

"Let's hope not."

She stomped her foot in the dusty street. "They're

ruining the Averells' reputations."

"I'm afraid there's little we can do at this point."

"We can go to the newspaper office and make them print a retraction."

Frank Buchanan volunteered to talk to the editor of the *Casper Weekly Mail*. They found the office closed, so they walked over to the Demorest Restaurant, which was crowded, the conversations lively. Everyone seemed to be talking about the hangings in Sweetwater Valley.

Susan choked on her food midway through the meal. "I can't tolerate any more of these lies." Rising from her chair, she said she was going to the hotel. Michael rose to accompany her but she insisted that he finish his meal. Before he had time to protest, she turned and hurried from the restaurant. The boardwalk was empty except for a cowpoke weaving his way toward her. Obviously inebriated, he grinned when she hesitated, and tipped his battered hat. "Going my way, little lady?"

"Certainly not."

"The lady's spoken for," Michael said as he possessively took her arm.

Trying unsuccessfully to wrench from of his grip, she said, "Spoken for, am I?"

Michael steered her into the hotel lobby where he lectured her as though she were a child. "Women may be legally equal to men here in the territory, but only soiled doves walk the streets unaccompanied after dark."

Susan felt heat rush to her cheeks. "You mean he thought that I—"

Michael nodded. "He had too much to drink and would have taken advantage of you if I—"

"Hadn't come to my rescue?" she finished for him.

He shrugged and changed the subject. "I'll bring your luggage to you as soon as I finish supper."

"As you wish, Mister O'Brien." Susan walked to the

front desk without another word.

<><><>

After breakfast the following morning, Gene returned to the livery stable to play with the puppies while the adults stopped at the sheriff's office to talk to Deputy Watson. The deputy said he had rounded up five of the suspected cattlemen and delivered them to the Carbon County sheriff. They were told that John Durbin had managed to sneak off to his elaborate home in Cheyenne to avoid arrest and have his hip wound treated; but when Judge Corn learned of his whereabouts, Durbin was arrested and taken to jail in Rawlins.

Susan wondered why the prisoners had been taken to Carbon County. Her homestead and that of the Averells were located in southern Natrona County. Watson said the hangings had taken place just over the Carbon County line. He'd received a telegram from the governor's office telling him to turn the prisoners over to Sheriff Joe Hadsell in Rawlins. Hadsell had taken custody of the cattlemen and released them during the early hours of the following morning after allowing them to post each other's $5,000 bonds.

"I thought murder was an unbondable offense," Michael said.

The deputy admitted that he thought so as well. "The Cattlemen's Association is still a mighty powerful organization in the territory. They either buy off witnesses or make 'em disappear."

Frank Buchanan told them that Bothwell had threatened that both he and Tex Healy would be hanged like Jimmy and Ella, if they didn't leave the country. Deputy Watson shook his head knowingly. "Bothwell told me when I arrested him that I'd find six or eight cattle rustlers hanging from trees between his ranch and Casper."

Susan gasped. "And did you?"

"No, ma'am. I think Bothwell has some spokes missing from his wagon wheels."

Michael's face grew even redder. "So the lynchers were all set free?"

"The trial's set for October, if they can round up the witnesses," the deputy said.

They all looked to Frank, who seemed to shrink inside his clothing. Where could he and the other witnesses hide until the trial? Susan pleaded with the deputy to convince Ralph Cole to leave the road ranch. Bothwell must be aware that Ralph was also a prime witness against the cattlemen. The deputy agreed to return to the road ranch the following day to check on Ralph Cole, although he couldn't force him to leave.

The trio then walked over to the newspaper office to talk to the editor, James Casebeer. Frank told them that Casebeer had published Jimmy's letters to the editor in the *Casper Weekly Mail*. He must sympathize with the Averells, unlike other newspapers in the territory, who published the cattlemen's lies.

"Am I glad to see you," Casebeer said when they arrived. "The Cheyenne rags are publishing worthless trash about James Averell and Ella Watson. Tell me what really happened."

When Frank finished telling him as much as he knew, Casebeer hauled out copies of other newspapers. He said from what he had learned from a friend's telegram, a Sweetwater rancher's foreman named Henderson happened to be in Cheyenne when he received a telegram telling him about the hangings. Henderson in turn notified the *Cheyenne Daily Leader* with the news. The newspaper, controlled by the cattlemen's association, then embroidered the facts to glorify the lynchers.

"The editor, Ed Towse, should be writing dime novels," the newsman said. "He and the foreman Henderson must have stayed up all night making up the story of how the evil homesteaders have been victimizing the poor cattlemen. And, of course, the other territorial newspapers picked up the news and reprinted the lies as gospel."

The editor unfolded a newspaper from *the Leader's* rival, *the Cheyenne Sun,* which labeled Ella Watson a prostitute who ran a rural brothel and accepted stolen calves in payment for her services. "That fat fool publisher has Ella Averell confused with Kate Maxwell, who caters to rustlers. Maxwell runs a dance parlor, gambling den and whorehouse in Bessemer Bend, twelve miles upstream from Casper. Kate robbed a Faro dealer and killed a man in Bessemer Bend. That's probably how Ella mistakenly received the label 'Cattle Kate' after she died."

Casebeer read an article aloud from the *Douglas Budget*:

Jim Averell has been keeping a low dive for several years and between the receipts of his bar and his women, and stealing stock he has accumulated some property. While on one of his drunks not long ago, he so abused one of the women that she tried to escape, Averell caught her and tore her clothes from her body, but she got away—

"Stop," Susan cried. "I won't listen to any more of these horrible lies."

"She's right," Frank said. "It's all pure hogwash. And I know for a fact that the only cattle on either homestead was bought and paid for by Ella, with money she earned while working as a cook at the Rawlins House. She bought her LU brand from Gene Crowder's dad before he left the valley. All her cattle had been branded just before she and Jimmy were hanged. But the cattlemen said they'd been rustled."

"That so?" Casebeer said he'd need proof that was true before he'd print it in his newspaper.

"Thank heavens," Susan said. "An honest journalist."

Frank frowned. "The Averells kept their valuable documents in a safety deposit box in Rawlins. That's where you'll find the papers."

"May I quote you on that, Mister Buchanan?"

"That and a whole lot more, if you have the time to listen."

Casebeer pulled a pencil from behind his ear and began to take additional notes. It was nearly dusk when they left the office.

"I wouldn't blame Casebeer and his partner Lombard if they put the newspaper up for sale," Frank said. "The cattlemen are liable to burn the place to the ground. *The Casper Weekly Mail* seems to be the only paper in the territory that doesn't print the cattlemen's lies."

Susan said, "What I don't understand is how newspapers in New York, Salt Lake City and Denver got the dime novel version of the hangings so soon."

"The Wyoming Cattlemen's Association news service," Michael replied. "I'll bet my money belt they sent out telegrams the minute they reached Sand Creek, the same time they sent one to Henderson in Cheyenne It's lucky they didn't spot Ralph when he rode into town."

Frank mulled that over for a moment before he said, "I think I'd better find me a place to hide until the trial takes place in October."

Michael agreed. "What about Tex Healy's place?"

"Don't think so. Bothwell threatened Tex the same as he did me. We both need to make ourselves scarce for a while."

"I'll keep Gene with me," Susan said. "We'd better get back to the livery. He must be hungry by now."

Michael had warned the boy not to leave the stable until

their return. Frank could take care of himself. When they reached the stable, Gene was nowhere in sight although they heard the puppies yelping in a cage at the rear of the building. They had forgotten to feed them. Michael asked the owner if he knew where Gene had gone.

"An older man came riding in not long after the boy arrived and they left together."

Susan gasped. "Did Gene put up a fight?"

"Not sure," the stable keeper said. "I was busy feeding the horses."

Michael told him to bring his horse around. He insisted that Susan return to the hotel while he searched for the boy. He refused to listen to her protests as he lifted a saddle onto the horse's back and tightened the cinches. Frustrated, she hurried back to the main street to search for Gene herself.

The boardwalks were crowded with shoppers, the main street filled with buggies, wagons and horses tied at the hitching rails. The stable owner had to be mistaken. Gene would not have ridden off with a stranger, without making a fuss. It then dawned on her that it could have been the boy's father, who had returned to claim his son. But wouldn't Gene have insisted that he let her know he was leaving? She knew he wouldn't deliberately cause her worry.

She thought of Johnny, worried that he may not have reached his destination in Steamboat Springs. And what of Ralph Cole? He was definitely in danger. They should have stayed at the road ranch until they knew the cattlemen were in prison. Susan hurried to the sheriff's office to report Gene's disappearance. Once there, Deputy Watson suggested that Frank Buchanan may have taken the boy with him to hide until the trial.

"Frank would have let us know they were leaving. And the man at the livery stable said an older man had ridden off with Gene. Frank is only in his late twenties." She then described him.

"Coulda been old man Crowder. Gene's the youngest of nine kids, so if he heard about the hangings, I'm sure he would have tried to protect the boy."

Susan nodded but the sick feeling in her stomach belied the deputy's explanation. She made him promise to let her know if he learned of Gene's whereabouts. She then left to search every store in town. When she failed to locate him, she queried people on the boardwalks, but everyone claimed not to have seen the boy that morning. Discouraged, she returned to the hotel.

Michael arrived at the hotel several hours later. He had ridden in all directions without success. Gene and the old man had vanished. She asked if Michael had located Frank Buchanan. Sighing heavily, he said Frank had also disappeared.

"This can't be happening. We'll be next to disappear." Crying uncontrollably, she allowed him to take her in his arms.

"We're safe, Susan. We were in Rawlins when the hangings took place. We're not a threat to the cattlemen."

"But Bothwell wants my land. And he knows that we know he's behind the murders."

"He also knows that we can't testify against them and the rest of the lynchers. Too many witnesses disappearing will be hard for Bothwell and his cronies to explain."

As they stood talking in the upstairs hall, Michael told her that he had met a rider from Cheyenne on the trail while searching for Gene. The stranger said that Ella's cattle had been shipped to the Cheyenne stockyard. *The Daily Leader* claimed they had been stolen by rustlers and would be sold at auction. The proceeds would go to the Cattlemen's Association.

If they were unable to locate Gene, Michael planned

to rent a building to launch his veterinary practice until his own could be built. They also needed somewhere to store Susan's building materials. He offered to buy them from her so that she could afford a train ticket home.

"You would do that for me, Michael?"

"Of course. This rough and tumble town is no place for a sensitive woman like you. I had no right to ask you to help me set up my business. It's too dangerous."

"What do you mean?"

He cited one example. "The feed store employees sleep in a bunker of grain sacks to protect them from stray bullets fired in the nearby saloons. And that's just the tip of—"

"I'm not as delicate as you may think, Mister O'Brien. And I keep my promises."

"Very well then. We'll search for Gene and Frank again tomorrow. Then we'll get started on the veterinary business. Don't ever say that I didn't give you an opportunity to escape."

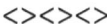

Susan declined Michael's invitation to supper. Worry about Gene had destroyed her appetite and she wanted only sleep. She would inquire about a room at the boarding house after they had exhausted their search for Gene. Sleep evaded her until the wee hours of the morning. Everything that had happened during the past week ran through her mind like her worst nightmare. Ella's sweet face plagued her as did Jimmy's smile. She pounded the mattress with her fists, her hatred for the evil cattlemen overpowering. How dare the authorities in Rawlins allow the cattlemen to go free on bond? They were making a mockery of justice.

When she at last fell asleep, she dreamed of faceless

men hanging from scaffolds in the Rawlins town square. A crowd of townspeople were cheering. Susan awoke with a start when someone knocked at her door. Light streamed through her window but she was too tired to roll out of bed. She then heard Michael's voice and remembered Gene Crowder. Forcing her legs over the side of the bed, she called that she would meet him downstairs. Splashing water on her face, she dried off and quickly dressed. Yawning, she left the room and made her way downstairs to the lobby where Michael stood waiting for her. He offered her his arm.

"Hungry, my lady?"

She managed a slight smile. "Not really but I'll eat something."

He escorted her to the restaurant where they discussed the territory they would cover that day in search of Frank and Gene. Michael thought that Frank may have returned to his friend Tex Healy's ranch on Fish Creek to warn him of the danger. After breakfast they talked again with the livery owner and rented a buggy from him. They had decided that Gene's father would have taken an eastern route to escape the cattlemen. However, if Gene had been kidnapped, his abductor would have taken him back to Bothwell. They would head east for a while, asking along the way if anyone had seen Frank or Gene.

Susan couldn't understand why Frank hadn't left a message that he was leaving. Had someone taken him prisoner or killed him to prevent him from testifying at trial? And what of Gene? If his father had taken him to safety, Gene surely would have insisted on leaving a note at the hotel. What if the same person had kidnapped them both? Scanning both sides of the trail with Michael's field glasses, Susan paused often to wipe moisture from her eyes.

They stopped that night at a sheepherder's camp along

the North Platte River. Michael shared a tent with the dark-skinned young man and Susan slept in his. The herder hadn't seen another traveler for several days. That evening he entertained his guests with his fiddle after a supper of mutton stew. Susan dropped off to sleep to the sound of water splashing over river rocks and the deep-throated croaking of frogs.

When asked the following morning if travelers might have taken another route, the herder shook his head, saying that most people followed the river and newly-constructed railroad tracks into Casper. Susan agreed that neither Frank nor Gene had come that way. The river ran south from that point so they headed north, after filling their canteens.

"I'm worried about Ralph," Susan said when the sun was overhead. "He's so close to Bothwell's ranch that it would be easy to make him disappear."

"I've been thinking similar thoughts. We're not having any luck, so they must be in hiding. We'd better return to Sweetwater Valley. I think we might be able to convince Ralph to come to Casper with us, at least until the trial."

Susan sighed. It was a day's trip back to Casper and another two and a half days to the road ranch. She prayed that Ralph was safe.

They spent another night with the young herder and enjoyed more fiddle music and mutton stew. Pulling Susan to her feel, Michael guided her into a two-step in the firelight. Their dance floor was small and uneven, surrounded by clumps of sagebrush. Laughing for the first time since the hangings, Susan didn't want the dance to end. She could tell that Michael was in a similar mood.

She slept soundly that night and awoke at dawn to the scent of boiled coffee. Michael was helping Jose cook breakfast over the campfire, the scent of bacon making her ravenously hungry. Michael paid the protesting young man when they finished their meal. They then climbed back in the buggy for the trip to Casper.

"I should have written to Ralph," she said. "He probably feels we've abandoned him."

"We practically begged him to come with us. What more could we have done?"

"I know, but—"

"He seems a resourceful young man. I'm sure he'll be fine."

"Ralph didn't look or act well before we left. I hope he's not ill."

Michael attempted to distract her by talking about the veterinary clinic. He had located an abandoned building on Center Street, not far from saloon row. He said it could serve as a temporarily location until his clinic was built to his specifications. Susan tried, but was unable to concentrate on what he was saying. She was reliving her final days with Ella and Jimmy as well as silently railing again at the cattlemen, whom she knew were going to get off scot free. The wealthy could buy their way out of anything, including the prosecution of murder.

"I'll never forgive myself if something happens to Gene or Ralph. Or Johnny and Frank, for that matter. They're the only witnesses to the hangings."

"I heard the two newspaper men at the *Sweetwater Chief* were standing on the roof of their office watching the kidnapping with field glasses."

"Then why haven't they come forward to tell what happened?"

"They probably fear they'll be killed by Bothwell and his men."

"We need to talk to them, Michael."

He said they'd have to store their equipment and building supplies before they left Casper. And find someone other than the livery owner to care for the puppies. He was sure the dogs had already worn out their welcome. They couldn't be happy cooped up in a cage.

Life had become so difficult. Why had she considered leaving home in Missourah and homesteading on her own? She wasn't as strong or independent as she originally thought. Susan glanced at Michael, who didn't seem quite so arrogant or overbearing. Maybe she should take him up on his offer to return home as soon as his clinic was up and running. At least she had that option.

They had a late supper when they reached Casper. Few people were present and Michael seemed unusually happy. Smiling, he asked when she would like to leave for Sweetwater Valley.

"As soon as we unload the wagon and find someone to care for the puppies."

"That shouldn't take long. When we return with Ralph, we'll set up the clinic. "

Susan listened and halfheartedly agreed. "We still don't know what happened to little Gene."

"He and Frank could be anywhere in the territory— hiding until the trial."

"Why didn't they let us know where they went?"

"Frank's probably afraid that we'd let the information slip and Bothwell would hear about it."

"I hope you're right, Michael."

They drove the buggy back to the stable and checked on the puppies. They were sleeping in a cage that had grown too small for them. The stable owner suggested they take them to the widow Hadley, who had a number of dogs of her own and could use the money.

Gathering the squirming pups in their arms, they

followed his directions and arrived at the Hadley home as the widow was feeding her brood. Taller than Susan and thin as a willow reed, she graciously invited them inside. Several dogs came bounding into the sitting room as they entered. Worried they would harm the puppies, Susan asked about their temperament.

"All females," Amelia Hadley said. "They've had young'un's of their own and they'll adopt these puppies and take care of them."

Relieved, Susan agreed to leave them in her care and Michael paid for a week in advance. They then walked back to the hotel, where Susan promptly went to bed. She didn't sleep well that night and was cross the following morning. Snapping at Michael when he arrived late to escort her to breakfast, she noticed the expression on his face and apologized. When he grumbled and turned away, she realized he was experiencing stress of his own.

After breakfast, they inspected the building he planned to rent. There was plenty of room for storage in the back as well as the animal clinic. Behind the building was enough space for several stalls to hold recuperating horses. Why construct a building when they could use the current one? She then remembered they weren't far from saloon row where shots were often fired when drunken men got into arguments. Maybe the location wasn't such a good idea after all.

She helped Michael unload her building materials and the veterinary supplies he purchased in Rawlins. They decided to partition off the storage area when they returned from Sweetwater Valley. Susan swept the floor before Michael locked the building. They exchanged weary smiles and walked back to the general store to buy food for the trip. Michael also bought an additional tent and canteen, saying that he was tired of sleeping in the wagon.

They needed to take the Averell's wagon to the

road ranch, and she wondered how they would return to Casper. She didn't think she could drive one of the wagons on her own. When she mentioned her worry to Michael, he promptly added a side saddle to his purchases. Before she could protest, he said he would take it out of her wages or save it for his next veterinary assistant. Mister Cunningham, the store owner, smiled knowingly, which didn't set well with Susan. But if Michael wanted to waste his money on a saddle, so be it.

Rain came that morning, little more than an hour after they left Casper. Michael had fortunately remembered to bring along a tarp, which they huddled under as the horses plodded forward. Peering at the sky from under the tarp, Susan was fearful of another tornado, but not even a hail storm developed. As with most high desert storms, the rain ended within an hour. The trail was a bit muddy but the wind dried it out before noon.

Susan worried they were driving into a death trap set by Albert Bothwell. Did he have guards posted along the trail to watch for them or did he think they'd left the country for good? Was Ralph safe or had they hanged him and taken over both homesteads? So many questions and no answers. Michael asked what was wrong when he noticed that she had twisted the skirt of her dress into a knot.

They encountered a horse and rider along the trail shortly before they made camp that evening. The cowpoke had ridden from the Sweetwater Valley and was on his way to Casper. His name was John Sapp and he had served as Albert Bothwell's foreman until he was fired for arguing with his boss about the hangings. When asked if he knew Ralph Cole, the lanky wrangler said he'd heard that Jimmy's nephew was sick with mountain fever and that he was being cared for by H.B. Fetz, editor of the *Sweetwater Chief.*

"He's not safe," Susan cried.

"It's worse than that," Sapp said. "Bob Conner, one of the cattlemen who hanged the Averells, has been sending whiskey to Fetz to give to Ralph to help with his back pain. He said it was orders from Doctor Haynes, the Natrona County coroner.

"Why's the coroner prescribing for Ralph?"

"He's a friend of Bob Conner."

Michael was livid. "We've got to save Ralph before it's too late."

Sapp look dubious. "Ralph's having seizures. I'm afraid it's already too late. I overheard Bothwell and Conner talking about putting small doses of strychnine in the whiskey to give to the Cole kid."

"No!" Susan gripped Michael's arm. "We've got to save him, if we have to ride all night."

"The horses won't make it, Susan. We've got to let them rest a few hours."

Sapp stroked his mare's neck. "My mount's done in too."

"Why didn't you tell Fetz about the strychnine?"

"Bothwell's gunmen escorted me off the ranch and halfway here. I was told I'd be shot on sight if I tried to go back."

"Was Fetz in on the plan to kill Ralph?"

"I doubt it. He seems a decent sort although he's cowed by Bothwell."

"When did Ralph get sick?" Susan asked.

"A few days ago. There was an epidemic of Mountain fever last year but it didn't kill many people, especially somebody as young as Ralph. I'm gonna stop in at the sheriff's office in Casper to report what the cattlemen are doing."

"You're welcome to camp here with us tonight," Michael

said. "We'll leave as soon as the horses are rested."

Sapp warned them to be careful. Bothwell and Connors were out to eliminate anyone who could testify against them. While they were eating bacon and canned beans, the foremen said he also heard that Ernie McLean, who had pushed Ella from the rock, had been seen the morning after the hangings blubbering on the doorstep of a local homesteader, confessing that he had taken part in the hangings. And that another homesteader had witnessed the Averells seated in Tom Sun's white-topped buggy escorted by five cattlemen on horseback. They had been riding down the stream bed instead of the trail to Independence Rock.

Michael said, "So there are plenty of witnesses to convict the cattlemen."

"They've been warned they'll wind up like the Averells, if they don't keep their mouths shut tight. Bothwell already got himself appointed postmaster to take Jim Averell's place."

"A murderer appointed postmaster?" Susan gritted her teeth. "The governor must be a cattleman."

"There's no making sense of it," Sapp said. "I'm leaving the territory after I talk to the sheriff. Bothwell's probably got my name on his kill list."

Michael gripped his hand and wished him luck. "Get a few hours' sleep. I'll stand watch while you do." He rose from his perch near the fire and walked to the wagon to retrieve his shotgun.

The night air chilled her as Susan sat by the fire and brooded. Would Bothwell allow them to see Ralph? In the unlikely event he would, could they take Ralph with them? And was it too late to save him?

Michael touched her shoulder and suggested she get some sleep. He had already set up the tent near the campfire and placed a pallet inside. Susan refused to move. She knew she couldn't sleep while worrying about Ralph. Where was Harvey Jones? Why wasn't he taking care of Ralph? John Sapp had already gone to sleep so she couldn't ask.

Who was next on Bothwell's list? Probably herself and Michael. Did they dare venture onto the Bothwell ranch the following evening? She imagined herself shooting her way onto the ranch and finding Ralph. Shaking her head, she knew rescue was impossible.

Michael picked her up when she fell asleep with her head on her knees. She protested when he placed her in the tent and covered her with a quilt, but soon went back to sleep.

Chapter Nineteen

They arrived at the road ranch as the sun was sliding behind the Seminoe Mountains. Michael jumped from the wagon and went inside the unlocked store. He shook his head when he left and rushed to the other cabins. When he returned minutes later, he said that Ralph was nowhere to be found. Nor was Harvey. Susan handed Michael a pair of field glasses and pointed to a freshly excavated mound on the Bothwell property. A lump in her throat prevented her from voicing her fears.

"It could be someone else, Susan. We can't assume it's Ralph."

A moment later she managed to say, "Would Bothwell prevent us from visiting the grave?"

Michael scanned the area with his binoculars. "I don't see anyone on horseback."

"Let's go before someone stops us."

Michael climbed back into the wagon and took the reins. Riding along the border of Jimmy's homestead, which stretched between Horse Creek and the Bothwell ranch, they searched the horizon for riders with rifles aimed at them in the setting sun. The wagon pulled through an unlocked gate on Bothwell's land and Michael climbed down and ran to the grave. Sinking to his knees, he crossed himself, bowed his head and said a brief prayer. Returning to the wagon, he helped Susan down.

"It's Ralph. Be quick with your prayers."

Blinded with tears, she allowed Michael to guide her to the grave. A roughly carved board stated Ralph's name but nothing more.

Michael clinched his fists and swore, "I'll see them all in prison, if it's the last thing I ever do."

Susan wiped her tears. "I feel the same, but there's nothing we can do here now."

"We have to find someone who isn't in cahoots with the cattlemen. Ralph's body needs to be exhumed and tested for strychnine."

Susan noticed someone riding in their direction. "Let's go," she whispered. "before we're accused of trespassing.

"Hold your ground and don't let on that we know about the strychnine."

Susan watched as the tall, neatly bearded man rode toward them and reined in just short of trampling them. "Aha," he said. "My new homesteading neighbor has returned. I wouldn't advise you to stay. We have a mountain fever epidemic here in the valley."

Susan bit her tongue to prevent herself from screaming at him.

Michael's voice was tight. "What happened to Ralph Cole?"

"He died late last night and we buried him here this morning."

"Have you notified his family?"

"As a matter of fact I have. Some of his things are at the newsmen's place and I assume the rest are at Averell's."

Susan found her voice. "What about Ella's family? Has

anyone notified them?"

Bothwell sat taller in the saddle. "I understand that Miss Watson's father will be arriving soon to hold an auction."

"Miss Watson?" Susan then remembered that Ella and Jimmy had kept their marriage secret.

"Yes, that woman living in sin with Averell, and running a bawdy house in her cabin." He swung his arm in the direction of Ella's homestead land.

"Thank you for seeing to Ralph's burial," Michael said. "We'll be on our way back to Casper."

The arrogant expression on Bothwell's face said, *See that you stay there.*

Michael escorted her to the wagon and they hurriedly climbed aboard. Flicking the reins, he drove them back to the road ranch store. When they arrived, Susan resisted going inside. She could feel the ghostly presence of her friends the moment she stepped across the threshold. The store had been ransacked, probably by Bothwell's employees. And a fresh skull and bones had been painted on the door.

"I didn't tell you about this before," he said, "because I was afraid you would scream at Bothwell, if we saw him."

"You're right. I would have and he might have prevented us from leaving." She wiped fresh tears from her face. "But why would Harvey leave Ralph alone? He promised he would stay to protect him."

"Harvey might have been frightened off, Susan. Or worse."

"Do you think they may have killed him, too?"

He nodded, suggesting they prepare something for supper in the cabin café, which hadn't been vandalized. Bolting the door behind them, he said they could clean up the store the following morning before they left for Casper.

Susan left the lantern burning in her room that night. Michael said he would leave his own door open so that he could hear her in the event someone tried to break in. She lay awake for hours, experiencing an eerie feeling that Ella and Jimmy's spirits were floating about the room.

When a curtain fluttered at the window, she gasped. Thinking it might be Ella and not a breeze filtering through a crack between the logs, she said, "I miss you my dear friend. Life will not be the same without you. I hope you and Jimmy are happy in heaven."

The curtain fluttered again and she was tempted to call Michael to witness what was happening. But she couldn't allow him to see her in her nightgown.

"We'll do everything we can to bring your murderers to justice, Ella. Michael and I won't rest until Bothwell's gang is in prison."

A rap at her door startled her. Michael's worried voice asked if she were calling him. No, she said, she was talking to Ella. The door burst open and he was standing there fully clothed.

Pulling the thin blanket to her chin, she shrieked, "How dare you come in my room uninvited?"

"For heaven sake, Susan. I thought someone had broken into your room through the window."

"Ella's here," she said, pointing at the fluttering curtain.

He looked at her as though she were losing her mind. Crossing the room to the window, he ran his hand along the sill. "It feels like an air leak. I noticed some newspapers in the store. I'll stuff them in the crack." He turned and left the room.

When he returned, he tore strips of newspaper and stuffed the offending crack in the frame. "There, now you won't have to worry about fluttering curtains." He promptly left again, closing the door behind him.

She waited several minutes before she said, "If you're

here, flutter the curtain, Ella." When the curtain refused to move, she sighed and lay back on her pillow. Her friend was gone but she was positive that her spirit had been there in the room. Or *was* she losing her mind?

Before they left next morning, Susan wrote a note to Ella's father, offering her condolences and asking that he get in touch with her. She and Michael then straightened up the store and whitewashed the door to cover the skull and cross bones. They knew it would be difficult enough for Ella's father, without finding the crude warning sign. Michael then saddled the horses, which had trailed behind the wagon for the return trip to Casper. Helping Susan mount her sidesaddle, he sat for a moment gazing at what had once been their friends' road ranch.

High winds swept across the prairie as they left. Susan would have been tempted to stay until the winds had calmed but the unoccupied road ranch was so depressing that she couldn't wait to leave. A last look as they rode past the store made her shiver. She could still feel the Averell's presence and that of Ralph Cole's. Fresh tears dried in the wind as she tried to concentrate on the tasks ahead. She was grateful for the job as Michael's assistant and hoped it would keep her mind occupied and off the murders. She still worried about Gene Crowder, Johnny DeCory, Frank Buchanan and Harvey Jones. Bowing her head, she prayed they were safe.

The return trip to Casper seemed to take twice as long as the one they'd made days earlier. They camped at the same location they had shared with John Sapp, and talked about the subject they'd been avoiding all day, Ralph Cole's death.

"He was clearly murdered," Susan said. "But how can

we prove it?"

"We'll have to find someone who's *not* under the cattlemen's thumb to check the contents of Ralph's stomach."

"But the Natrona County coroner—"

"I know, Susan. He's obviously in cahoots with the lynchers."

"Then who—?"

"We'll ask James Casebeer. He used to be the postmaster and I'm sure he'll know who to contact."

She nodded. "Yes, the honest newspaper editor."

"We'll stop there as soon as we reach Casper."

James Casebeer was locking his newspaper office when they arrived. When told of Ralph Cole's death, he unlocked the door and invited them inside.

"I've received other disturbing news," the editor said. "Deputy Watson and Tex Healy were arrested on the charge of horse theft by the sheriffs of Converse and Crook counties. And Frank Buchanan's in protective custody in Cheyenne."

"Cheyenne?" Michael said. "That's the cattlemen's headquarters. How could the Carbon County officials allow that to happen a month before the trial? Unless they're in bed with the cattlemen."

Casebeer shook his head. "My thoughts exactly. That's not all. Watson and Healy's arrest on trumped-up charges of horse thieving will cast doubt on their testimonies as witnesses at trial."

Susan's heart began to pound. What had happened to Gene Crowder, if Frank had been taken to Cheyenne? Gene was an important witness to the Averells' kidnappings.

"We can only hope that it was his father who took him

from the livery stable," Michael said.

Casebeer glanced at the clock on his office wall. "I have an appointment in a few minutes. We can talk about this later."

They agreed and left the office to lead their horses to the livery stable. Michael then escorted Susan to the boarding house, where she secured a room. It would be a busy day tomorrow and she needed a good night's sleep. But how could she sleep with so much on her mind? Witnesses were disappearing, dying and arrested. Were she and Michael on the cattlemen's list? And what had happened to Gene and Johnny? Had they been poisoned like Ralph Cole?

Susan drifted off to sleep with her handgun beneath her pillow. When someone knocked next morning, she drew her gun and aimed it at the door.

"It's Michael. I'll wait for you downstairs."

Groaning, she forced herself out of bed. What she needed most was sleep, but she knew how much work awaited them at the clinic. Dressing in her oldest clothing, she pulled her hair back and fastened it with a clip. Yawning, she left her room and descended the stairs. Michael stood at the foot wearing a disarming grin.

"Breakfast awaits, my lady." Offering his arm, he led her out to the boardwalk and down the street to the restaurant.

He protested when she ordered a small bowl of porridge. When told that she was running low on money, he said that her wages would begin that day. He also said that he planned to open the clinic by the end of that week.

"Are you certain, Michael? There seems a lot of work to do before—"

"Quite certain. I'll order the signs made today and a carpenter will arrive this afternoon to begin work on the counter and a desk for each of us."

Susan remembered the animal cages and examining table stored at the back of the building along with her building supplies. Would it ever be possible to return to her homestead? Her future depended on whether Bothwell and the other cattlemen were convicted of murder.

Later that morning while she was sweeping the clinic's planked floor, James Casebeer stopped by to tell them the latest news. "I thought you'd want to know that I just received a copy of the Rawlins newspaper. It seems that Thomas Watson—Ella's father—traveled incognito from Kansas to her homestead with George Durant, the property administrator. They're auctioning off his daughter's property as well as Averell's."

Susan groaned. "We must have just missed them." She hoped Ella's father wasn't in danger, so close to the Bothwell ranch.

"You may have heard that Ella's cattle were shipped to Cheyenne to be auctioned off," Casebeer said. "The proceeds will go to the cattlemen's association because they claim the cattle were mavericks stolen by rustlers."

"But Ella paid for them," Susan said. "The papers are in her safety deposit box in Rawlins."

"So you've said," Casebeer replied as he was leaving. "I'd planned to track down Deputy Watson to see if he had access to the papers you mentioned. Now he's in jail and the Rawlins officials had the first coroner's inquest of the hangings ruled invalid. They also said that the lynchers are persons unknown, although Bothwell and Tom Sun admitted to Deputy Watson that they took part in the hangings."

"Is there no law and order in this territory that the cattlemen don't control?" Susan asked.

Casebeer shook his head. "When you've got a cattleman in the governor's office, you'd best not cause the association any problems."

"We're indebted to you for your editorials defending

our friends," Michael said. "Please be careful. The cattlemen seem to be targeting everyone who speaks out against them."

He patted the revolver riding on his hip. "My partner and I are putting the newspaper up for sale. In the meantime, we're watching each other's backs."

Susan sighed. Would the new owners support the cattlemen? *The Casper Weekly Mail* was one of the few newspapers in the territory brave enough to rail against the cattle interests.

Before the newsman left, he agreed to run an advertisement for the veterinary clinic. Michael paid for the ad, shook Casebeer's hand and opened the door for him. Once the editor left, Michael asked Susan's opinion of where to place the counter and office furniture. When she ventured an opinion, he began unpacking the supplies he'd purchased from the retired veterinarian in Rawlins. Handing them to her, he asked that she sort them and place them in piles on the floor. Already weary, Susan lamented the fact that they had no chairs. Smiling, Michael took her arm and led her down the street to the general store where he had her select two desk chairs. He then carried them back to the clinic, telling her to have a seat until the carpenter arrived.

Susan gratefully sank into the chair, thinking that traveling to Wyoming Territory was the worst mistake she'd ever made. What was she going to do after Michael's veterinary clinic was operational? Accept his offer to buy her building materials and take the train back home? Perhaps she could start a business of her own in Casper. But all she really knew was horticulture. On second thought, she didn't think people would buy flowers when they could grow them in their yards. And where could she grow them during the frigid winters? She mentally scratched that possibility from her list.

She would have to decide before the first snow. Should she work for Michael until spring with the hope that Bothwell and his cronies would be imprisoned? She wondered if the court had set the trial for October to insure that unknown witnesses would be unable to travel to Rawlins during a snowstorm to testify. The thought made her shiver.

The carpenter arrived early and he and Michael discussed the length and location for the counter. She suppressed a smile when they settled on the exact spot that Susan had chosen.

The clinic door opened and a petite older woman poked her head inside. Susan rose from her chair to invite her in. She introduced herself as Miss Anna Webel, Casper's first school teacher. Handing a newspaper to Susan, she said, "You're one of the few respectable women in town and I thought you might like to read the new ordinance."

Susan accepted the copy of the *Casper Weekly Mail* and read the following:

It shall be unlawful for any woman to frequent or remain in the barroom or saloon between the hours of 7 a.m. and 10 p.m. Upon conviction thereof, shall be fined in any sum not less than five dollars or more than twenty-five dollars. It shall be unlawful to use any vile, profane or unlawful language, or to act in a boisterous or lewd manner, or shall smoke any cigar, cigarette or pipe on any street in Casper, she shall, upon conviction, be fined in any sum not to exceed twenty-five dollars.

"Why are you showing me this?"

"I thought you would appreciate the new law that protects us from all those evil women on David Street."

"Oh, you mean the soiled doves." Susan turned to glance at Michael, who tried to hide his amusement.

"Some people call them that. They've come here in droves to entertain—" Miss Webel's face reddened and she quickly changed the subject. "I'm so glad that a nice young couple has moved to town to care for our animals."

"Oh, we're not a couple. I've just been hired as Doctor O'Brien's assistant."

"But you've been traveling together and I thought—"

News certainly gets around in a small town. Miss Webel will probably decide to classify me with the soiled doves. Susan offered her the other chair and apologized that she didn't have a cup of tea to offer her. Michael needed to buy a wood stove for the clinic before the weather turned cold.

She asked the teacher about her background to deflect further questions Miss Webel might have. Soon the hammering was so loud that the spinster took her leave, promising to return the following day. Susan groaned, hoping that she would be so occupied with paperwork that she wouldn't have time to visit with her. She didn't want to talk about her adventures in Sweetwater Valley or the hangings.

Most of the town's residents dropped by to visit that week, including the mayor, George Mitchell. The handsome young man with a handlebar mustache spent so much time talking to Susan that Michael took him aside to discuss the town's ordinances. She later heard the mayor laughing about how Casper had won the county seat over its neighboring rival town of Bessemer Bend.

"When the ballots were counted, Bessemer's votes totaled 677, more than four times the number of residents," the mayor said. "Casper's ballots totaled 304, which was also more than the eligible voters who live here. The election judges knew there was gross ballot box stuffing but they gave the county seat to Casper, because there were fewer dishonest votes and more people in residence."

Michael wondered aloud what had happened to the people of Bessemer Bend.

"Most of them packed up and moved downstream to Casper."

More dishonesty, Susan thought, shaking her head. How was she going to trust anyone? When the mayor left, she asked Michael if he planned to extend credit to his customers. He thought for a moment before he said he hadn't decided. There seemed to be a disregard for integrity in Wyoming Territory. If customers didn't pay their bills, he would soon be out of business.

Susan smiled. "I've heard that the local doctor takes produce and eggs for his services. Perhaps you should consider doing the same."

"Good idea. Then I can pay you in kind. But that might make it difficult for you to pay your rent at the boarding house."

Susan fretted for the rest of the day. Should she sell her building supplies to Michael before he ran out of money? Returning home to Missourah still didn't set well but staying in Wyoming was placing her life in danger. What should she do?

Later that day, James Casebeer stopped by to tell them that Jimmy Averell's younger half-brother was in Sweetwater Valley interviewing witnesses to the hangings. "It seems that Willie Cahill traveled from Spokane, Washington, and has already found five witnesses who can testify that the cattlemen hanged the Averells."

"Then his own life's in danger," Michael said. "Someone needs to warn him."

"I'm sure he's been warned. All the newspapers in the territory have published little else since the hangings—most if it lies although some truth has come of it."

"The only truth is in your own newspaper, James. Have you been threatened?"

"If you call a skull and crossbones painted on your front door a threat, then, yes, my partner Lombard and I have been threatened."

Susan gasped. "Is that why you're selling the newspaper?"

"That and a few other things. I've decided to take a vacation trip to Yellowstone Park next week. I need a rest from all the bad news."

"Can't say I blame you," Michael said. "I wouldn't be surprised to find something painted on my office door. It looks like the cattlemen are going to get away with all their crimes."

"At least most of the other newspapers have begun to rail against the cattlemen and the false reports from the Cheyenne rags. They finally realized they've been duped by Editor Towse of the *Cheyenne Leader*, who made up the story about the Averells and dubbed Ella "Cattle Kate.""

"He should stand trial for libel," Susan said.

"Who's going to sue him? The Averells?" Casebeer bade them goodbye and left.

Susan decided to walk to the post office to see if she'd received a letter from her mother. She was handed a short note from Ella's father, Thomas Watson, instead. Ripping open the envelope she read:

I received your note telling me that you were my daughter's friend. I've been hearing such terrible stories about her that I've come to believe that she was living in sin in Sweetwater Valley. My family will be forbidden to mention her name again.

Susan felt as though her heart had stopped beating. How could a father believe those terrible lies about his own daughter? She rushed back to the clinic to reply to Thomas Watson, but realized that she didn't know where to send the letter. There was no return address on the envelope.

Chapter Twenty

By the following afternoon the counter was in place and Susan's desk was ready for occupancy. Michael had purchased a ream of writing paper at the print shop, along with pencils, pens and ink bottles. The printer had already installed the sign out front which read: O'Brien's Animal Care Clinic. When Michael's desk and the supply shelves were finished, they would open for business.

Susan thought of her own animals and decided to pay them a visit. She couldn't afford to board the puppies much longer and wondered whether her new boss would mind housing them at the clinic.

James Casebeer stopped by late that afternoon to tell them that Fetz and Speer had packed up their printing equipment and moved to Rawlins. "*The Sweetwater Chief* and town of Bothwell no longer exist, except in Bothwell's mind."

"I'm surprised that Bothwell allowed them to go," Michael said. "They're witnesses to the kidnappings."

"If I were them, I'd travel a lot farther than Rawlins to set up shop. I don't think the cattlemen will allow them to live much longer, knowing what they witnessed. And speaking of leaving, my trip to Yellowstone begins tomorrow."

Worried, Susan asked if Casebeer were traveling alone. When he acknowledged he was, she warned him again to take precautions.

Susan awoke the next day with James Casebeer on her mind. Sitting on the edge of the bed, she said a prayer for his safe return. While she was getting dressed, Michael knocked at her door to make certain she was ready for their grand opening. He told her when she had descended the stairs that he had also moved into the boarding house and that breakfast awaited them. They joined other boarders at a large mahogany dining table laden with platters of eggs, bacon and hotcakes.

She was uncomfortable when she realized that she was the only woman present. Several unkempt men appeared not to have taken a bath in some time. She hoped that Michael would set a good example with his neat suit and freshly shaved face. On second thought, they might consider him a dandy.

Breakfast over, they walked to the clinic where a poster in the front window announced the grand opening. Before long several women appeared with small animals, one a white, long-haired cat; the others unleashed, pampered dogs. Susan wrote down their names and asked that they seat themselves on the unpainted pine benches at the front of the building. It wasn't long before the woman with the cat was holding it above her head as the dogs jumped in an attempt to reach the feline. Shrieking, the cat and its owner left the clinic before Michael had time to examine his patient. Susan wondered if each dog would have to be placed in a cage as soon as it arrived.

Once the cat was gone, the dogs began fighting among

themselves. Michael asked the owners to return at specific times with their animals restrained on a leash. Susan hurried to her desk to write it all down but not before she tripped and fell over a prancing mutt who stood as tall as her knees. Michael helped her from the planked floor and inspected her scratched palms. Applying antiseptic reserved for the animals, his expression was one of exasperation.

Susan flinched at her desk as she wrote down the various appointments, wondering if the customers would actually return. The veterinarian had his first patient perched on the examining table and was inspecting the dog's ears. The anxious adoptive parent stood close by smiling at Michael as though he were someone special. How could anyone bat her eyes that often without losing her lashes?

She looked back at the appointment schedule and noticed that their current client had Miss before her name. She was not much past her teens and must be husband shopping. Perhaps she would be interested in Susan's job, if she decided to return home.

When Miss McIntyre left with her dog without paying, Susan raised a brow and stared at her boss. "Extending credit already, Doctor O'Brien?"

"She promised to return tomorrow to pay her bill."

"Oh, I'm quite sure she will."

The clinic door opened moments after Miss McIntrye left. The matronly woman with the white cat ignored Susan as she handed her feline to Michael. Her beloved Mimi had an injured paw. Michael removed a small twig and applied a bit of the same antiseptic he's spread on Susan's palms. While the cat's owner fumbled in her reticule to pay the fee, she invited Michael to supper that evening. "A small feast with my husband and two daughters."

Michael cleared his throat and glanced at Susan, as though he needed help. Taking her cue, she rifled through the appointment book. "You already have an engagement this evening, Doctor O'Brien."

He smiled, a grateful expression flitting across his face. When he apologized and thanked his second client, she turned on her heel, paid her bill, and left, apparently in a huff.

"It appears that you've become a prize, Michael. Should I start a social engagement calendar?"

He grumbled and started for the back of the clinic when the door opened again. This time the lady had her dog restrained with a rope. It seemed that Susan would be kept busy braiding leashes for their patients. She recognized this patient as the dog that had tripped her up, and decided to keep her distance.

"Bisbee has fleas," Miss Carter said in a lilting southern drawl. Obviously dressed in her finest—as were her predecessors—the young lady was all smiles as she described her canine's scratching habits.

After he examined the dog, Michael retrieved a bottle of medicinal soap from his freshly built shelves. Told to bathe the dog once a week, Miss Carter drew back as though he had suggested she eat from her dog's dish. When he noticed her revulsion, he said, "Or have someone else do it."

Smiling sweetly, she said, "I thought that you—"

"We don't have the facilities here to bath animals," he said. "Place him in a large tub and scrub him down with this soap."

Susan breathed a sigh of relief. For a moment she feared that Michael would ask her to bathe his patients. She envisioned fleas crawling over her body and wondered whether her own dogs were infested with them.

The customer left with a displeased expression and Michael appeared to be questioning his decision to open the clinic. Susan returned to the appointment schedule and declared that it was time for their noon meal, so they closed up shop and walked two blocks to the boarding house. The enticing scent of chicken and dumplings wafted on the warm breeze. Half the boarders present for breakfast were seated at the table engaged in lively conversation about the Sweetwater hangings. Michael gave Susan a warning look not to take part in the debate, but she couldn't hold her tongue when one of the men called Ella "Cattle Kate."

When she'd had her say, a man whipped out a copy of the *Cheyenne Leader.* An editorial written by Towse said in bold type: LET JUSTICE BE DONE. He read the beginning paragraph to those seated at the table:

All resorts to lynch law are deplorable in a country governed by laws, but when the law shows itself powerless and inactive, when justice is lame and halting, when there is failure to convict on down-right proof, it is not in the nature of enterprising western men to sit idly by and have their cattle stolen and slaughtered under their very noses.

"So you're saying that cattle rustling should be punishable by vigilante law?" Susan said heatedly. "What you don't seem to understand is that the cattle in question were bought and branded legally. They weren't stolen."

Exasperated, Michael decided to join in. "Haven't you been reading the *Casper Weekly Mail*? And are you aware that the witnesses to the hangings have died or disappeared?"

"Everybody in Casper knows that Averell was a friend of Casebeer and Lombard. So of course they would defend him in the newspaper," the balding merchant said.

Michael rose from the table and took Susan's arm. "Back to the clinic. Don't waste your breath on people who believe everything they read in the Cheyenne newspapers."

Susan heard the man say as they were leaving, "The news report was also in the Dublin, Ireland, paper so it must be true."

"Dublin?" Susan questioned. "How in the world—?"

"The Cattlemen's Association must have friends abroad. They might even own the newspaper."

"That's frightening, Doctor O'Brien. The Dublin newspaper might belong to your relatives."

"You can confine your formalities to the clinic, Miss Cameron."

Her employer said nothing more as they walked back to the clinic. A middle aged woman waited impatiently at the door holding a long-haired dog small enough to fit in her reticule. Susan reached to pet the dog and had her hand bitten for her trouble. Tiny spots of blood appeared on her index finger and she yelped as loud as the dog.

"Maybell doesn't like strangers," the woman said. When Michael unlocked the door, she pushed past Susan to follow him inside. The veterinarian's assistant watched the woman waddle to the examining table. Their client didn't appear happy when Michael sterilized and bandaged Susan's finger before he looked at the dog.

When Missus Blankworthy described the dog's complaint as a "queasy stomach," the veterinarian smiled for the first time that day.

"What have you been feeding Maybell?" he asked.

"Dumplings, stew and table scraps."

"Put her on a chicken and rice diet until she's feeling better. Then feed her meat."

"Kill my chickens?"

Michael retrieved a small bottle of tonic from his supply shelf and told her to spoon it into the dog twice a day. Another disgruntled customer left the shop moments later.

"Well, at least she paid her bill," Susan said. "By the way, what kind of dog is Katie?"

"A Havanese. It's the national dog of Cuba and probably

arrived with the Spanish colonists during the sixteenth century. The elitists and wealthy landowners adopted the dog and emigrants brought it with them to this country."

"Fascinating, Michael. But how did someone in Casper acquire such a dog?"

"Wealthy cattlemen. The Blankworthy woman is obviously from a monied family."

"With no manners. She didn't even apologize for her dog biting me."

"Don't pet the animals, Susan. It's likely to happen again."

The clinic door opened a moment later and a young man resembling Jim Averell stepped inside. He introduced himself as Willie Cahill and said he was in town to talk to them about the hangings. Michael immediately offered him a chair and posted a closed sign in the window. Asked when he'd arrived in town, he said less than an hour earlier.

"How did you know where to find us?" Susan asked.

"I talked to Thomas Watson in Rawlins. He told me about the note you left him. He said his daughter was a prostitute and that she and Jimmy were running a"—he glanced at Susan and hesitated. "A bawdy house. The old man even believes the lies that Ella was a rustler."

"Unbelievable." Susan said.

"I told him that wasn't possible. My brother would never—"

Susan was quick to agree. "Ella was a good woman. She wouldn't submit to other men."

"Bothwell wants the Averells' land. That's it, pure and simple," Michael said.

"How did he get the other cattlemen to go along with the hangings?"

Michael's voice sounded angry. "Homesteaders are a threat to the cattle businesses. I guess they thought that hanging Ella and Jimmy would scare the rest of the settlers away, leaving Sweetwater Valley as free grazing land."

"Looks like they're getting away with it."

Michael leaned against the edge of the counter, his arms crossing his chest. "We read in the Rawlins paper that you talked to five other witnesses."

Willie sighed. "That's an exaggeration. I talked to a farmer who was plowing his field when the buggy with Jimmy and Ella passed by, escorted by the cattlemen. I also talked to the editor and his assistant who ran the *Sweetwater Chief*—after they moved to Rawlins."

"Are they willing to testify?"

"They're afraid to after what happened to the other witnesses."

"What do you plan to do now?"

"I'll keep nosing around until I find someone that's not afraid to testify."

"I hope you realize, Willie, that you're placing your own life in danger."

"Somebody's gotta do it."

A slender woman stood at the window and knocked—one who had been there earlier. Michael told Willie to stop by at five o'clock and the three of them would have supper together at the restaurant. He then lifted the closed sign and opened the clinic door. When Willie exited the building, the woman breezed in leading her mixed breed dog on a chain.

"I thought I had my appointment time mixed up," she said, smiling.

At long last, a patient with a nice owner, although Susan felt sorry for the dog on the chain. Asking the woman to release her dog, Michael lifted him onto the examining table, where he noticed wounds on the animal's back.

"He was attacked by a larger dog," his owner said, "and the wounds won't heal."

While Michael was retrieving ointment, the woman

said, "I hear that Deputy Watson and his accomplishes were arraigned for grand larceny and posted bail in Sundance."

"Witnesses dropping like flies," Michael muttered as he spread ointment on the dog's back.

"And that's not all. My cousin, who's clerk of court in Sundance, says Deputy Watson will be sent to prison."

"How convenient," Michael replied. "And how quickly the wheels of justice turn when they need to."

"My Charley says that we're lucky we weren't all murdered in our beds while he was patrolling the streets. Phillip Watson must be related to that awful woman, Ella Watson, who was hanged."

Michael stopped what he was doing to say, "No, they were not related and they're both innocent as charged. You can tell your Charley that we've known them both personally."

"Honest, hardworking people," Susan added.

Missus Coleman hesitated before she said, "Charley has a subscription to the *Cheyenne Leader* and—"

Michael smiled. "That explains it. Cattlemen control the *Leader* and they print whatever the association tells them."

She left with a puzzled expression on her face, but at least she had paid her bill. Michael suggested they refrain from taking part in further discussions about the hangings with customers. It was sure to get back to the cattlemen.

Chapter Twenty-One

Editor Lombard appeared briefly the following morning to tell them the latest news. "The paper won't be out for a few days but my partner asked that I keep you informed."

No customers were present so they stopped what they were doing and invited him to sit. The newsman's demeanor was gloomy "Ralph Cole's body was exhumed and his stomach removed to test for poison."

"Who's conducting the test?" Michael asked.

"Doctor Haynes."

"Haynes?" Susan said. "Isn't he the coroner who treated Ralph for mountain fever? And a friend of the cattleman, Robert Conner?"

"One and the same."

Michael scowled. "Talk about allowing the fox in the hen house."

Lombard nodded. "The good doctor sealed Ralph's stomach in a jar and says he'll send it to a competent chemist in Chicago to analyze."

"But will he?" Susan said.

"That remains to be seen." The lanky, middle aged newsman rose from his chair saying, "By the way, the

Averells weren't hanged. They strangled."

"Strangled?" Susan shrieked and covered her lips.

Michael gripped the editor's arm. "What are you saying?"

"They didn't fall far enough to snap their necks."

"So the cattlemen stood there are watched them strangle to death?"

"I'm afraid so."

Susan hurried to her desk crying.

"May they all rot in hell."

"That I'm sure of, Doc."

Not long after the newsman left, a rough-appearing cowpoke entered the clinic. His horse was ailing and he asked that the doc take a look at him. The gelding was standing at the hitching rail just outside the clinic door. Michael hesitated. The man looked vaguely familiar to Susan and from Michael's expression, he also seemed wary.

"I'll be with you in a minute." Michael walked back to the storage room and returned a moment later. Susan noticed an unfamiliar bulge in the veterinarian's pocket as he followed the man out the door. She watched anxiously through the window as Michael parted the horse's lips and peered at his teeth. He then looked at the ears and felt around the stomach area. Pulling a mercury thermometer from his pocket, he moved to the horse's rump.

Susan retrieved her revolver from a desk drawer and, holding it within the folds of her skirt, returned to the window to watch. The two men entered the clinic moments later, both of them laughing. Hurrying to her desk, she sat with the gun still hidden at her side.

"Stanley Ryan, this is my assistant, Susan Cameron," Michael said. "We met him at the livery stable last week. Remember?"

Susan nodded and released the breath she'd been

holding. "Of course. Mister Ryan. I knew I'd met you somewhere."

The cowpoke dipped his head and asked how much he owed the doc. Michael gave him some tonic and said it was on the house. When Ryan left, Susan glared at her boss. "You can't stay in business that way, Michael."

"Did you notice how bedraggled the poor man is? He needs new boots and his saddle must have been built during the Revolutionary War."

"How are you going to pay the rent on the building and my wages?"

Michael smiled. "Don't worry your pretty little head about your wages. I have savings to tide us over."

"Us?"

"Pay your wages is what I meant."

Of course that's what you meant.

There were few patients that day, so she was told to take the afternoon off, with pay. She decided to visit the puppies, who were romping in Amelia Hadley's fenced yard. How she wished that she had her own yard. Her dream of homesteading was fading fast.

The Hadley widow invited her in for a welcome cup of tea after Susan had worn herself out playing with the puppies. They were growing so fast that they would soon be full grown dogs. Alex's handsome head nearly reached her knees. What could she do with them? She would ask Michael to fence in a yard for them behind the clinic. Why hadn't she thought of that sooner?

Stanley Ryan returned the following week to tell them what he'd heard from cowpokes on the range. Susan offered him a cup of boiled coffee from the wood stove Michael had installed a few days earlier.

"I know you folks were friends of Jim Averell and would like to know ..." He paused to take a sip from his steaming cup. "The young boy who was livin' with 'em died of Bright's disease and they said his body was fed to Bothwell's wolves."

Susan gasped. "Which boy? John DeCorey or Gene Crowder?"

"The tow-headed boy. Can't remember his name."

"Oh, no. It must have been Gene. Are you sure?"

"Yes, ma'am."

Michael steadied her as though he thought she would faint. "Children don't die of Bright's. That's a kidney disease usually suffered by older people."

"That's what Bothwell's tellin' ever'body."

When Ryan left, Susan sat down heavily in her chair with tears in her eyes. "Dear Lord, who are they going to kill next?"

"Frank Buchanan and John DeCorey are the only witnesses left other than the *Sweetwater Chief* newsmen and the homesteader Willie Cahill says he talked to."

"And us, Michael?"

"We weren't anywhere near the scene of the hangings."

"I don't think that matters to the cattlemen. I'm sure Bothwell wants my homestead as well as the Averells."

"If that's true, you'd better pack up your things and board the next train back to Missouri."

Susan sighed. "I doubt I'll even be safe there unless I turn my homestead over to Bothwell."

"I don't think you can do that until you prove up on your land."

"But I can vacate it."

"Yes, and give up your dream."

Wiping a tear from her cheek, she said, "I can homestead somewhere else when I earn enough money. It took three years the last time."

"I'll loan you the money, Susan. You can pay me back when you can afford to."

"That's awfully generous of you, Michael, but I can't accept your offer."

"Why? There are no strings attached."

She took a step back to look at him. "You must be independently wealthy."

"Let's just say that I'm not worried about starving."

Susan's tears resumed. When Michael asked what was wrong, she said she was thinking of poor Gene Crowder. He didn't deserve to die any more than the Averells and Ralph Cole. How could Albert Bothwell and the others sleep at night? They should be imprisoned for life or hanged from the same tree as Jim and Ella.

The door to the clinic opened and a stranger walked in. He said his cattle were suffering from anthrax and asked that Michael ride with him to the ranch to take a look. Susan's frightened expression must have changed his mind because the veterinarian said he didn't treat cattle and suggested one in Rawlins.

When the angry man left, Michael said, "No trips away from the clinic unless I know I can trust the man."

"I'm glad you turned him down. We can no longer trust anyone."

They found a skull and crossbones painted on the clinic door when they arrived at eight the following morning. Michael hugged Susan to his side as though protecting her from an evil curse.

"It must have been that stranger who came here yesterday," she said.

"I agree. He probably works for Bothwell or Conner. We'd better report this to the sheriff and stop in to see

Lombard. Hopefully, Casebeer has returned from his trip to Yellowstone."

There was a chill in the air as they walked arm in arm to the sheriff's office. He wasn't in so Michael left a note. They proceeded to the *Casper Weekly Mail*.

Lombard stopped what he was doing to offer them a cup of strong coffee. When asked about his partner, he said he was surprised that he hadn't heard from him. He was due to return in two days. Offering them a seat, he showed them a copy of the latest newspaper, which headlined the sentencing of former sheriff's deputy, Phillip Watson, age 30. He had been sentenced to six years in the penitentiary at Joliet, Illinois, for his conviction on the charge of grand larceny. His alleged horse stealing partner Tex Healy had skipped the territory after posting bail.

"Can't say I blame Tex," Lombard said. "As far as I'm concerned, they were trumped-up charges brought by the cattlemen."

Michael told him about the skull and crossbones painted on his own door, and Lombard said that he and Susan should take a vacation—somewhere away from Wyoming until after the trial. Doctor O'Brien glanced at his assistant and reluctantly agreed.

"Maybe a train trip to Missouri *is* a good idea," he said.

Susan hesitated. "If there was something we could do to bring the cattlemen to justice I would stay, but they apparently control the entire territory. That skull and crossbones is fair warning, Michael. I think we should leave. But what about the puppies?"

"I'll pay for several months' boarding for them while we're away."

Susan frowned but agreed. "Alex won't know me when he sees me again."

"Sure he will. Dogs are like elephants. They never forget."

"Then let's lock up the clinic and pack for the trip."

Lombard offered to keep an eye on the clinic while they were gone. They thanked him and left. They then debated whether to paint over the skull and crossbones.

"I think we should leave it," Susan said, "along with the closed sign so that people will know why we're no longer here."

"I'm sure Lombard will write a story about it, so we won't have to explain what happened when we return."

"When *you* return, Doctor O'Brien. I have no desire to homestead in Wyoming now."

"What about the puppies?"

"I'm sure they'll be happy in a yard behind the clinic."

Michael appeared shocked. "All three of them?"

"You can send Alex to me on the train when I'm settled on my new homestead."

Michael's face fell. "Whatever you decide."

After the clinic had been secured and the closed sign in place, they walked back to the boarding house. They were shocked to find a similar skull and crossbones haphazardly painted on the door.

"Why didn't we notice it this morning when we left?" Susan said. As she spoke one of the boarders rounded the building carrying a brush and paint container.

"Musta been some kids out pranking last night," the stout man said. "I hear they got your place too, Doc."

Michael shook his head. "I don't think it was kids. We need to keep watch for strangers."

"That so? You think it's got something to do with the Sweetwater trouble?"

"Yes, I do. Miss Cameron and I are likely targets and will be leaving town for a while."

"Can't say as I blame you. You don't think they'd try to burn down the boarding house, do you?"

"Not after we're gone, but they might set fire to the clinic."

Michael followed Susan into the boarding house and urged her to hurry her packing. The train to Nebraska was due to leave in two hours. "I feel like such a coward leaving like this, but it isn't safe for you to travel alone. The boarding house must have been targeted because we're staying here."

"You needn't come along, Michael. I can take care of myself."

"I'd rather not be in their crosshairs. There are so many of them that I'd be suspicious of my own clients."

"As I was when Mister Ryan came to the clinic, and the man who said his cattle have anthrax," Susan said. "But what will happen to your clinic while you're gone?"

"I'm not sure, but, like you I can always start over."

Susan hurried upstairs to pack as Michael did on the ground floor. She had purchased two new dresses to wear at the clinic but had neglected to buy another valise. She thought stuffing her clothing in her old bag was akin to stuffing sausage and she was afraid of ruining her clothes. They wouldn't all fit so she decided to rush down to the general store to buy new luggage, without disturbing Michael.

The general store was two blocks from the boarding house where Mister Cunningham waited on her. When asked where she was going, Susan hesitated before saying she was taking the train to Nebraska the following day. She trusted the store owner but knew he liked to gossip with customers. It was best that he didn't know her destination.

"I noticed that Doc O'Brien closed up his clinic early today."

Crossing her fingers, she said, "Yes, he's going home to see his ailing mother."

"I noticed the skull and crossbones on his door. Doesn't have anything to do with you both leaving, does it?"

Susan avoided the question. "Do you know who put it

there?"

"No, but one of my customers was coming home from a saloon early this morning when he noticed somebody on a paint horse loitering around the clinic. It was after midnight so he didn't get a good look at him."

If you want to know what's going on in town, ask Mister Cunningham.

Hurrying back to the boarding house, Susan climbed the stairs to her room to repack her clothing. Looking about, she spotted a simple necklace Ella had woven for her, which was lying on the washstand. Lips trembling, she pulled it over her head. She still couldn't believe that her friend was gone.

Was leaving the right thing to do, or should she and Michael arm themselves and carry on at the clinic? She felt that the two of them were fighting an entire army with Albert Bothwell leading the charge. Her homestead land wasn't worth risking her life. She was only twenty-four and had her entire life ahead of her. But who was going to make sure that the guilty men were convicted of murder? They seemed to have everyone in authority in their pockets.

The situation was hopeless.

Susan continued packing. Moments later Michael knocked, asking if she were ready. Sighing, she picked up her reticule and opened the door. Her two bags were setting nearby and he carried them downstairs, where his own luggage waited. One of the other boarders offered to help with their bags and they started off together to the station.

"Do you feel that someone's watching us?" she whispered.

"I'm sure they are. Don't turn around to stare. Whoever painted the skulls and crossbones must be laughing up his sleeve right now, thinking he scared us away."

"He did, actually."

"But not for long."

"Are you thinking of returning right away?"

"As soon as I see you safely home."

"But, Michael, there's nothing you can do. There are too many of them."

His chin rose defiantly and he said nothing more. Susan watched as he paid for their tickets and the man for his help carrying their baggage. They then boarded the train. Once seated Susan gazed from the window at the town she was leaving behind. She doubted she would ever see it again and wasn't sure she wanted to return. When the whistle blew and the train jerked forward, she felt a tear make its way down her cheek. Glancing at Michael seated next to her, she noticed his stony-faced stare at the end of the coach. He didn't seem to want to watch their departure from Casper. She realized that he might be giving up his own dream as well, all because of the cattlemen's greed. She bit down on her lip until it bled.

Michael reached for her hand and gripped it gently as the train pulled from the station. She resisted the urge to pull away, feeling comforted that he cared enough to accompany her home. But what would happen to the veterinarian when he returned to Casper? Would the clinic still be standing or would he also be forced to start over elsewhere?

Some forty minutes into the trip, the train began to slow. When it jerked to a stop in the midst of the sagebrush-covered plain, the passengers leaned out the windows to have a look.

"Probably animals on the track," Michael said. But a moment later, two armed men entered the coach and Susan placed her reticule beneath the seat. There wasn't time to hide what little money she had left or to rummage in the bag for her gun. She was surprised when the bandits made no demands on the other passengers. She watched as they made their way toward her, while glancing at each passenger on either side of the aisle. When the men reached their seats, she and Michael were pulled to their feet and told to exit the train.

The man who clutched her arm was taller than Michael and a great deal heavier. Dressed as cowhands wearing bandanas to hide their faces, one of them pulled her toward the exit. She could hear Michael cursing behind her and a scuffle taking place. Turning, she saw the second bandit place his gun to Michael's temple and heard the click of the hammer pulled back.

"No," she screamed. "Don't kill him."

"Then you'd better do exactly what we tell you, little lady."

Shoved from the coach, they were forced to walk with guns at their backs to the river bank where two saddle horses were tethered to a cottonwood limb. A two-seated wagon hitched to a pair of matched horses was parked nearby. Why the wagon if they were going to be hanged? There were plenty of large cottonwood trees along both sides of the river. She knew Michael was armed because she'd seen him hide his short-barreled Colt under his jacket. Why didn't he shoot them? Or had the kidnappers taken his gun? Her own revolver was hidden in her reticle beneath her seat in the train.

Glancing back at the train, she noticed passengers peering at them through the open coach windows. Were they afraid to fire at the gunmen for fear of killing their prisoners? She was pushed into the wagon, followed by Michael, and one of the men took the reins. The wagon jerked forward into the sagebrush and turned back in the direction of Casper.

The train whistle blew but didn't start forward. Logs had been piled on the tracks and the trainmen must be waiting for the wagon to disappear before they left the train to clear the tracks. Susan's heart pounded as she envisioned Ella and Jimmy in similar circumstances.

The second man rode behind the wagon with his gun aimed at her. Was that why Michael sat so impassively?

"Why are you doing this?" she yelled. "If you want my land, you can have it."

The filthy man driving the wagon simply laughed.

She heard the train start forward and knew they were at the mercy of Bothwell's gunslingers.

Seated behind the man with the reins, Michael whispered for her to keep talking as he slowly unbuttoned his suit jacket and eased his hand onto his gun.

"How dare you kidnap us," she shouted. "We haven't done anything wrong."

"What're you doing?" the man on horseback yelled as he rode alongside Michael.

"Chest paints," Michael gasped, leaning forward. "I'm having a heart attack."

"You're too young—"

In one swift movement, Michael pulled his gun and fired, hitting the rider in the chest. Before the man fell from his horse, Michael hit the surprised driver over the head with the butt of his gun. The gunshot startled the horses and they bolted and ran. Susan screamed as Michael attempted to grab the reins. The driver fell from the wagon as it bounced over uneven ground, the reins ripped from his hands.

"We're going to overturn," Michael yelled, wrapping her in his arms to protect her with his body. A moment later one of the wagon wheels caught on a sage plant and tipped onto its side. They were thrown free as the horses continued to run, dragging the wagon with them. Susan groaned when he released her from his embrace.

"Are you hurt?"

She blinked several times, feeling pain in her ribs where he had held her. "I'm all right. Are you, Michael?"

Attempting to sit upright, he said, "I think I landed on a rock."

Susan crawled around him to have a look. "Yes, a small one. Did you hurt your back?"

"I'm fine. We've got to catch the horses. I dropped my gun in the wagon when I grabbed for the reins. The one I hit on the head will be here soon and I'm sure he still has a gun."

"Why didn't you shoot him too?"

"I should have, but I don't like shooting people in the back."

"Have you shot anyone before?"

Michael blew on his right hand. "No, but I've practiced shooting targets."

Susan noticed a horse standing nearby grazing, although the saddled gunman's mount had raced off into the prairie.

"Look," she said. "That must be the driver's horse."

Michael plucked the top from a sage plant and stealthily crept toward the horse, holding the plant in front of him. When the mare raised her head and snorted, he stopped and continued to offer the plant. Curious, the horse moved forward and Susan knew that Michael was holding his breath. She dared not move or breathe herself. Slowly, the mare continued to move in Michael's direction until she was able to sniff the sage in his hand. When she began nibbling his offering, he grabbed her reins and mounted. Beckoning to Susan, he lifted her behind the saddle, insisting she hug him around his waist. Then, gently kicking the paint's ribs, he urged her in the direction the other horses had taken.

It wasn't long before they heard a gunshot. Michael ducked low over the mare's neck and yelled for Susan to flatten herself against his back. Kicking the horse into a gallop, they raced away from the scene. Susan knew the horse's owner wouldn't risk killing his own mount but she was still frightened he would attempt to shoot them. She was relieved to see his rifle secure in the saddle scabbard.

Nearly an hour passed before they came upon the wagon still attached to the horses. Heads down, they were grazing. Michael ground-reined the paint and crept over to the team. Susan could see that the wagon was ruined and knew she would have to ride astride the paint to wherever Michael decided to take them. She was still worried about the man on foot behind them. If he was able to catch his partner's horse, he would soon be within firing range.

"Hurry, Michael, before that man catches us."

He nodded and unhitched the horses from the twisted wagon frame. Rushing back to the mare, he lifted Susan down from the horse's back and up into the saddle. Then, quickly sizing up the horses, he chose a gelding to ride bareback. Grabbing the mane, he mounted the skittish horse. Unaccustomed to riding astride, Susan gripped the reins and saddle horn, hanging on for dear life. She was too frightened to care that her ankles and calves were exposed.

"Which direction are we going, Michael?"

"East toward the railroad tracks. If we're lucky, we can catch up when the train stops to take on water."

"What about your gun?"

After a quick inspection of the wagon, he said, "It must have fallen out. Let's go."

Chapter Twenty-Two

She followed as he rode across the high desert, his long legs wrapped securely around the gelding's ribs. Nothing appeared to be moving in the distance. Maybe the second man's shot had frightened off his partner's horse. She bowed her head and said a short prayer.

The sun was setting when she noticed a column of smoke rising ahead. Was it the train? Michael pulled up smiling. His nod said her prayers had been answered.

"We need to stop the train," he said. "If they don't recognize us, they'll use us for target practice."

"They'll think we're trying to rob the train, Michael."

"Loosen your hair and let it blow free."

Susan removed the clips from her hair before she asked, "Now what?"

"We'll ride ahead of the train and stand on the tracks so they'll stop."

"It'll soon be dark. They might not see us."

"I have a better idea. We'll gather sagebrush and set fire to it on the tracks."

"What if they think we're bandits trying to rob the train?"

"We'll stand behind the fire and jump and wave our arms. If the train doesn't slow down we'll jump off either side of the tracks."

"And then?"

"I'll climb onboard and tell them to stop."

Susan closed her eyes and shook her head. "You could be killed trying."

The horses were tiring and she wondered whether they could catch the train, let alone get ahead to set a fire. She was in awe of everything Michael had done that day and would have to trust his judgment. She didn't want to even think about what would happen if he failed. And what if the fire burned the wooden planks between the rails. Would it cause the train to derail?

Michael's horse seemed to be limping. A moment later he stopped and dismounted. Holding the gelding's leg, he examined the hoof. When she came alongside, he told her to hurry to stop the train. "Hold both your arms up when you reach the engine. With your hair flying behind you, they'll know you're a woman and not trying to rob them."

She wanted to scream, but did as he said. Riding low over the horses' mane, she gripped the saddle horn with one hand, the reins in the other. She could see the train in the distance but didn't think she could reach it before dark. The mare seemed to sense her urgency and managed a burst of speed.

"Please, Lord," she cried. "Help us stop the train."

When she was within shouting distance, she noticed someone waving a large white cloth from the small rear platform. Was it a table cloth or someone signaling her? She frantically waved at the man and a moment later he waved back.

"Stop the train," she screamed. But the door closed and nothing happened. The train must be making too much noise for the man to hear. The wind had changed directions, whipping hair into her eyes. When her horse drew alongside the first coach, she noticed several people peering out the windows at her. She continued to yell for them to stop the train until her voice grew hoarse.

They were waving back at her. Did they think she was playing a game? The horse was now even with the third car behind the engine, the coach she had been riding in. Would someone recognize her? Riding as close to the coach as she dared, she continued to scream, although there wasn't much left of her voice. Someone stuck his head out the window and nodded yes. Did that mean the dark haired man was going to stop the train? Or was he simply acknowledging her?

The face disappeared as she continued to ride forward toward the engine. Smoke made her cough and she felt the sharp sting of cinder when it burned her face. The saddle horn bit into her stomach and she cried out in pain. As she reached the engine, a shrill whistle blew and the train began to slow. Her breath came in great gulps as she allowed the horse to slow as well. When the conductor left the train and came toward her, Susan breathlessly told him about Michael and the men who had kidnapped them.

"One of the passengers recognized you, Miss," he said. "Come aboard and I'll get you something to drink."

"But my friend—"

"A trainman will ride your horse back to help him."

"Hurry. One of those awful men is after us."

Helping her aboard, the conductor rounded up a sturdy looking fellow and told him to ride back to rescue her friend. He made sure the man was well armed. When Susan peered from the window, she spotted Michael in the distance leading the limping horse in the fading light. No one else appeared on the horizon, although blowing sagebrush made her gasp more than once.

A waiter arrived with a large glass of ice tea which

she gulped down halfway. Still breathing heavily she watched the trainman mount her former steed and ride in Michael's direction. The coach buzzed with excitement about the kidnappings and the fact that they had been able to escape. If only Ella and Jimmy had been able to do the same. There had been too many lynchers and Michael wasn't there to save them. Envisioning how he had foiled the kidnappers, she felt a warm glow spread throughout her body. She knew she had been too hard on him, but he was interfering with her plans. Her dream was all but lost.

It was dark by the time Michael came aboard and the train resumed its trip. Smiling wearily, he thanked her for her efforts to stop the train.

"Didn't think I could do it, did you?"

"I knew you could, but I was afraid the horse would step in a prairie dog hole and break a leg, or throw you. I don't think even you know how fast you were traveling."

"You're right, I didn't, but it wouldn't have made a difference. I knew our lives depended on my stopping the train."

"You're a special woman, Susan Cameron."

"And you, Doctor Michael O'Brien, are a remarkable man. I think I'll write a dime novel about you someday."

"I didn't know you're a writer."

"I've penned a few things but I haven't shown them to anyone."

"I'd like to read them."

Susan smiled. She was peering out the window when a bullet shattered the glass inches from her head. Michael dived from his seat, pulling her to the floor. After he made sure she hadn't been hurt, he said, "That fool is probably shooting at us with my own gun."

"Everyone down on the floor," someone yelled and diners immediately obeyed.

Trembling, Susan said, "Heaven help us if the train

stops again." She then remembered her reticule and they crawled forward to the connecting door. Two coaches later, she found her former seat and drawstring bag. Retrieving the gun, she handed it to Michael and they made there way back to the dining car. Another shot had broken a gas lamp affixed to the wall. Their attacker was fortunately a poor shot.

"Sit still," he said. "I'm going to crawl back until I can get off a shot at him."

Susan held her breath as she watched him push past passengers crouched in the aisle. Several people glared at her and she knew they blamed the two of them for the shootings. She then heard Michael's harsh low voice demand that everyone stay down. A window was partially open and he used the frame as cover. Peering into the darkness, he raised the barrel of her gun to fire. An instant after the concussion reverberated inside the coach, she heard a man cry out in pain.

When Michael crawled back, he said the interior train lights provided enough illumination to spot the rider on horseback. He had seen him fall from his horse, but he didn't know if the man was alone. Turning his head, he reminded everyone to stay where they were for a few additional minutes. When no further shots were fired, the passengers grumpily got to their feet, still glaring.

One of them, however, walked forward to slap Michael on the back. "Mighty fine shootin', Doc. I couldna' done better myself."

Susan recognized him as one of their customers. The lanky farmer had brought in a sick horse, which Doctor O'Brien had successfully treated. What in the world was he doing on the train?

"Goin' to Chadron to see my ma," he said. "She's nigh onto eighty-five and livin' alone."

Susan inquired if he were planning to take her back

with him to the farm to stay with his family.

"Too dangerous, Miss. It ain't safe in Wyomin' no more. I'm puttin' my place up for sale and movin' back home."

Michael said, "I can't say I blame you. But when the cattlemen are convicted of murder, the Casper area should be a safe place to live."

"Maybe you're right, Doc. I'll wait and see how it goes."

They nodded their understanding and returned to their coach. Taking their respective seats, Susan sank back into hers thinking what a day it had been. No wonder the territorial government had enfranchised women more than twenty years earlier. It was the only way they could get them to stay in such a wild and wooly place.

Dangerous and deadly were better descriptions of life in Sweetwater Valley. She wondered if Michael actually planned to return to his clinic after he saw her safely home. Moments later she drifted off to a series of nightmarish replays of all that had happened since the train's departure in Casper.

Susan awoke with a start when the whistle blew and the train stopped to take on water. The early morning sun shone through her window and she turned to search for Michael, who had reclined in the seat across the aisle. She noticed a large bruise on the side of his face and when she mentioned it, he told her not to worry. He could take care of himself. Where had she heard that remark before? He was as stubborn and arrogant as she was. The realization made her blanch. If not for Michael, she could have been killed long ago. How was she going to make it up to him?

It was then she noticed a short, neatly-dressed man enter the front of the coach. Her hand instantly dived into her reticule. When the young man came closer she recognized him as Jimmy Averell's half-brother, Willie Cahill. Beckoning to him, she lifted a finger to her lips to silence him. She then scooted next to the window and patted the seat she had just vacated.

"I'm surprised to see you" she whispered once he was seated.

"No more than I am to see you," he whispered back.

"We're hiding from Albert Bothwell's gunmen." She nodded at Michael across the aisle.

Willie did a double take and turned back to ask, "Is that Doc O'Brien?"

"Don't let on that you know us," she whispered. "Now tell me why you're on this train."

"Probably the same reason as you. I've been followed and thought I'd throw them off the track, so to speak."

Susan smiled. She appreciated his play on words. "When did you leave Casper, Willlie?"

"Two days ago. I sneaked off the train at Douglas 'cause I spotted them in the next coach. I boarded again this morning."

Susan patted his hand. "I'm glad you're leaving Wyoming."

"Before I left Casper, I talked to the editor Lombard at the Weekly *Mail*. He said his partner, James Casebeer, had disappeared on his trip to Yellowstone. He thinks Bothwell's gang killed him so he'd stop publishing stories against the cattlemen."

Susan gasped and closed her eyes. Tears soon burned her cheeks.

Michael must have overheard their conversation because he beckoned Willie to his side of the coach. Susan heard their low-pitched voices but couldn't understand a word they were saying. If James Casebeer had also been murdered, her life and Michael's were still in danger, as was Willie's.

Susan scanned the other passengers before peering out the window, shading her eyes against the morning sun.

She would keep her hand in her reticule and shoot through it, if necessary. Just let another one of Bothwell's gunmen try to kidnap them. Biting her lip, she wondered whether someone had followed Willie when he boarded the train in Douglas. Her heart pounded unevenly and breathing became difficult when a tall, well-dressed man entered the coach and immediately made eye contact with her.

"Morning, ma'am." He tipped his hat and smiled when he came opposite her in the aisle. "Mind if I sit next to you?"

Susan gripped the handgun in her bag tighter and raised her chin defiantly. "I certainly do mind. I'm planning to take a nap and I need all this space to lie down."

"Begging your pardon." His stride quickened and he opened the rear connecting door. She sighed when she heard the sound of wheels clicking on the tracks and felt the rush of air, which ruffled the skirt of her dress. Leaning, she held it down.

"Good thing he left when he did," Willie said. "I was fixing to show him the door, myself."

Willie's such a nice man. It's a good thing he left Wyoming when he did or he may have reached his destination in a pine box. She knew it could happen to herself and Michael as well. Scrutinizing the other passengers again, Susan tried to determine whether they had visible weapons or seemed to be eavesdropping on Michael and Willie. No one appeared interested in anything happening in the back of the coach, so she relaxed against the seat and eased the tightness from her spine.

Willie slid back into his former seat beside her to tell about his trip to find witnesses to testify against his brother's killers. He feared that he was marking each one for death by simply talking to them. Susan replied that she didn't hold out much hope that the cattlemen would be convicted.

"I'm afraid I agree with you, Miss Cameron. When I realized I was being followed, I made sure I was in a crowd of people, even if I had to stay up all night."

"It probably saved your life, Willie."

He leaned to peer around her and out the window. "We're not out of trouble yet. Doc said the two of you had been kidnapped. It could happen again."

Susan tensed, knowing he was right. "Keep your gun handy. We might need it."

Someone gently shook her shoulder in the middle of the night.

"You all right, ma'am? You was screechin' in your sleep."

Susan gasped. Squinting, she noticed a black man standing over her dressed in a white jacket and dark trousers.

"I'm a porter, ma'am, just checkin' to make sure—"

"Darkies aren't allowed to touch white women," a passenger said. He was seated ahead of Michael and Willie. "I oughta have you strung up."

"Sorry, suh, I didn't mean no harm."

Alarmed, Susan sat upright. "It's all right. I was just having a bad dream. Thanks for checking on me."

From the corner of her eye she noticed Michael leave his seat to escort the porter from the coach. When he returned he stood looking down at her. She guessed that he was thinking what a problem she was and how relieved he would be to leave her in Missourah.

"What was the porter doing in our coach?" she whispered.

"One of the Pullman passengers requested some tea. The porter was on his way back from the dining car when he heard you cry out in your sleep."

"Poor George. He seemed frightened when that passenger called him out."

"George?"

"Isn't that what all porters are called?"

"Yes, I think you're right. They're treated badly by a few asinine passengers. That's why I walked him back to the Pullman coach."

The same male voice yelled, "Pipe down back there. We're trying to get some sleep."

Michael patted her shoulder and returned to his seat. She noticed that Willie had switched seats with him and was snoring with his mouth open. It was a long while before Susan drifted off again and daylight arrived too soon. The train had slowed to pull into another station when Michael asked if she were hungry.

Nodding sleepily, Susan agreed when he said he would bring her something back from the dining car. When he left, she pretended to sleep while watching the other passengers until Michael returned.

"May I share a pastry with you, ma'am?" Michael said in an Irish brogue that nearly made her laugh. "I noticed that you haven't eaten this morning?"

"This hayseed bothering you, ma'am? I'll have him thrown off the train." Susan recognized the voice as the man who threatened the porter. Well-dressed but bulging at the seams, the gray haired, middle aged man fingered a long gold chain which hung from one vest pocket to the other. She knew that one of them held a gold watch.

"Hayseed indeed. This gentleman offered to share his breakfast with me and I'm going to accept."

"Don't get your dander up, ma'am. I'd be pleased to escort you to the dining car and buy you a good breakfast."

Susan thanked him and dismissed him. She then turned to Michael, who was grinning at her. "It appears the lady *can* take care of herself," he whispered.

Unwrapping a large sweet roll, he handed it to her along with a cup and small carafe of coffee, some of which had spilled on his clothing. No wonder the distasteful man had called him a hayseed. The stains on his dirty clothing didn't make him appear respectable. She looked down at her own clothing and cringed.

"Aren't you going to eat, Michael?"

"Not hungry and don't call me by name."

Susan glanced about the coach before she said, "Thank you, kind sir. May I inquire of your name?"

"Zebinezer Gladstone, ma'am. You can call me Zeb. May I be so bold as to ask your own name?"

"Elvina Ripple. That's *Miss* Ripple."

Heads turned in the coach but she ignored them. Michael was attempting to hold back his laughter as she dabbed her mouth with the napkin he'd given her, to hide her own amusement.

She was daintily nibbling the roll when they pulled into the station at Chadron, Nebraska. Moments after the train arrived at the station, a sheriff's deputy boarded their coach and escorted them onto the platform at gunpoint. Complaining that their luggage was aboard, they were told to walk to the jail for questioning. Willie Cahill grabbed his bag and trailed along after them. When they entered the small sheriff's office, Michael was outraged when the deputy relieved him of Susan's gun.

"Are you aware of what's going on in Wyoming Territory?" Michael asked the scrawny, red haired young deputy.

"We got a telegram saying you were on your way."

"From where and who sent it?"

The deputy ignored the question. "You two are suspects in the shootings of Frank Buchanan and George Henderson."

Susan gasped. "Frank Buchanan's dead?"

"They found his body shot fulla holes in the desert

northwest of Rawlins, Wyoming."

Michael pounded his fist on the desk. "The cattlemen sent two killers to take us off the train. You can ask anyone in our coach what happened."

"The train already left for Omaha."

The office door opened and Willie stood staring at them. Michael briefly told him of the two men's deaths and filled him in on the charges against himself and Susan.

Turning to the deputy, Willie said, "You're joking, aren't you? Miss Cameron and Doc O'Brien wouldn't kill anybody."

Susan cringed, remembering the kidnapper Michael shot on the prairie.

Ignoring Willie, the deputy scowled at Michael. "I'm gonna have to lock you two up till the sheriff checks out your story."

"Telegraph the editor at the *Casper Weekly* Mail or Casper's mayor, George Mitchell. They'll vouch for us." He then told the deputy about his veterinary practice and insisted that they could prove they weren't anywhere near Rawlins at the time of the shooting.

"Who's George Henderson?" Susan asked.

When the deputy shrugged, Willie said, "Henderson was a foreman for a rancher named John Clay. The lynchers sent him a telegram telling him about the hangings."

Michael's face took on an even angrier expression. "John Clay's a member of the cattlemen's association. I remember now. Henderson went to *the Cheyenne Leader* to tell them lies about the hangings. The cattlemen must have had him killed to shut him up about his role in the conspiracy."

The deputy smirked as he looked over Michael's disheveled clothing. "So it's Doctor O'Brien, is it?"

Michael nodded.

"There are plenty of people in Casper who will vouch

for us," Susan said, her own rage building. "You have no idea what we've been through. The cattlemen are trying to frame us and steal my homestead land."

The deputy retrieved a set of keys from the desk drawer. "Tell your stories to the sheriff when he gets back." Opening a cell, he nudged Susan into it. She cringed when she smelled the cell's interior, which she sensed hadn't been recently cleaned.

Michael straightened to his full height, towering over the young deputy. "That's uncalled for."

"Sheriff's orders."

"Find the sheriff and get him over here," Michael demanded.

The deputy backed against the only desk in the small office. "He'll be here in a few minutes."

"You can place me in a cell, but you're going to have a lawsuit on your hands for incarcerating this fine young lady."

Susan looked down at her torn, filthy dress and knew what the deputy must be thinking. "It's all right, Michael. My Uncle Jacob is a federal judge in Omaha. When he learns what's happening here, he'll make sparks fly as far as the nation's capital."

Michael smiled. "Why didn't you tell me—?"

Before she could answer, the deputy said, "He can't do a thing if he doesn't know where you are."

Susan placed both hands on her slender hips, and glared at him. "Uncle Jacob is planning to meet us in Omaha. When he finds out you've arrested us, you can say goodbye to your job." She hated to lie but drastic measures were necessary under the circumstances. She envisioned herself and Michael traveling in chains in a prison wagon.

Willie left to send a telegram to Susan's uncle, after repeating his protest that she and Michael were innocent. Nearly two hours later the balding, potbellied sheriff arrived, weaving a bit in his stride. Susan left her narrow, lumpy cot to glare at him.

When he approached her cell he said, "Haven't seen you before. Which wappi drug you into town?" Gripping the bars he leaned in close to leer at her. The stench of alcohol made her retreat to the back wall.

"Miss Cameron is the niece of Federal Judge Jacob Bentley," Michael said from the adjoining cell. "When he hears that you've imprisoned her—"

The sheriff's guffaw echoed inside the small office. "Now I've heard it all. This so-called *lady* looks like she's been drug through a hog pen."

"Actually," Susan said, "We were dragged from the train at gunpoint."

"Bandits?" The sheriff eased himself from the bars and took a seat at his desk.

Michael told him all that had happened since the hangings as Susan watched the sheriff's face for some sign of disbelief. When Michael finished, the sheriff glanced at his deputy, who shook his head in agreement. Retrieving a telegram he'd placed on the sheriff's desk, he read aloud, "Confirmed. Susan Cameron niece of Judge Bentley. Will meet train in Omaha."

"I also wired the mayor of Casper." Appearing pleased with himself, the deputy picked up a second telegram. It says here, "O'Brien and Cameron upstanding citizens. Worked at clinic till two days ago." He handed the wire to the sheriff, who looked it over and remarked that it had been signed by George Mitchell, Casper's mayor.

Susan sighed with relief. Thank heavens everyone in Casper knows when someone leaves or arrives in town.

"Why'n hell didn't you turn 'em loose," the sheriff roared.

The deputy ducked his head saying, "Waiting for you, sir." Before the sheriff could reprimand him further, the deputy hurried to unlock Susan's cell. He then did the same with Michael's.

The sheriff waved his hand for them to leave. When they had collected their possessions, Michael took her arm and led her out to the boardwalk to look for Willie.

Susan insisted, "First a trip to the general store, which should be open by now. We can buy new clothes and bathe at the hotel."

Michael nodded and peered up and down the main street until he spotted a mercantile halfway down the block. A man who appeared to be the proprietor was arranging merchandise in the window when they arrived. After a moment of inspection through the plate glass window, he ignored them and went back to work. Michael retrieved a hundred dollar bill from his wallet and held it for the man to see.

The door opened and the proprietor said, "Morning, folks. What can I do for you?"

"We were accosted by robbers and need to replace our clothing."

The large man wearing a long gray apron lifted a heavy brow as he glanced again at the money Michael was holding. "Looks like they didn't make off with your cash."

Susan said, "My friend fought them off." Wasting no time she headed for the clothing department but not before she heard the proprietor ask, "You two traveling together?"

She smiled when she heard Michael say, "Our chaperon is at the hotel arranging for our rooms." So he *was* concerned with her reputation. She knew women in Nebraska weren't liberated like those in Wyoming, but at least they weren't hunted down like animals. She spotted a silk dress with leg of mutton sleeves that appeared to be her size. The primrose color wasn't to her liking but she could dispose of the dress when they retrieved their luggage. What would Uncle Jacob think when he met them at the station? And was it safe to board another train? She didn't think the gunmen dared follow them further into Nebraska, but one of them could have been watching when they left the jail.

Michael found clothing that didn't quite fit but he wasn't fussy about his appearance. The plaid shirt and overalls made him resemble a farmer. What a contrast they would make, with her silk dress, which he insisted on buying, and him in laborer's clothing. Susan laughed and the two men laughed with her. It was only until they reached Omaha, and hopefully anyone following wouldn't recognize them in their new duds, especially if they wore hats to disguise themselves further.

Susan chose a large airy hat with a trailing feather, which swept down the side of her face. They decided that Michael should wear a wide brimmed straw that was several sizes too large. She laughed again when he tried it on. The veterinarian's expression was one of determination as he pulled Susan's gun from his battered suit jacket and placed it in the overall's s pocket. "If we've been followed this far, they're in for a surprise."

Susan shuddered at the thought, suggesting that Michael buy another gun. When he handed back her own, she looked about for a new reticule to accessorize her dress. She would also buy a heavy shawl. She found a gray silk drawstring bag, hoping the outline of her gun wouldn't be apparent in the clinging material. Sighing, she realized that she no longer cared if anyone knew she was carrying a weapon. She only wanted to reach Missourah without another kidnapping attempt.

When they had collected their purchases in a large canvas bag, Michael moved to the window to check for anyone who might be loitering in the street. A moment later he motioned for Susan to follow him onto the boardwalk. Was someone waiting in one of the buildings with a rifle aimed at them?

They reached the hotel without incident and Susan released the breath she had been holding. The hotel clerk looked at them curiously when Michael asked for adjoining rooms.

"Buggy accident," he said. "My sister and I were thrown free when the horses ran off."

The elderly clerk adjusted glasses that slid down his narrow nose. Scrutinizing Susan with a disbelieving expression, he said, "We don't allow—"

"Judge Bentley is meeting us at the station in Omaha, and we have a sack full of new clothes to replace the ones lost when the horses ran off with our luggage." Michael lifted their canvas bag and retrieved Susan's new dress for the clerk to see.

"She doesn't look like your sister."

"Different fathers," Michael said heatedly. "Our room keys now, if you please."

Susan tripped and nearly fell as they climbed the stairs to the second floor. She had been craning her neck to observe the lobby's luxurious oriental rugs and red velvet upholstered furniture. The hotel was quite a contrast to the lodgings they'd had during the past several months. When they reached her room, Michael insisted on testing the beds in both rooms so that she would have the most comfortable. Telling her not to answer her door until he came for her; he left, but not before he reminded her of the connecting door.

"I won't be opening that door and neither will you, Doctor O'Brien."

"For heaven sake, Susan. If someone tries to break into your room, you can escape into mine."

Chagrined, she followed his instructions to securely lock her door. When he left, she undressed and took a sponge bath from the wash basin, while listening to sounds outside her window. She wondered why hotels were built so close to the saloons. There didn't appear to be as many taverns as in Casper, but some of Bothwell's men could be drinking in one of them, waiting for them to emerge from the hotel.

A banging noise awakened her early next morning, accompanied by Michael's voice. He asked that she hurry before they missed the next train to Omaha. Had she actually slept all night? The events of the previous day came rushing back as she slipped into her new dress and pinned up her hair. Leaving the bed unmade, she hurriedly opened the door where she found a farmer leaning against the railing, his straw hat tipped to hide his face.

"Put your belongings in here," he whispered, holding open the large canvas bag. "Follow me down the street to the depot. I'll pretend not to know you. That should confuse anyone who might be watching."

Susan smiled. "Agreed, Michael. A good plan."

"Don't acknowledge me until we reach Omaha."

She nodded and followed five stairs behind. When they reached the lobby, he glanced about before heading for the door. Susan spotted two wranglers standing at the front desk and wondered whether Michael had seen them. Glad that her hat's swooping feather hid that side of her face, she strutted as though a grand lady to the hotel entrance. When she reached the boardwalk, she realized that Michael was nowhere in sight. Holding her breath, she withdrew the pistol from her reticule and held it within the folds of her dress. She then heard a bell tinkle as the hotel door opened, and turned to see the two men on the boardwalk behind her. One of them said, "That's her."

Susan's heart pounded as she raised her gun and pointed it at them.

"Ah, now, little lady, you wouldn't shoot two cowpokes out lookin' for a good time."

"Turn around and keep walking or I'll shoot you both dead."

They laughed and continued toward her. Susan hesitated. Could she kill them without knowing what they were up to? Her hands trembled as she pulled the trigger, aiming at the stocky man's feet. He howled in pain and dropped to the boardwalk. His companion drew his own gun before Susan could recover from what she had done.

"Put your gun down," a familiar voice said from somewhere behind her. Two guns against one must have convinced the scruffy man to do as he was told. Placing his pistol on the boardwalk, he backed away.

"Put your gun away," Michael told her as he scooped up the weapons. "I'll meet you at the station." When she hesitated, he gently nudged her on her way.

From the corner of her eye she noticed the sheriff's deputy running toward them. She hoped Michael would be able to persuade him that they were only protecting themselves. She dared not look back until she reached the station. Once there, she turned to watch what appeared to be a farmhand gesturing with both hands as he talked to the deputy. A small crowd had gathered around them.

Should she take the train if Michael were arrested? She knew that's what he'd want her to do, but could she leave him behind to take the blame for the shooting? Susan wrung her hands as she watched someone drag a mail bag onto the platform. Hurrying over to him, she asked when the next train for Omaha would leave. The stooped older man retrieved a watch probably as old as himself from his vest pocket.

"'Bout an hour's time, missy. Take a seat in the depot till the train pulls in. Ain't necessary to stand out here in the cold."

Susan pulled the heavy shawl about her shoulders and did as he suggested. Several people were seated on wooden benches and she sat as far away from them as possible. She didn't want them asking questions. What had happened to Michael? Was he sitting on a lumpy mattress inside his former cell? She decided she couldn't leave him to take the blame and promptly left the station. Once outside the door, she felt a firm hand grip her shoulder and propel her back toward her seat.

"All taken care of," he whispered. "I'll sit across from you."

Susan's knees trembled as she glanced down at the overalled legs and work boots. She wanted to ask how he had talked his way out of trouble, but didn't dare. The other potential passengers were scrutinizing Michael's clothing and inching away from him. Her former seat was taken, so she had to sit next to him. He frowned when she smiled at him, so she removed a dime novel from her drawstring bag. She felt secure that Doctor O'Brien would keep a close watch on the others as she concentrated on her book.

"Feels like winter's coming on," said a handsome, well-dressed man seated opposite her.

Susan dropped the book to answer him. "Indeed. It feels like a touch of snow in the air."

Michael removed his straw hat and told the other man that he was a veterinarian and Susan's traveling companion.

The two male passengers facing Susan filled the small station with laughter.

"It's true," she managed to say. "We're escaping the lawlessness in Wyoming."

The laughter faded and they waited for an explanation. Michael must have thought them trustworthy because he briefly filled them in on what had happened, without mentioning their direct involvement. The man sitting opposite her said that he had been reading about the Averell's deaths and was shocked that a woman had been hanged. The other passenger said he was a cattle buyer and acquainted with A. J. Bothwell. Susan caught her breath, frightened he might telegraph the cattleman of their whereabouts.

He must have sensed her fear because he assured her that he had no intention of getting in touch with the murderous cattleman. "I met Bothwell in Cheyenne and disliked him on sight. He's a little tin god in his own domain. I wouldn't buy his steers if they were the last—"

The other passenger cut in. "John Maples, Cheyenne merchant." He extended a hand to Michael. "I'm afraid most people in my area believe whatever they read in the *Leader*. However, there *are* some of us who know the cattlemen's connections and that the editor, Ed Towse, prints whatever they tell him. So I'm inclined to believe your story."

Susan insisted, "Everything Michael told you is true, and he didn't tell it all. If he had, you would probably not believe him."

"I'm sure the cattlemen will be charged with murder and hanged like their victims," Maples said."

"Not without witnesses," the cattle buyer told him.

"That's true," Michael said. "I doubt there are any witnesses left."

"*The Sweetwater Chief* editors." Susan reminded him.

Her companion scowled. "If they've got any brains, they'll leave the territory."

The merchant sat back in his seat. "The trial's set for next week, weather permitting."

Michael said. "Good point, Maples. Why'd they wait so long to hold the trial? The court docket can't be that full. I think the date was set to discourage other possible witnesses who might testify. October snowstorms can be deadly."

"That's why I'm getting my traveling done for the year.

A fall blizzard can happen any time."

The cattle buyer laughed. "Try shipping steers in October. I've had some cattle sidelined on snowbound tracks for days, losing half a carload before the rails were cleared. Cattlemen are afraid of losing everything after the recent hard freezes."

"That coupled with losing their precious Cheyenne Club," Maples said, "must be the reason for the hangings."

"That's no reason to kill innocent homesteaders and run them off their land." Susan's voice was louder than she had intended.

"Pure greed," Michael told them. "Albert Bothwell's the ring leader. He managed to convince the other cattlemen that the Averell's small herd was rustled because they'd been freshly branded with Ella's LU brand."

"Legally bought and branded," Susan said. She was feeling better now that her anger had been released, although fearful that word would get back to the cattlemen.

"Sounds cut and dried," the cattle buyer said. "I hear the hangmen were arrested and released on bond. You think they'll show up for trial?"

"Who knows? They seem to have the governor in their pockets."

Maples said, "I'm afraid a range war will erupt before this is over."

Chapter Twenty-Three

Susan stared through the frosted window, wondering what had become of Willie Cahill. Had he rented a horse to ride the remainder of his trip, or connected with a stage line? She didn't want to consider the possibility that he had been waylaid by Bothwell's men.

Michael sat next to her, his straw hat tipped forward as he dozed. Sighing, she closed her eyes.

Uncle Jacob would lecture her when he met the train in Omaha. He'd warned her not to homestead in Wyoming Territory. She thought back to her graduation from the university. Smiling, she envisioned the gift her uncle brought with him on the train. A panda bear of all things, with a pouch filled with silver dollars. He said the bear would comfort her whenever she was lonely. Glancing sidelong at Michael, she wondered whether he had been sent to replace her bear.

He must have sensed her scrutiny. "Hungry?" he asked.

"No, Michael. Just wondering what's ahead for us both."

"I've been wondering the same. Have you decided where you'd like to try homesteading again?"

"No. Any suggestions?"

"How about Kansas or Nebraska?"

"The land's too flat. I love the mountains."

He thought for a moment. "Montana has beautiful mountains, as does Colorado and Utah."

"I'd like someplace warmer and I don't condone polygamy."

Michael laughed. "I think you're running out of choices."

"There's still land on the West Coast. I've been considering California."

He smiled. "What a coincidence. I've been thinking of the golden state, myself."

It was Susan's turn to laugh. "You're incorrigible, Doctor O'Brien."

The whistle shrieked as the train jolted to a sudden halt. An instant later the coach was catapulted onto its side. Michael had been seated next to the window and she regained consciousness lying across his body, surrounded with broken glass. Unable to move, she heard groaning elsewhere in the coach, thinking she was in the midst of a nightmare.

Michael tried to lift his head. "Hide," he whispered. "If someone wrecked the train, they'll be looking for us."

"I'm paralyzed."

"Can you move your arms?"

Susan found that she could raise her left arm.

"Smear my blood on your face and pretend you're dead."

She gasped when she felt a sticky substance on Michael's face. Patting her bloody hand on her own face, neck and bodice, she closed her eyes and strained to listen. How badly was Michael hurt and would she ever move again? The groaning in the front of the coach had stopped and an eerie silence settled over the wreckage. She heard men's voices in the distance and held her breath as a barrage of gunfire took place.

Someone wearing spurs seemed to be climbing the

overturned coach, so it wasn't a trainman. Perhaps a passenger from another coach. She dared not open her eyes or attempt to turn her head.

"If that wasn't them in the first coach, there's a couple in here in the last seats," a gruff voice yelled. "They're covered with blood so they must be dead."

Another man said they should be shot for good measure. But before the first man could reply, the sound of gunfire sounded again. Susan heard spurs rattle as the coach trembled slightly under the man's weight.

"Let's get out of here," the gruff voice yelled as he apparently returned fire. A moment later she heard the sound of fading hoof beats.

She returned her attention to Michael, who groaned in obvious pain. "Are you badly hurt?"

"My face is cut and I can't see out of my right eye. Are you all right, Susan?"

She tried to move but could only feel her toes. When she told him, he said she was suffering from temporary trauma. She could feel Michael's feeble attempts to pull himself upright and the resulting pain down her spine as his body moved beneath her. Relieved, she knew the pain meant she wasn't paralyzed.

"Anybody still alive in there?" an unfamiliar voice called. "Them train wreckers hightailed it outa here."

"Help us," Susan cried.

"Hold on, lady. I'll get some help."

It seemed hours before she heard the sound of someone climbing the side of the coach. She could also hear groaning from injured passengers further down the aisle. Thank heavens they were still alive.

The sound of breaking glass startled her. Whoever was trying to rescue the passengers must have broken the upraised window, or cleared away remaining chards of glass. Why hadn't they entered through the connecting doors? When she moved, pain surged throughout her body. Had she broken her bones?

Michael told her to lie quietly until help arrived. He had managed to position himself to free his right arm so that he could wipe blood from his face. She sighed with relief when he reported that he now had vision in both eyes. Susan was also regaining the use of her own limbs and she hugged him as though he were her panda bear.

"Give the rope some slack," their rescuer said a moment before he landed on the inside wall. Placing a hand on her shoulder, he said, "Can you move, ma'am, or do I need to carry you?"

Susan struggled to right herself, with the man's help, and was soon standing among the debris. Their Good Samaritan helped Michael to his feet and she glimpsed the gash on his forehead. She found her reticule and removed a handkerchief which she used as a temporary bandage. Pressing it to his face to stop the bleeding, Michael insisted they help the other passengers.

Their rescuer led the way. A heavy woman was wedged between the seats and the middle aged cowhand, who introduced himself as Randal Begley, yelled to someone outside the coach. "We need a pry bar in here. Drop it through the window if you can find one."

A young, dark haired woman across the aisle was holding her arm and crying. Susan tried to comfort her while Michael conducted a preliminary examination. He said he thought the arm might be fractured.

"We need cloth strips to wrap your arm and use as a sling," he said, pulling a knife from his boot. "A petticoat would do."

The young woman lifted the hem of her dress with her uninjured hand. "Use mine."

Punching a small hole in the cloth, Michael ripped a long strip along the edge from seam to seam. When he had wrapped her arm, he tore another strip to hold her arm securely in place. She screamed in pain when he tied the sling behind her neck. He then helped their rescuer push the seat back to extract the woman from her cage. Their efforts failed and they decided to wait for a leveraging tool.

"Good thing there weren't many passengers on the train. Looks like nobody else made it," Begley said.

Susan shuddered. "Are you sure? Maybe they're unconscious." She carefully avoided viewing the bodies.

"I helped doctors in the war and I know dead people when I see 'em."

"The War Between the States?"

"Yes, ma'am. Let's get you two ladies outa here. Then we'll pry this woman loose." As he spoke, his partner yelled. "Look out below," as a metal bar landed beneath the open window, clattering on the coach wall. The man then yelled, "Need my help in there?"

"We got 'er licked. Keep watchin' for them varmints in case they come back."

Susan said, "I heard a lot of shooting. Was that you and your partner shooting at the train wreckers?"

"We saw them killers shooting at the trainmen and passengers in the other coach before we got into firing range."

Michael asked if the two men had been riding the train.

"No, sir. We was ridin' to our next cattle job when we saw the dead heifer on the tracks just before the train ran into her. Them no-goods was sittin' their horses just waitin' for the train to wreck."

Susan gasped. "Are there any other survivors?"

"None that we could find, but we'll take another look soon as we get the four of you outa here." He turned to glance back at the wailing woman stuck between the seats. Shaking his head, his expression said extracting her was in doubt.

Michael reached for the lariat hanging from the window and tied it around Susan's waist. "Passenger ready to evacuate," he yelled. She screamed when the rope jerked upward, cutting into her waist. Michael steadied her ascent as she was lifted into the chilling air. The lanky man on the overturned wall grinned as he pulled her onto what was now the roof, warning her about the glass. He looked enough like his companion to be his brother.

Once they were on the ground, he said he was Randal's cousin, MacKenzie. "Call me Mac, ma'am. I hope you're not as badly hurt as you look."

She glanced down at her hands and remembered her blood-smeared face. Staring into his dark bulging eyes, she told him it was her friend's blood and that it had probably saved her life. She didn't say *again* because she was in no mood to retell the past. She knew if she ever wrote about her adventures, no one would believe they were anything but fiction.

"I think your partner needs you inside the coach to help the other passengers," she said. "I'll stand guard out here, if someone will hand me my reticule."

Mac shot her a questioning look before he looped the end of the lariat to the underside of the coach. He then climbed inside.

Susan could hear banging noises and wondered what was taking place. A few minutes later Mac tossed her reticule to her

"They're tryin' to pry the door open," he said before his head disappeared back inside.

The men must have pried the woman loose from the seats and decided she was too heavy to lift through the window. Susan looked about before she pulled the gun from her bag. What had happened to the girl with the injured arm? She noticed Mac climbing back over the side of the coach and positioning the rope for another survivor.

Moments later, the young woman was pulled shrieking onto the temporary roof. Susan reached to help her down

When her tears subsided, she said her name was Callie Moore and that she was on her way to Omaha to visit her parents. Tears streaked her face as she gingerly touched her arm. The two women heard a loud cracking sound and another woman cry out in pain. Unnerved, Susan urged her companion to accompany her as she skirted the end of the train. When they reached the coach's opposite side, they noticed the door had been pried open and a large woman was attempting to crawl outside. Randal Begley crouched on the upraised side, his hands outstretched to hers, urging her forward.

How would the six of them reach civilization? She then remembered the cowhands' horses. Susan walked forward to peer at the engine, which was also on its side, its smoke still belching from the stack. A small section of track had been pried up on one side, a rock wedged beneath it. The dead cow was inches further down the track. No wonder the train had capsized. Had the entire train crew perished? She was afraid to look. She'd experienced enough death and destruction to last a lifetime. No one would believe that Albert Bothwell was responsible for all the deaths, if, indeed, he was. Who else wanted her dead so that he could take over her homestead land?

Michael called to her and she saw that the older woman was standing on the ground. Rushing back, she tried to comfort her but the woman was inconsolable. "Why did they wreck the train?" she wailed. "And why didn't they hold me for ransom?"

Ransom? Who is this woman? Susan lowered her head, a deep feeling of guilt enveloping her.

Randal Begley averted his gaze from the woman they had just rescued. "We can ride double to the nearest ranch."

"We'll wait for you to bring back help." Michael gazed at the afternoon sky and must have wondered how they would stay warm in the chilling wind.

"The two young ladies can ride along," Mac Begley said.

"We'll wait here," they both answered at once.

"Suit yourselves."

Susan watched as they rode off, wondering if they would actually return. If not, maybe someone at the next station would send out searchers when the train failed to arrive.

Michael surveyed the wreckage and began searching for other survivors. When he returned, his expression told them that none had been found.

"Looks like they robbed the mail car while they were at it."

"Were we unconcious that long?" Susan said.

"Maybe they had accomplices."

Susan frowned. "It's too late to ask our rescuers."

Michael looked about for something to shield them from the freezing wind. Susan joined in the search. There wasn't much to serve as shelter, so Michael climbed back into their former coach. After a while, he yelled for everyone to stand back as he threw objects from a window that was now on the roof. First came a dark brown furry object resembling a large bear rug. Next were a couple of coach seats followed by two more, which landed with soft thuds in the sandy soil. Several pieces of luggage followed, which the hefty woman claimed.

Susan hoped that Michael was able to locate their own canvas sack of clothing. Righting the coach seats in the sand, she invited the other women to sit. Thank heavens they were on the leeward side of the train, which helped to protect them from the bone chilling wind. Gazing skyward she noticed dark clouds on the horizon, the wind hinting at snow. Would they be rescued before the storm?

Callie followed her gaze and gasped. Susan knew the

young woman's coat was somewhere in their former coach. She cringed, envisioning Michael stumbling over bodies in his efforts to locate their possessions. They might have to climb back inside the train to escape the coming storm. Glancing at the older woman, she knew that wasn't possible. All they could do was pray for rescue before they died of exposure.

Michael tossed down their canvas sack along with a large amount of luggage, one of which belonged to Callie. Her coat soon followed. How would they get her into it, with her arm in the sling, without hurting her? Susan draped the coat around Callie's shoulders.

The wind had calmed and the first flakes of snow began to fall. She helped Michael form low walls of luggage against the roof of the overturned coach. He sliced their canvas bag to form a tarp over their heads, securing it between the top layers of baggage. He then built a small campfire from sagebrush within the enclosure to help keep them warm. What would they have done without him? Susan had come to depend on him, despite the freedom and independence she originally sought.

The veterinarian crawled into the dining car and returned with biscuits and a few pieces of fruit in his overall pockets as well as a container of water. The storm soon brought snowflakes the size of silver dollars. Susan shivered as she hugged young Callie to her side.

Michael urged them to crawl into their baggage cave and the two young women complied, slipping into their crowded seats. The older woman followed, still grumbling about the train wreck. Thank heavens she didn't know the reason for their dilemma.

Susan glanced down at her bloody hands and reached for the container of water. Pouring a small amount of water on the hem of her petticoat, she scrubbed the blood from her hands and face. It was to cold to wet her bodice.

The wind had resumed, flapping their canvas roof until Susan feared it would blow away. Icy wind filtered in, chilling the back of her neck. Pulling her collar higher, she attempted to protect her ears. Where was her knit cap?

Moments later Michael crawled into the enclosure with a small bucket of coal from the tender car, which he fed to the dying fire. When sparks flew in her direction, the heavy woman shrieked that they would set her coat on fire. Laughing, Callie suggested that she remove the fur or leave their makeshift barrier.

The woman glared. "Insolent young pup."

Susan came to Callie's rescue. "She's in pain and we're in serious trouble. We need to keep our spirits up."

Michael agreed. "It's going to be a long night. I suggest you all get some sleep before it gets too cold."

Exhausted, he dropped into the remaining seat and soon fell asleep. Susan smiled when the rotund woman said, "How can you stand his snoring?"

"It's music to *my* ears," Susan said, smiling. "We couldn't survive without him."

Callie agreed.

The middle aged woman grumbled and pulled her fur coat about her.

Susan studied her for some sign of compassion for her fellow travelers, but none was found. She then asked her name.

The woman mumbled, "Gertrude Hightower."

"I've heard of the Hightower clan," Callie said, wincing when she moved her arm. "Bankers, or so I've been told."

Hightower's flabby chin rose as she eyed her young companion. "My husband is an attorney at law with offices in the recently built New York Life building in Omaha. He's under consideration to serve on the state supreme court."

Callie giggled and covered her mouth with her good

hand. She was obviously unimpressed. The woman's fur coat was large enough to shield the three of them from the storm but she seemed not the sort to share, no matter the circumstances.

Callie fell asleep, her chin resting on her chest. Susan glanced at Gertrude, who still glared at her companions. The young woman made whimpering sounds in her sleep as Michael crouched to leave the enclosure. Would help arrive by morning? A sinking feeling in her stomach told her no one would come to their rescue. They would all die among the wreckage with the other passengers.

Chapter Twenty-Four

Susan awakened during the night when she heard Gertrude complaining about the smoke, although a hole had been cut in the middle of the tarp to allow the fumes to escape. The woman's sleep was obviously more important than keeping her companions alive.

The gash on Michael's face was a deep red in the dim light. Susan felt a flutter in her chest as she watched him stoke the fire. When she inquired of the time, he pulled a watch from his pocket. Holding it near the fire, he whispered that it was a quarter past three, too early to rise. When the fire had been rekindled, he said, "By the way, Miz Hightower, you snore like a sawmill."

"Certainly not, young man. Ladies don't snore."

"What do you call it?"

"I occasionally breathe heavily."

Surprised by Michael's sarcasm, Susan knew that his nerves were as raw as her own. She was glad that Callie was a sound sleeper. She knew the young woman would have further antagonized their fellow survivor. Gertrude sighed and pulled the fur coat over her double chin. Slumping in her seat, she said nothing more.

Susan slept little the rest of the night, worried the killers would return. When the sun rose next morning, she left her seat to determine how much snow had fallen. Ice crystals had sifted in around the edges of the tarp, leaving a fine white coating on their grumpy *diva*. She wondered who would take the blame for damaging her coat, and how many minks had died to provide enough fur to cover her ample body.

Michael's head appeared under the tarp to announce a wagon's approach. Reaching for her reticule, Susan retrieved her gun.

"Stay inside," he warned, "and remain quiet."

She could hear the creaking of the wagon as its wheels bit into snow. Were they rescuers or more of Albert Bothwell's men? Susan soon heard men's voices and was tempted to peer outside. She whispered a warning to Callie, whose frightened brown eyes seemed as large as a barn owl's. From the corner of her own eye, she noticed the Hightower woman pull the fur over her head. She resembled a huge fur ball in the early morning light.

A conversation was taking place outside the enclosure but Susan was unable to understand what they were saying. Michael must have met the men at their wagon. Her palms were moist and she laid the gun in her lap. Wiping palms on her dress, she picked up the weapon and aimed it at the opening they used as an entrance. She then heard Michael's voice.

"Put your gun down, Susan. Help has arrived."

"Are you sure they're not Bothwell's men?"

"As sure as my name's Michael Beircheart O'Brien?"

"Beircheart?"

"It's Gallic for Benjamin. My grandfather was French."

She grasped his offered hand and crouched to leave the enclosure. Several inches of snow crunched underfoot and she slipped and would have fallen if Michael had not caught her. Chagrined, she looked up to see two men standing beside the wagon, watching her. Who were they and why hadn't Randal and his cousin Mac accompanied them? When they noticed her staring, both men focused their attention on the horses. Was Michael wrong about them? Susan dug in her heels when he urged her forward to meet the Campbell brothers.

"Don't forget me," Callie called.

The luggage wall moved aside, collapsing the canvas roof. A shriek from inside told them that snow covering the tarp must have fallen on their grumpy companion. Callie laughed and extended her hand to Michael. It was then Susan realized how pretty the young woman was. Smiling, Michael helped her from the enclosure. He then untangled the Hightower woman from the icy cave.

Susan returned her attention to the wagon, its wheels mired in snow. The tracks seemed to lead in the direction their original rescuers had taken. She turned to help Michael spread the tarp in the wagon bed, overhearing the men offer to help load the luggage. A chill of fear sliced down her spine as she surveyed them. They appeared harmless enough but were they? And was Michael a good judge of character? She was beginning to wonder.

A moment later the brothers accompanied Michael to the pile of luggage. Gertrude followed, insisting that their benefactors place her huge portmanteau on top of the rest as well as under the tarp. Everyone exchanged glances when Michael grudgingly agreed to her demands. Sighing, Susan made her way back to the pile of belongings that Michael had placed on the frozen ground. Carrying them back to the wagon, she rolled them in the tarp, despite Gertrude's protests. She couldn't wait to continue their journey, with one less traveling companion.

When they finished loading the supply wagon, she asked why Randal and Mac had not accompanied them.

One of the men explained that the cowpokes had arrived at their ranch asking that they rescue the train wreck victims. They feared they'd lose their wranglers' jobs if they got there too late.

Michael shrugged, telling them all they required was a ride to the nearest train station. He would be glad to pay them for their troubles. Refusing pay, they agreed to his request. Someone needed to notify the railroad as well as the nearest sheriff. The train wreck victims would be frozen so there was no need to form a burial detail until after the sheriff arrived. Fortunately, the train had only two passenger coaches.

Susan was convinced that she and Michael were the intended victims. Why had only passengers in their coach been spared? It didn't make sense that others had died instead. Had they all been shot while they lay unconscious or had the train wreck actually killed them?

The three men padded an area in the bed of the wagon with coats the deceased no longer needed, along with the soft luggage. When they were all seated as comfortably as possible, the wagon jerked forward and they were at last on their way. Hightower immediately complained that she should be seated beside the driver. Susan had to restrain Callie from striking her. It was going to be the wagon ride from hell.

It wasn't long before they met three men on horseback, who had been sent to investigate the train's delay. When told of the wreck, one of the men, who sat taller in the saddle than the rest, retrieved a note pad and pencil from his saddlebag. He then wrote down the survivors' names.

"Gertrude Hightower, wife of Harold Hightower, Esquire," she said before anyone else had time to answer. "You must get word to him to meet me at the nearest station."

The railroad agent's lips set in a firm line. "We've got

more important business to attend to, ma'am. You can notify your husband by telegram from the next station."

Susan shook her head to dislodge the disturbing image of the three men burying victims. Or would they return to the station to recruit more people to bring the bodies in? It was cold enough for the ground to freeze, so burying victims would present a problem. How far was the next station? She didn't think she could stomach her annoying wagon mate much longer.

"It's not a far piece," one the Campbell brothers said when she asked. "Coupla hours, maybe."

She noticed Callie grimacing and holding her injured arm. Hopefully it wasn't broken. Michael moved closer to the young woman and felt the area above her wrist. When she screamed in pain, he frowned, saying he was sure the arm was fractured. A doctor in the next town could wrap it securely so that it would properly mend. Placing an arm around her, he hugged her to his side and kissed her hair. Was he simply being compassionate or was he interested in Callie? He might be deliberately trying to make her jealous. Susan bit down hard on her lower lip and turned to survey their back trail.

Nearly three hours later they arrived at a small railroad town where they informed the station master of the train wreck as well as the ordeal they had experienced. Gertrude Hightower insisted that his first order of business was to telegraph her husband and get her on the first train to Omaha.

Apparently exasperated, Michael said they needed to talk to the sheriff and that Callie needed a doctor.

"Sheriff's in another part of the county," he said. "Unless you want to stay here for a few days, I'll fill him in on what happened and who you suspect caused the train wreck. As for a doctor, old Doc Williams died last week and we don't know when we'll get another. I hear they've got a doctor in

Valentine, but he's rumored to be a drunk."

"Valentine?" Susan repeated.

"Yes, ma'am. Heck of a name for a town sitting in the middle of the Sand Hills with no vegetation and trees. Only fit for coyotes."

"No," Callie wailed.

The short, balding man removed his glasses to wipe them clean. "I hear there's a good doctor in Norfork. Back in sixty-five a group of German Lutherans settled there from Wisconsin."

"How far by train?" Michael asked.

"Two days depending on the weather."

Michael glanced at Callie, who shook her head yes. "Are you sure you can stand the pain?"

The station agent said, "You can get the young lady some powders at the apothecary down the street."

Michael nodded. "And a better sling."

Susan knew he was worried that waiting too long to properly attend to Callie's arm could result in permanent damage. He must be weighing his options as they trudged off down the snow covered street to the local apothecary. The building was small, the shelves lined with bottles of various descriptions. A short middle aged man behind the counter glanced at Callie and pulled a bottle of laudanum from the nearest shelf.

Michael frowned. "I'm not sure the young lady should take that. It's tincture of opium with morphine and alcohol."

Apparently surprised, the druggist insisted that opium was a vegetable compound. Turning back to the shelves, he retrieved a small bottle of white powder. "Surely," he said, "you don't object to an ounce of cocaine."

"Indeed I do. Cocaine has driven men insane and I certainly wouldn't give it to a young lady."

While the druggist sputtered his objections, Michael

scanned the dusty shelves.

"Give me that bottle of Sloan's Liniment."

"But that's for horses."

"Yes, but it doesn't cause other ailments. It'll work just fine."

Callie stood with her mouth open, shaking her head. Before she had a chance to agree with the druggist, Susan took her good arm and steered her out of the shop. Once on the boardwalk she said, "Michael knows what he's doing."

"But—but he's a veterinarian. Not a people doctor."

"For your information, Callie, most men who call themselves doctors are nothing more than charlatans, with no medical training."

"That can't be true."

"I'm afraid Susan's right," Michael said as he closed the apothecary's door. "Anyone can set up shop and call himself a doctor these days."

A tear slid down Callie's face. "But you're going to treat me like a horse."

He placed an arm around her shoulder. "The liniment takes away the pain and has been used on cowpokes and horses alike. It'll ease your pain until we can find a medical doctor in Norfork or Omaha."

Seemingly pacified, Callie leaned into Michael's side and smiled up at him. Susan gritted her teeth as she followed them down the boardwalk to the general store where they could buy luggage. She could hear the train's whistle in the distance when they left the store.

They discovered Gertrude Hightower sulking in a corner of the small station, wrapped securely in her mink coat. They ignored her when they seated themselves on a wooden bench near the door. Susan watched as Michael opened the bottle of liniment and moved closer to Callie. Untying her sling, he gently rubbed liniment over her wrist and lower arm. Tears ran down her cheeks as she gazed at him adoringly. Susan looked away as Doc O'Brien wrapped her arm and fitted Callie with a new sling.

"Passengers bound for Valentine, O'Neill, Norfork, West Point and Omaha, please step onto the boarding platform," the station master called.

Getting to her feet, Susan cast a quick glance at Hightower, wishing she wasn't going to board the train. Fortunately, their coach was filled when they took the last seats at the front of the coach, and Hightower was forced to board the following car. Smiling, Susan had taken the seat next to Michael and across the aisle from Callie, whom she knew was traveling all the way to Omaha. Callie was obviously experiencing a school girl crush. Did Michael have similar feelings? She told herself she didn't care, but why the sick feeling in her stomach?

Chapter Twenty-Five

Before they reached Valentine, high winds created an opaque sandstorm, which coated the windows and blocked her view. Glancing at the other passengers, Susan noticed frightened expressions as they huddled in their seats. Shivering, she recalled her last train ride. Would they arrive safely in Omaha?

Their train waited on the tracks for nearly two hours before the storm finally subsided. She would have to telegraph her uncle concerning the delay, which she knew would displease him. Uncle Jacob was a bulldog when it came to maintaining schedules. The longer he had to wait, the angrier he became.

Thank heavens Gertrude Hightower was riding in another coach. Susan envisioned her holding court at the front of her own coach, telling the other passengers how badly she'd been treated. Her husband would probably sue the railroad.

A shrill whistle sounded as the train jerked forward, forcing Susan against the seat. Looping her arm through Michael's, she smiled up at him and laughed at his surprised expression. Across the aisle Callie groaned and gripped her arm.

Leaning around Susan, he said, "You'll be fine, Callie. Just be careful that you don't bump your wrist."

Smiling sweetly, she said, "I think I need more liniment."

Susan reached to open Michael's valise and extracted the liniment. "I'll be glad to help," she said as she leaned across the aisle. Callie's expression said she wasn't pleased but she submitted to Susan's nurturing. When her arm had been rewrapped and the sling again in place, Callie said she wouldn't need more medicine until she reached Omaha.

Susan smiled. "Great stuff, this liniment. It's amazing how quickly arms can heal."

The young woman turned to talk to the man beside her, seated next to the window. Susan felt sorry for her, remembering her own first crush. Professor Hensly must have realized how Susan felt about him because he transferred her to another classroom. Was Michael wise enough to do the same? From the corner of her eye she noticed him attempting to hide a smile.

The train ride seemed interminable. When they reached O'Neill, Susan insisted that she send telegrams to both her mother and Uncle Jacob. Callie chose to remain on the train while Michael accompanied Susan to the telegraph office.

"She's sulking," he said. "We should have insisted she come along."

"She'll get over it. When I was her age—"

"You had a crush on—?"

"So you know."

He chuckled. "Awfully hard not to. And, by the way, you're not much older than she is."

"Old enough to know what would happen if I marry."

Michael stopped in his tracks. "So you think I would

dominate you? Make you my domestic slave?"

"Most men are domineering. They think of women as second class citizens. That's why I wanted to homestead in Wyoming, where women have some rights."

"You still might be able to, Susan. If memory serves me, the trial for the lynchers was supposed to begin yesterday. I'll find a newspaper while you send your telegrams."

Susan gasped. "How could I have forgotten?"

"The train wreck and kidnapping probably distracted you."

"We'd better hurry before the train leaves." She decided to ask the telegrapher if he'd heard about the trial.

He had. "They let them go," the short, freckled-face young man reported. "Received a telegram yesterday afternoon saying they'd been set free."

"But how could that have happened?"

"The newspaper office put out a special edition this morning. Might be a good idea to read it, if you're interested."

Michael walked in the door as she was paying for her telegrams. Holding a rolled newspaper, his face said he knew about the dismissed trial. Taking her arm, he suggested they read about it on the train.

The whistle sounded before they reached the station, forcing them to run to catch the train. Breathless, Susan took a seat and reached for the newspaper. She couldn't believe what she read.

"They dropped the charges because the witnesses all disappeared or were found dead."

Michael shook his head sadly. "That in itself should have been grounds for a murder investigation. Bothwell and his fellow lynchers got off because cattlemen own Sweetwater Valley. There's nothing more we can do."

"We can travel to Washington and report them to congress and the president."

"We'd be wasting our time, Susan. Harrison's a Republican who will probably side with the cattlemen, and congress is full of lawyers who don't much care about the rights of lowly homesteaders. Too bad Cleveland lost the election, although I doubt he'd get involved."

"Doesn't anyone in government care about the homesteaders?"

Michael sighed and shook his head. "Well, at least Bothwell has no need to kill us now. He's off the hook and can do whatever he wants with the land. He and his cronies can turn the entire Sweetwater Valley into grazing land."

"What are you saying? That we should return to Wyoming?"

"Isn't that what you want most in life? To be free, to own your own land, and have the right to vote and hold office?"

Susan chewed her lower lip. "Yes, but is there anywhere safe in Wyoming, or as beautiful as Sweetwater Valley?"

"I doubt that Bothwell's influence extends much farther than the valley and the governor's office in Cheyenne." Michael rattled the newspaper as though shaking the bad news into space. "The territory will become a state next year. That should help to bring law and order to Wyoming."

"I'm still not convinced. I love the Sweetwater Valley, but I know that I can no longer live there. Not just because of living in fear of the cattlemen. I could never look at the road ranch again without crying."

"The Wyoming side of the Black Hills is beyond beautiful. I know you'd like it there."

"What about you, Michael? What are your plans?"

His laugh was mirthless. "I'll find a wife and settle down wherever a good veterinarian is needed. It doesn't matter where."

"I'm sure Callie's interested," she whispered.

Michael snorted. "Stop playing games with me, Susan."

Shocked by the intensity of his words, she sat back in her seat to think. *Was* she playing games? She knew he wanted to marry her and she didn't want to lose him, but fear that she would be squashed beneath his thumb had her emotionally paralyzed. Perhaps they could negotiate. Sitting tall in her seat, she said, "May we talk more about this when we reach Omaha?" She thought she saw a slight smile. "I can't imagine why you'd want a woman who's so contrary and has treated you badly."

"It's because I admire your spunk and determination. Maybe because you're attractive in a different sort of way—"

"Define different, Michael."

He thought for a moment. "Not quite beautiful but delightfully pleasing."

"Not plain as an unbuttered biscuit?"

"Whoever told you that should be horse whipped."

"I think I love you, Michael."

"I know I love you. How does Missus Susan O'Brien sound?"

"Let me think about it. We need to talk about so many things before I decide to give up my freedom."

"You won't have to forsake your freedom. We'll live as equal partners in Wyoming's Black Hills. If we build a house and clinic in the northeast corner of the territory, we can cross the border into the Dakotas or Montana, if the new state remains lawless."

Susan smiled. She wondered what her family would say if she introduced Michael as her future husband and said they would live in the Black Hills. She cringed, imagining Uncle Jacob's reaction. Michael was a veterinarian, not a member of the bar. Would he think him unworthy?

Balderdash. I'm my own woman and can do as I please. At least as long as I remain in Wyoming. If we marry before we reach Omaha, there's nothing Uncle

Jacob can do. When she told Michael, his face lighted like a candelabra, one feature at a time.

"Are you serious, Susan?"

"Absolutely."

"Then let's leave the train in Norfork and find a justice of the peace." His smile faded. "Are you sure you won't mind passing up a big wedding?"

"I have no desire for pomp and circumstance."

Michael stood and slipped by her to kneel in the aisle on one knee. "Will you do me the honor of marrying me and making me the happiest man on earth?"

Susan laughed. "Yes, if you agree to my conditions. Now get up and brush off your knees. How will it look for the bridegroom to have dirty overalls?" She heard Callie's wail across the aisle as well as the cheers and applause of other passengers. How could she have forgotten they were riding in plain view of everyone on the coach? She glanced at Michael and could have sworn that he blushed.

"We still have details to work out before the ceremony," she said, "and I want them in writing."

"In writing?"

"Indeed. Uncle Jacob taught me well."

"Can I take back my proposal?"

"Not with all these witnesses present. I'd have to sue you for breaking my heart."

"Hush woman. I'm about to kiss a future Wyoming governor."

ABOUT THE AUTHOR

Jean Henry Mead is a national award-winning pho-
tojournalist and author of 19 books, including her western
historical novels, Logan & Cafferty mystery/suspense
series, Hamilton Kids' mysteries, and nonfiction history
and interview books. She's a former news reporter
published domestically as well as abroad, who has served
as a news, magazine and small press editor. The California
native lives on a Wyoming ranch with her husband and
Australian Shepherd. You can visit her webpage at:
www.jeanhenrymead.com.

www.ingramcontent.com/pod-product-compliance
Lightning Source LLC
Chambersburg PA
CBHW070700280626
47159CB00022B/1013